# Partnerz in Crime

# Partnerz in Crime

*Kareem*

*www.urbanbooks.net*

Urban Books, LLC
300 Farmingdale Road, NY-Route 109
Farmingdale, NY 11735

Partnerz in Crime Copyright © 2017 Kareem

ISBN 13: 978-1-62286-492-8
ISBN 10: 1-62286-492-1

First Trade Paperback Printing June 2017
Printed in the United States of America

10 9 8 7 6 5 4 3 2 1

*This is a work of fiction. Any references or similarities to actual events, real people, living or dead, or to real locales are intended to give the novel a sense of reality. Any similarity in other names, characters, places, and incidents is entirely coincidental.*

Distributed by Kensington Publishing Corp.
Submit Orders to:
Customer Service
400 Hahn Road
Westminster, MD 21157-4627
Phone: 1-800-733-3000
Fax: 1-800-659-2436

MAY - - 2017.

# Partnerz in Crime

by

*Kareem*

# Part 1

# Chapter 1

## *Time Served*

### Korey

I could hardly believe that I was actually on this Greyhound bus on my way back home after having given the Feds some of my best years behind steel doors and concrete walls. I loved the fact that I was now a free man again. But I didn't know whether to feel happy about it or feel angry as I did well over a decade ago when I was sentenced. After all, I surely felt that I had done too much time for nothing, literally.

As I rode on this bus and thought on the anger that I honestly wanted to feel, I thought also on how I had worked so hard to rid myself of this anger while inside the joint. I took anger management classes to help me overcome the anger and deep hatred that had built up inside me for the criminal "justice" system. A system where "justice" is often delayed and usually denied to blacks and Hispanics and even some whites.

I felt that it was the whites in "high places" who wisely designed it to be this way. While in the joint, I had read that it was the CIA, run by whites in the eighties, who were responsible for cocaine being placed in the black communities, starting with poor black communities on the West Coast first, before making its way to the East Coast.

I, and so many of my thug associates, were blind to the trap and fell right into the mutha! Before many of us knew it, hustling crack cocaine had made us hood rich, with more cash in our pockets and stash spots than we had ever dreamt of having. My thug associates and I were doing it big in those days, buying big whips, the finest sneaks, gators, clothes, and cribs to live in. Then, boom! Here come the Feds, busting hustlers everywhere and hauling us off to a new reality. Federal penitentiary! The judge dropped twenty years on my codefendant and me. Twenty got'dayum years!

I was so enraged that, had one of my thug associates been able to slip me a burner in that courtroom, I would have shot the white prosecutor, the white judge, and the white female attorney who represented me! My attorney promised that she could get me an acquittal, being that absolutely no drugs were ever found on my person or at my place of residence. Not to mention the prosecuting attorney never proved beyond a reasonable doubt, as is required by law to establish guilt, that I even touched drugs! My codefendant never ratted. The government's only witness was a cat who took the stand claiming that, on numerous occasions, he purchased fifty grams or more of crack from me and my codefendant. I told my attorney that the government's witness was lying like the devil! But her ass raised no objection to the untruthfulness of this rat. It was enough for the jury to come back with a guilty verdict.

"Mr. Taylor, I apologize, but that's just how our judicial system is. You win some, you lose some," my attorney turned to me and said after all was said and done.

"Bitch, fuck you!" I looked in her ocean-colored blue eyes and barked, wishing like it was my birthday that I could have killed her ass! That's how angry I was at that time in my life.

I entered the penitentiary hot mad for us getting judicially lynched, my codefendant and me.

I was twenty years old at the time, and I didn't know if I was gonna make it. I found myself acting in a manner that was conducive to the hate and anger that I had built up inside me for the system and many whites. Every white officer who worked for the system who looked at me wrong while in the pen, whether male or female, I went out of my way to argue with them and call them derogatory names. I stayed in and out of solitary confinement as a result.

"Young blood, I know you hate what happened to you in that courtroom, but you have got to find a better way to channel your anger, or you're gonna find yourself doing some serious hard time," an elderly brother pulled me to the side and advised me on one occasion. He had seen me about to have it out with a white male officer for shaking my cell down and leaving it a complete mess.

"Man, I hate them muthafuckas! I wanna kill 'em all!" I told him.

"I know you do," he shot back. "That's your problem, young blood—"

"Nah, I don't have a problem! They're the damn problem!" I cut him off.

"You do have a problem!" he jacked me up. "You are allowing the hate you have for them to cause you to act irrational and stupid. Look, man, hate destroys the hater! Don't give them white folks that much power over you. Think, brother. Think!" he spat, before turning me loose and walking away, seemingly mad at me for continuing to act in an emotionally stupid way.

His words carried a lot of weight, for they repeatedly echoed loudly within me every time I felt like cursing out a white person or causing one harm. *Hate destroys the hater!"*

I found out who this man was to think enough of me to give me wisdom that could help me exercise better judgment. I discovered that he was out of the Windy City and was a major shot-caller for one of Chicago's largest and most notorious gangs. He was serving fifty-five years for having to put in mad work for his crew. But now, after serving over twenty years, he had reformed and was teaching an anger management course, which I took from him advising me to. From then on, the old man became one of my chief counselors, aiding me in my growth and development toward positivity. Before I knew it, I realized that my true enemy was not the white man or anyone else outside of myself. My enemy was me not being able to control my negative emotions.

"Never let your emotions override your intellect and better judgment," the old man planted deep inside my head. I made up my mind that anger and hate would never control my actions again.

Now, I was on the bus on my way back home to Charlotte, North Carolina, also called the Queen City, or "Baby Atlanta" because of its growth and business opportunities. I hadn't been in my city for twelve long years due to my incarceration. Neither did I think I would see my city anytime soon, being that I had to do 85 percent of my twenty-year sentence. Surprisingly, due to a recent change in the crack law, I received some very good news.

"Mr. Taylor, we're gonna need you to pack your property. Your prison sentence has been reduced to time served."

"Say what?" I replied, wide-eyed and excited at my case manager delivering me the news.

"Mm-hmm, yep. They want you up in R/D with your property and ready to go in thirty minutes. Congratulations!" he said and shook my hand.

Six months prior, I had received a letter from my codefendant, Hammer:

> *Yo, my nig,*
> *I'm home and, boy, it feels good to smell the fresh air of freedom again! I guess them crackas felt sorry for the many of us they gave long prison sentences to for petty-ass crack offenses. Your boy out here doing his thing, though. I can't wait to see you. Matter fact, I don't know why you weren't released when I was released, but I know I should be seeing you soon. Make sure I am the first nig you call the moment you are released. I got a big surprise for you. Also, I sent you $500. It should hold you down for a minute. I love ya, my nigga!*

While riding home and listening to Sam Cooke's "A Change Is Gonna Come" on my MP3 player, so many thoughts were running through my head. Thoughts like, *what in the hell am I going back home to?* My tenth year in prison I lost my mother to breast cancer. She could have survived it, but she depended on divine healing. She completely abandoned medical treatment from the doctors. "A nice-sized lump was discovered on the left side of my breast, son. The doctors say they're gonna have to operate. I can't let them do that. I came into this world with all of my limbs and body parts, and that's how I'm going to leave. But, baby, don't think Mama crazy. Mama just don't like the medicines of man," she shared with me. I cried like a baby when, fourteen months after speaking with her on the matter, she passed away.

I was on my way back to my city without a mother to hug and love on. This brought tears to my eyes. Other things came to my mind as well. Like losing my girl, who was also the mother of our daughter, Olivia. I knew the day would come when I would have to face her telling me that she couldn't do twenty years with me far away from her. Thing was, she didn't tell me shit! She just stopped writing and stopped sending pictures of her and our daughter. It killed me inside to not know how they were doing. Doing time without my girl and without knowing how my daughter was taking to growing up without a father was harder than accepting the fact that I had twenty years to give the federal government.

Moreover, I thought about how I needed to find me a job, a place to stay of my own, and some transportation. One thing was for sure, I knew shit wouldn't be easy for me trying to do things the right way this time. Thank God I was not on any probation; I got time served.

# Chapter 2

## *I'm Home*

I stepped inside the Greyhound bus station after my long seven-hour ride had ended. I looked in search of a payphone. After my eyes searched the station, I spotted one and made my way to it. I retrieved my address and phone book to phone Hammer. I wiped the phone with a napkin. I always did this in the joint to avoid germs. I dialed Hammer's number.

"Helllll-looowah," some female answered after the third ring, stretching the word "hello" very soft and sexy-like.

"Yeah, may I speak with Hammer, please?"

"May I ask whooooozzz calling?"

"Tell him it's his brother, Korey."

"Killa Korey?" Her voice got excited, like she knew me.

I thought before I responded. I wasn't Killa Korey Taylor anymore. Just Korey. I didn't have time to go all into this with a stranger, so I conceded. "Yeah, it's Killa Korey."

"Oh, hey, Killa Korey! I'm Hammer's sweetheart. I have heard so much about you!"

"Okay, what's up, Ms. Hammer?" I replied. Hammer never mentioned having a sweetheart but, hell, he loved women, so I wasn't surprised that he had one answering his phone.

"Nothing much. Hold on. Hammer, your brother on the phone!" she yelled. "He is gonna be so happy to hear from you, Killa Korey. You are all he talks about! Here he is now."

"Yo, what up?"

"What's the business? This your brother, Korey. I'm home, fam."

"Korey, don't play with me, my nig. Are you home for real, yo?"

"In the Queen City at the Greyhound bus station as we speak."

"Oh, shit! How long you been out?"

"Just stepped off the bus, fam. You are the only one who knows I'm home. What's up?"

"Maaaan, oh shit! I can't believe my nig out. Oh, shit!" Hammer sounded like he was going hysterical. "Look, stay right where you're at. Someone will be by to pick you up shortly. You hear me?"

"I hear ya, fam."

After disconnecting the phone with Hammer, I went and stood outside with my belongings in a duffle bag. My G-Shock watch read a quarter 'til 7:00 p.m. It was in the middle of December, and it seemed like I was the only person outside of this bus station without a jacket or coat on. The only clothes I had on to warm me from the slight chill factor were my prison-issued light brown button-down, heavily starched, and creased shirt and pants, with top and bottom thermals underneath, and my black leather steel-toe boots.

I saw three fine-ass chicks step out of the bus station carrying luggage. They walked past me slowly. Two of them looked back, one after the other, checking me out. I heard one of them say, "Dayum, that red nigga sexy and glowing!"

"Mm-hmm," the other replied, smiling. "Must be one of them military brothas."

"Or one of them guys just coming home from prison!"

I cracked a smile, having taken in an earful of their conversation regarding me. I almost stepped to them to get a name and perhaps a number. But when I heard 50 Cent's "I Get Money" pumping hard through the high-amped speakers of a black Lexus coupe with dark-tinted windows and chrome rims pulling up, I knew this had to be my dawg, Hammer. 50 Cent was his favorite hip hop artist.

The car pulled into the lot of the bus station and parked. Seconds later, a fine-ass red bone with long, flowing black hair emerged, walking toward me in a long leather trench coat that was tied at the waist and matching black leather stiletto boots.

"Is this you?" she stopped in front of me and asked, showing me a picture of myself.

"Unless you were sent by the Feds to arrest me for something I've done in the past or are here to kill me, it is." The picture, which had been taken in the joint, was one of me I had sent Hammer.

"Well, I'm not a cop, and I'm definitely not a killer. Heard you were, though."

"Can't believe everything you hear, cutie."

"I don't. But I do believe some things, especially coming from a reliable source. Hammer is a reliable source. Now, are those your bags?" She looked down at my belongings that were resting on the concrete.

"Yeah, they are." I reached to pick up my duffle bag.

"I got it. Just follow me to the car." She grabbed my duffle bag and started walking. We got to the car where she pressed a button on her keychain, causing the trunk to lift. She placed my duffle bag inside. Then she looked at me and smiled with a beautiful set of pearly whites. "By the way, I'm Keisha; and I've heard a helluva lot about you, Korey," she said before walking over to the passenger's side to open the door for me like I was a king she'd been sent to cater to.

"Well, Keisha. I just hope that whatever you've heard about me is all good."

"Good is like beauty. It's in the eye of the beholder," she replied.

I took a seat inside, and she shut the door. Keisha hopped inside the car and ignited the engine, which caused the 50 Cent CD that was playing earlier when she pulled up to start playing through the high-amped speakers. "This is your brother's CD, not mine. I like rap, but not a lot. I was told you love Stevie Wonder. Is that correct?" she asked, retrieving something from the console.

"Stevie Wonder's my favorite," I confirmed, trying to figure her out in my head.

"Mine too." She hit a button on the CD player, causing the 50 Cent CD to eject. "I think Mr. Wonder's a musical genius! How about this, Korey?" She put the CD that she'd retrieved inside the CD player. Seconds later, "Ribbon in the Sky" was making love to my eardrums.

"Now that's what I'm talking about." I nodded, looking over and into her eyes. They were a very pretty light brown, and I thought it very sexy that her eyebrows were arched sexy thin.

"You like that, huh?" She smiled, reminding me of a lighter version of the model Tyra Banks: very, very beautiful. I couldn't believe I was sitting next to such a beauty. But here I was.

"I love it."

"Again, your brother told me you would. He told me you would love this as well." She untied her coat at the waist, then zipped it down. She opened it up while we were still in the bus station's parking lot. Thank God no one could see inside this Lexus because of the heavy, dark tint on the windows. A nice, healthy set of double-D perky titties greeted my eyes, eyes that hadn't seen tits up close and personal in years! I bit down on my bottom lip in admiration of her very lovely set of twins. She reached for my hand and guided it gently over them. They were warm and soft as the loveliest cotton. She felt my nervousness.

"You like how soft my breasts are, Korey?" she asked, looking into my eyes and continuing to guide my hand farther down.

"What man wouldn't like how soft your tits are?"

"I know it's your first day home, playboy. But relax. Relax and finger this pussy," she said, gapping her legs and placing my hand between her soft, smooth thighs.

I thought before I dared to react. The guy who taught me "hate destroys the hater" also taught me that men leaving prison have got to stop wanting to fuck the first woman we meet. He taught me that you should take your time and get to know a woman first, and let her get to know you, so that something other than a "fleshy" relationship can surface, something everlasting like love. Having practiced and practiced and practiced self-control, I reluctantly removed my hand from between Keisha's warm, soft thighs.

"I'm a'ight right now, Keisha," I told her.

She cocked her head, surprised. "Dayum. You sure?" She gave me one of those "you're not gay, are you?" type of looks.

"Yeah, I'm straight. Just wanna take it slow right now. That's all."

"Your brother seemed to think that this is what you wanted."

"There's a lot about me that my brother don't know. People change. You are a very beautiful woman, though. What do you do for a living?"

"Well, thank you." She blushed. "I'm an attorney. I'm sure your brother will tell you all about me." She pulled out of the bus station's lot and hit the road. "One thing's for sure: he's got an ass kicking coming to his crazy ass!"

"Why is that?" I looked over at her pretty face and smiled.

"'Cause his ass knows I could have been doing something else. Instead, he coerced me to come pick you up, dressed like this! That's why!"

"Yeah, that's him. Still crazy."

"Well, that makes two of us," she shot back, then turned the volume up on the Stevie Wonder CD.

After riding for about twenty minutes and vibing to that Stevie, we pulled into this nice-ass middle-class neighborhood and drove up to the driveway of this big two-story brick home. Parked outside was a milky white Corvette with chrome rims, a gray BMW, and a black Range Rover.

"Well, Korey. We're here," Keisha said, shutting the engine off.

We both stepped out. She popped the trunk and retrieved my belongings.

"I'll take those, Keisha," I said, reaching for my property.

She dodged my attempt. "Told you, your brother sent me to take care of you. So I got this."

"Take care of me?" I chuckled. "What am I? A kid?"

"I don't know," she replied, looking down at my crotch area. "Your brother sent a real woman, and you didn't respond. Not like most men would, anyway."

She walked inside, smiling, with me following close behind.

# Chapter 3

## *I Got a Surprise for You*

"Killa muthafuckin' Korey! My nig is home. Oh, shit! What's up, dawg?" Hammer greeted me with open arms the moment I walked through the door behind Keisha.

"What is up, bruh?" I embraced him. I had never seen him smile as hard as he was smiling. Keisha walked past us, shaking her head and smiling at us carrying on.

"Man, it's good to see my dawg," he said, justifying his reason for cheesing so hard, and he hugged me again.

"Good to see you too, bruh. I didn't think we were ever gonna get out of the joint."

"Me either, dawg. Guess them crackas felt sorry for a mu'fucka."

"They should have. How you gon' give out twenty, thirty, forty years, and in some cases life, to cats who were petty-ass coke dealers? C'mon, bruh, you know they were wrong from the start. We weren't mu'fuckin' kingpins!"

"Well, fuck them." Hammer waved that subject off with a dismissive wave of his hand. "We're home now. And, dawg, it's on. I'm telling you!"

"Word, bruh?"

"That's on my solid, my nig. Check this out, though," Hammer said out the side of his mouth, not too loud. "Did KeKe take care of you?"

I looked around for signs of Keisha, but I didn't see her. She had disappeared into another room in this huge, spacious house. "In what way you mean that?"

"You know what way I mean." He poked my chest with his index finger, smiling. "Did she give you some of that wet, wet?"

"Nah, bruh." I shook my head. "I'm straight."

"What? What'chu mean, you straight?" Hammer looked at me like I'd lost my mind.

"I just got out, man. Plus, I don't know shorty like that!"

"Killa. Killa Korey, man. Stop it!"

"I'm serious, yo. I gotta take my time—"

"Take your time?" Hammer interrupted, locking eyes with me. "Are you kidding me? My nig, we took our time when that judge dropped twenty on us! It's time now to take our throne! And what's a king without a fine-ass queen helping him do that, my nig?"

"All of that will come, bruh. Once I get me a job and feel how shit moving out here."

"Once you get a job?" Hammer backhanded the side of my head, cutting me off like I said something totally stupid! "Look around, my nig. Does it look like I work for somebody? If I don't work for nobody, there is no way my partner in fucking crime and brother is gonna work for somebody out here! Are you kidding me or what, K?"

"So what'chu saying? Apparently you know something I don't."

"I do, trust me. But first, I need for you to meet somebody."

"Who?"

"You'll see." Hammer placed his arm around my shoulder and walked me upstairs to a huge master bedroom, where I saw a fine redbone who looked just like KeKe. She was sitting on the edge of a queen-sized bed, touching buttons on a remote she had pointing in the direction of a huge wide-screen television mounted on a wall directly in front of the foot of the bed. On the screen was *Kings of New York,* which was Hammer's favorite movie back in the day. He and his girl must've been watching it together before KeKe and I pulled up.

"Kolanda, sweetheart. C'mere a minute." Hammer motioned with his head to the beauty sitting on the bed. "Sweetheart, you know who this green-eyed cat is?" he asked her, smiling and pointing at me.

"Of course. That's your brother, Killa Korey," she replied, revealing a healthy smile. She was wearing an all-white skin-tight full-body suit. It revealed every single curve God gave her body. It didn't take me having twenty-twenty vision to see and know that she and Keisha were twins. The only visible difference was the way they were wearing their hair. Keisha's was long and hanging down to the middle of her back. Kolanda had hers high up in a ponytail that came down to her buttocks. My dawg Hammer had really scored a beauty with this one. "How could I not know who this guy is after you have shown me countless pictures of the two of you in prison together?" Kolanda said further after looking me over.

"I know, right, sweetheart?" Hammer shot back, still cheesing from ear to ear. He was just glad to see me out of the joint and home with him.

"Right." She nodded. "Korey, you are all my husband talks about."

"Husband?" I interrupted her, surprised. "What'chu mean, husband? You married?" I looked at Hammer and asked.

"I was gonna wait to tie the knot until you came home, dawg, but my baby insisted that we marry without delay. I married her my first day home. We went straight to the courthouse and handled our business."

"Sure did. I wasn't taking any chances with this one here, Korey!" Kolanda locked her arm with Hammer's in an intimate fashion and blushed.

"Hey, it is what it is. Congratulations, though, bruh. I'm happy for the two of you. And, Kolanda, it's a pleasure meeting you. I know you're making my brother real happy!"

"Well, thank you, Korey. And I bet you made my sister reeeal happy!" she said with her eyes checking out my crotch area. "Where is KeKe anyway?"

"She's downstairs," Hammer told her.

Kolanda left us to go find her. Hammer placed his arm around my shoulder and walked me over to a bar that was also inside this huge master bedroom. "I got a surprise for you, my nig," he whispered.

"What kind of surprise?"

"Just have a seat and, tell me, what will it be? Brown or white?" He went behind the bar where there was nothing but bottles of liquor. All kinds.

"I'm good on the liquor. Just give me some OJ on ice."

"OJ? On ice?" Hammer folded his eyebrows and looked at me strangely. "My nig, it's your first day home. You better take a drink wit'cha dawg. Now, what will it be, Killa? Brown or white?" He held up two bottles.

"I don't drink anymore, bruh."

"I didn't ask you to get drunk, Killa! All I'm asking you to do is sip on one with your dawg. Besides, you're gonna need a drink after I show you what that surprise is. Now, what will it be, playa?"

"OJ on ice. That's my final."

"You trippin'." He grabbed me a clear glass, put some ice cubes inside it, and poured me what he had that was nonalcoholic. "How about this grapefruit juice?"

"That'll do."

"Here's to you being home, my nig. I love you!" We touched glasses then downed our drinks. I saw him look past me all of a sudden, a sign that someone was approaching. I turned around and, lo and behold, it was KeKe wearing a full-body black silk spandex pant-suit with black leather knee-high stiletto boots. *Lord, have mercy!* I said silently. *This woman drop-dead gorgeous!* I then silently began praying for strength!

"Excuse me a second, Korey. I need to speak with Hammer," KeKe said, stepping behind the bar and inter-rupting our moment of toasting to my freedom.

"No problem."

She stepped to Hammer and began whispering some-thing in his ear. As she was doing so, he looked at me and smiled, then looked back down, then at me again. He whispered something in her ear after a few seconds of her speaking in his. I knew they were talking about me. I felt it. She then walked away without looking at me. I turned my head to see what that booty looked like in that outfit of hers. That thang was wiggling and jiggling profusely! She had to be wearing a thong!

"My nig, my nig, my nig! What in the hell has gotten into you?" Hammer said, hitting his fist in his palm. "Did you see all of that?"

"I saw it," I replied. "Who am I, Stevie Wonder?"

"Nah, but you act like you don't have a dick between your legs, Killa!"

"You trippin', yo." I waved him off with my hand.

"I'm dead serious, my nig! Keisha was gonna give you the pussy!"

"Told you I don't know shorty like that."

"Don't matter, dawg! I sent her to you. You my dawg, my partner in crime, my brother! You know I wouldn't send any chick at you knowing you just got out fresh and clean. Do you know what I had to do to even get her to come at you like she did?" Hammer said then paused to look me in the eyes.

"What'chu do, pay her?" I took a guess.

"Pay her? Keisha and my wife got cake, dawg! They don't need money! I had to make a deal with her."

"You had to make a deal with her?"

"Yeah, my nigga. I had to make a deal with her. But I'll share that with you later. Listen, though, Killa. Keisha grade A, my nig. She's not like them hood hoes we used to holla at back in the day, chicks who'll fuck for nothing! Her pussy hasn't been tatted with all type of niggas' dicks! Feel me? She has only had one lover, my nig. He was a white cat who recently broke her heart and shit when she found out he had an affair on her ass! You know how us men do, dawg, be cheating and shit, not realizing we got a good thing 'til it's gone! Now, she's feeling like a slut because she normally doesn't expose herself like she did to you. I'm disappointed with you on this one, Killa!"

"Hey, Ham, like I said, I don't know her, and she doesn't know me. Not like that, anyhow. Maybe we'll get to know each other later. I mean, what's the rush?"

"No rush. She's just a little embarrassed, that's all. Anyways, put this up." Hammer changed the subject, turning from me to do something.

"Put what up?" I shot back, seeing him looking into a drawer attached to the bar.

"This. Put this up." He handed me a white envelope.

"What's this, bruh?" I asked.

"DPs, what'chu think? Now get to counting because that ain't shit. I got something else to show you."

I knew from Hammer saying that DPs were in this envelope that he was speaking in code like we used to do when we were street hustling prior to our incarceration. DPs stood for Dead Presidents, as in a lot of cash! I opened the envelope and couldn't believe my damn eyes. "Man, how much bread is this?"

"Twenty."

"Whut?" I looked at him like "where in the hell you get this kind of cake from?"

"Killa, dawg, that ain't shit!" He picked up on my facial expression. "I told you, for the surprise I have for you, your ass shoulda took a drink. I know it's your first day home, but your brother been working, baby. And, you right on time. Now put that little bit of cake away and follow me."

"Little bit of cake?" I repeated to my brother. "Man, you know how long it's been since I had this much bread in my hands?"

"Dawg, that ain't shit but something for you to go shopping with tonight. Trust me."

# Chapter 4

## *I'm Not Trying to Go Back to the Joint*

I placed the twenty Gs that Hammer had given me inside my front pocket and followed Hammer to a room right across from the one we were in. This room was nearly vacant except for having a well-made queen-sized bed, a ceiling fan, and a large-screen floor-model television and entertainment system. Hammer shut the door behind us and led me to a huge walk-in closet where there was a very large safe.

Hammer spun the combination lock to open it. "Take a peep at this shit, Killa Korey."

I squatted to look inside. "Damn! What's that? Keys of coke?"

"Nah, dawg. That's her big brother, heroin! The same shit that made Nicky Barnes and Frank Lucas and them cats filthy rich back in the day. My nigga, we about to make a whole lot of cash! Matter fact, as you can see, I've already started! And, Korey, yo, business is booming like fuck! Why you think I couldn't wait for you to come home, yo?"

"Hammer. Hold on, bruh. What do you mean, 'we'? I'm not going back to the joint, Hammer! I can't fucking do that place for the rest of my life. I can't, yo." I shook my head and put on my serious face.

"Neither can I. We just gotta play our cards right, K—"

"There's no such thing anymore," I cut in. "The Feds got it on lock out here! It ain't the same. Cats telling on their own mothers to avoid going to the joint, Hammer. Are you kidding me?"

"You ain't telling. I'm not telling. So we straight. Fuck the Feds!"

"Nah, bruh. Fuck going back to the joint!" I locked eyes with my brother to show my seriousness.

"Killa Korey, you killing me with this 'I ain't trying to go back to the joint' crap! Listen, man. You know what I'm not trying to go back to? I'm not trying to go back to hustling on a block for chump change! Shit, I went to the joint broke. We both did after them lawyers drained what little we had! And, K, I damn sure ain't trying to work for white folks who don't give a damn about a nigga who just came home from the joint with a felony on his record. Man, fuck that!"

"We don't give a damn about our people either, bruh, if we gon' sell this shit to them and throw rocks back at the penitentiary!" I countered, trying to get my dawg to think.

"Korey, when we were selling drugs, which one of us ever put a gun to a buyer's head and demanded that he or she purchase our work? Which one of us ever did some shit like that, huh?"

"I know where you're going with this, but—"

"Nah, keep it real, dawg," Hammer cut me off. "What I'm saying is, babies are not buying this shit. Grown folk are, Korey! Grown folk make their own got'damn decisions, playa! If they want that work, it's their own choice. We just happen to have what mu'fuckas want out here to make them feel good. And I'm trying to get it to them!" Hammer shut his safe. "You in or out?"

"I'm through with the streets, bruh. And you can call me soft, stupid, whatever. But next to me not going back, I can't leave my little daughter hanging again to grow up without her father."

Knock, knock, knock! Someone interrupted, banging on the door. "Ham, telephone. It's important!" Hammer's wife yelled.

"I'm on my way right now, sweetheart!" he shouted back before standing directly in front of me and placing his hands on my shoulders. "Killa Korey," he said, not too loud, "you are my brother, for whom I would run through hell with gasoline drawers on if need be and burn like a mu'fucka. I trust you. And, dawg, I love you. I'm not asking you to get knee-deep back into the streets like we were before doing time. All I'm asking you to do is honor those nine words we took our Partnerz in Crime oath on. Remember those nine words, my nigga? 'I will back my brother's play, come what may.'" Hammer reminded me, counting the words on his fingers as he uttered them. "We promised one another back in the days, you and me, that we would never go back on those words. I'm just asking you to be there for me. Who the hell else am I supposed to trust out here?" Hammer said, then walked away to open the door where his wife was waiting with the telephone in her hand. He took it and walked into their bedroom.

"Sorry to disturb what the two of you were discussing, but Hammer was expecting this call."

"Oh, no problem. I'm cool. By the way . . . ahh, Kolanda, right?"

"Right."

"You don't have to call me Killa Korey. Just Korey, that's fine."

"Oh, okay, my husband didn't tell me that." She smiled. "Well, Kooooorey," she said, stretching my name, "you know my sister is downstairs waiting on you, right?"

"She is?"

"Mm-hmm." She nodded. "She's taking you to the mall."

"Ay, Korey, c'mere," Hammer yelled, interrupting his wife talking to me.

I walked into his bedroom with his wife not too far behind me. "What's up?"

"C'mere a minute. I got something for you." Hammer motioned with his hand for me to come over to the bar. As I walked over, I saw him retrieve something from the same drawer he'd handed me the twenty Gs from. "I forgot to give you this. This is your phone. Please, man, whatever you do, don't go anywhere in this city without it. I gotta be able to keep contact with you, you feel me? At all times."

"I gotcha."

"Only my wife, KeKe, and I have your number. Speaking of KeKe—"

"I know," I cut him off. "She's downstairs waiting on me. Your wife told me already."

"Precisely, my nigga. She's gonna take you shopping, which I know you can't wait to do."

"Hell yeah. I gotta get out of these prison threads and boots."

"Well, you got enough loot to buy whatever you want. You heard me? So do you, yo. My wife and I will be taking care of some biz while y'all doing that."

"Cool. But peep this, Ham, we got to have a serious talk."

"'Bout what, K?"

"What you're into. Man, it's too much, too fast. I don't like it."

"Man, K. Forget about that for now. We'll talk about it later. Just go have yourself a ball shopping, my nig. And look, yo, I love you, man. Nothing means more to me right now than you being home and us being together, living like we supposed to. Like kings! I don't see nothing else right now. Nothing, my nigga!"

"I hear you. But, like I said, I ain't ever going back to the joint. I hate that fucking place. So I plan to snail pace every move I make."

"Nothing wrong with taking it slow. You know I feel you, K. Now, fuck what I'm into right now and go have yourself a ball at the mall! And I'll see you and Ke when y'all return."

# Chapter 5

## *Shopping*

Keisha drove me to South Park Mall. She talked to Kolanda damn near the whole way there while I listened to my man Stevie Wonder.

I must've blown at least five stacks while shopping. I bought all type of Jordan sneaks and matching Jordan Retro II herringbone jackets with the Jordan Retro II pants. I bought Timberland boots, the latest jeans and white tees, and a black leather quarter-length coat that tied at the waist.

"Now that really looks good on you, Korey," Keisha complimented me when she saw me try on that black leather coat and pop the collar.

"What about this?" I tried on an all-black nylon Adidas sweat suit with the black old-school shell-toe Adidas, Run-D.M.C. style.

"Hell yeah!" Keisha said, nodding her head. "Try the money green one on with the white stripes and the matching green Adidas. Not the money green leather shell-toe ones. The suede green Adidas with the white stripes," she said. Keisha had an eye for style.

"You like this money green one, Keisha?" I tried it on for her to see me in it as she recommended. When she saw me in that money green, her facial expression changed. Her eyes squinted, and she bit down on her bottom lip and shook her head slowly like she was thinking something freaky. "Let's go before all the girls who work here be throwing their panties at you!" She reached for my arm to lead me out like I was her man.

"You crazy, Ke," I told her, smiling. "Keisha, peep this," I said, gently placing my arm around her neck. Keisha is a shorty, like five feet five inches. I'm six feet two inches. "If you had a li'l girl, what would you get her for Christmas?" I asked, thinking of my daughter, Olivia, and seeing that it was near that time of the year. Christmas regalia was being displayed and hanging everywhere inside this mall. And Christmas carols were being played in every department store we entered.

"What do you mean by li'l girl? I mean, how old is she?"

"Thirteen."

"Thirteen? I don't know, Korey. Some money. Just give her some money."

"Some money?"

"Yeah, that way you won't be disappointed if you brought her something that she could do without! Girls are different these days than they were prior to you getting locked up. You never know what they want, Korey."

"You got a point."

"However, some jewelry wouldn't hurt. Girls love jewelry. And, guess what?"

"What's that?"

"There's a Kay Jewelers store right there." She pointed ahead of us. We walked toward that store. While on our way, I took notice of a Victoria's Secret store. I saw European and chocolate mannequins in the window dressed in some sexy lingerie, which I loved seeing a woman in.

"Hold up a minute, Keisha. Let's step inside VS a minute. I need to grab something for someone special."

"Really, Korey?" Keisha suddenly gave me this jealous look.

"Yeah. Watch my bags a minute while I holla at VS personal."

"Wow, she that special?"

"I think she is." I kept it real. I went and made my purchase and we bounced. But Keisha put on like she didn't want to move all of a sudden, seeing that I made a purchase for a woman.

"Yo, c'mere with your pretty self." I pulled her close to me like we'd been intimately involved for years. "Why you curling your eyes all up at me and frowning like you mad at me? You a'ight? I just had to get a present for someone. It's all good, ma. Don't be making that pretty face of yours frown like that."

"I hear you. She must be really special for you to have it packaged with a nice red bow on top of the box!"

"She is."

She pushed me when I said that and she rolled her eyes at me. I put my arm back around her neck, and we walked into the jewelry store like girlfriend and boyfriend.

Keisha picked out a nice sky blue tennis bracelet for my daughter. Sky blue was her favorite color. I dropped $788 on that bracelet for her.

"I hope she likes it, Keisha," I said to her as we wrapped our shopping up and stepped out of Kay.

"Oh, I'm sure she will. Told you, girls love jewelry."

"Excuse me but, if you're wrong, Korey gon' spank you."

"Oooo, boy, don't say that. Hell, I might like it." She looked at me all sexy-like, biting her bottom lip.

"I bet you would," I shot back. I then smacked her on the booty, but not too hard. It was soft and wiggled in my hand.

"Dayum, K. You and Ke back already, my nig?" Hammer looked up and saw Keisha and me entering his bedroom, where he and his wife were at the bar counting more money than I'd ever seen.

"Yep. And I can finally get out of them prison clothes. Never to put them on again!"

"I know that's right, Korey," Hammer's wife said, smiling and counting money.

Then Hammer looked at Keisha and said, "Ke, count the rest of this money for me with Kolanda while I holla at Korey about something important, will you?"

"You gon' pay me?" Keisha put one hand on her hip and held out the other hand, palm up.

Hammer sucked his teeth and playfully pushed Keisha at her shoulder. "Stop tripping before I body slam you up in here in front of Korey."

"Yeah, right. Whateva."

I laughed along with Hammer's wife. "I know, Korey. They a trip. They stay at it," Hammer's wife said, shaking her head while counting mad loot.

Hammer wrapped his arms around Keisha quickly in a bear hug fashion.

"Kolanda, will you get your husband!" she said, while Hammer had her up in the air, squeezing her.

"Ham, please leave her alone so we can get this done."

Hammer put her down. He stuck his chest out and spread his arms. "I'm the man up in here!"

"Whateva! You ain't nothing but a big kid!" Keisha said, then went to help her sister finish counting the money.

"Peep this, though, Korey." Hammer placed his arm over my shoulder and walked me into the same room he had walked me into earlier, the room with the safe in the closet. "You can shower and dress after this, because you, me, my wife, and Keisha going out to eat later. Shit, it only a quarter after ten," Hammer said, looking at his watch. "We got plenty of time. Check this out. Guess what just happened, my nig?"

"What's that?" I gave Hammer my undivided attention.

"Just had to put a nigga in serious check."

"'Bout what, yo?"

"Looking at Kolanda all sideways."

"Word?"

"On my solid. Pulled my burner and everything!"

"What happened?"

"She and I had to handle some business over on the west side, Burger King off Freedom Drive, you feel me? While inside handling my biz and shit, a nigga looks at my babe and shit, seeing me with her, and was like, 'Dayum, that bitch got a fat ass!' That's when I looked at this cat and was like, 'Nigga, what the fuck you say about my wife's ass?'"

"Word up, Ham? I know you blanked on that cat," I said. Like me back in the day, Hammer had a quick temper and would pull his burner and shoot someone for trying to play him for a sucka. I saw his temper hadn't changed.

"Before I knew it, my burner was at this cat's head! 'Bitch-ass nigga, I will split your fuckin' coconut for disrespecting my wife!' I told him. He cowered down and apologized. I was so close to shooting that nigga, though, bruh."

"Man, these cats out here bold like that now, yo?"

"This one was. Until I fuckin' put the fear of God in his bitch ass!"

"Man, I gotta be seriously careful. Especially if I'm out with Keisha. Cats was checking her out tonight at the mall, though. Can't blame 'em, either. Hell, she stack like that! Long as cats don't say or do something out the way."

"Yo, dawg, them girls got onions!" Hammer exclaimed, referring to Keisha's and his wife's bodies.

"And bell peppers!" We both laughed. "Check this, though, Hammer. What's with Keisha?" I whispered.

"What'chu mean?" He shrugged his shoulders and looked toward the door.

"Man, she started tripping on me in the mall!"

"About what, dawg?"

"I went and bought something out of Victoria's Secret. And she put on like she was jealous."

"She's that type, K. Real sensitive, my nig. She been hurt. Told you that already, though."

"Yeah, but you didn't elaborate."

"I'ma get around to telling you about it. But Keisha was fuckin' with a white cat. An attorney like her. He probably was the first to suck her pussy and fuck her. Had her head spinning and shit, feel me? She busted his ass in his office kissing and making out with his secretary and shit."

"What?" I responded in disbelief and shock. *As fine and sweet as Keisha is, how could any man mistreat her?*

"She's still scared behind that shit, man. You gotta be real easygoing and shit with her. She good people, though, K."

"I can see that. Check this, though, Ham. This cat you pulled your burner on, you think we'll see him again?" I began to slightly worry. "You know Charlotte ain't but so big. I would hate for us to be in the city and run into somebody we got beef with." I told Hammer that because I was the type who liked to handle my business right where it started, so that I wouldn't have to be confronted with it again. I knew Hammer was the same way.

"He had an out-of-town license plate. We won't see him again. The nigga was so shook, he couldn't wait to get on about his business. If we do happen to see this cat again, he better not even look my way. I'll drop his ass on the spot!"

"Yo, it's crazy out here." I shook my head, feeling where Hammer was coming from. "I'ma take my shower and get out of these prison clothes, Hammer," I told him.

"A'ight, K. Do that. Holla when you get yourself together."
We heard someone coming up the stairs. Hammer peeped
out, then said in nearly a whisper, "Here comes Keisha. I'll
holla at'cha."

"Oh, hey, Ke. What's up?"

"You left your bags downstairs. So I decided to bring
them up for you."

"Thanks, Ke. Got caught up talking to my brother." I
took the bags from her hand.

"No problem," she said, then turned to leave.

"Wait. This is for you." I handed her the gift I bought
from Victoria's Secret.

"The Victoria's Secret box? It's mine? Are you serious?"
She grabbed it, smiling. "You bought this for me?"

"Of course I did. Open it."

She opened her gift: a hot pink upper-thigh-length
nightie with SEXY written in white in big cursive letters
across the breast area.

"Ohhh," she said softly, holding it up for viewing.
"Thank you, Korey. You didn't have to do this." She gave
me a hug.

"You're welcome. You got another one in there."

"I seeeee." This one was royal purple with pink cursive
letters that read SPECIAL. "I really appreciate this, Korey.
Thank you." She hugged me again with watery eyes.

"I know that I don't know you like that personally,
Keisha. But I do know enough to know that you're special.
And I would be a cold-blooded liar if I didn't tell you that
you're sexy. You got that one hands down!"

"You so crazy!" She showed all her pearly whites and
playfully backhanded my shoulder.

"I'm serious, ma. You really are."

"You gon' make me cry, boy."

"And you gon' make me take a cold shower." I looked
her up and down as if searching for a flaw on this per-

fectly fashioned body of a goddess of a woman. From her cute face to her voluptuous breasts, small waist, curvy hips on down, she was a gift for sore eyes to behold. She was flawless.

"Well, I'll let you shower now. Bye." She waved her hand at me, then turned to leave. My eyes went straight to that soft, luscious booty of hers. She looked back and caught me checking it out. She cracked a smile and shook her head.

# Chapter 6

## *You Fly*

Having showered and gotten dressed, I felt so much better and free now that I was out of those prison-issued clothes. I was rocking a money green satin Adidas suit with the white stripes and matching green shell-toe Adidas sneaks with white stripes. I was smelling like the manly aroma of Eternity for Men.

"Yeah, nigga, you fly," Hammer said, stepping in unannounced as I was getting myself together.

"What up, bruh?" I turned from checking myself out in the mirror to acknowledge his presence.

"Chillin'," Hammer replied. "A nigga see you still love that old-school shit," he said, referring to my outfit and sneaks.

"For sho you know me."

"Like the back of my hand." Hammer bent over and, with his finger, wiped his white Air Force Ones, which complemented his saggin' dark blue jeans and button-down shirt, which was white with blue and light gray stripes.

"Speaking of me being fly tonight, you shinning yourself!" I told him. Hammer resembled comedian and actor Chris Rock! He had brown skin and was six feet two inches. He was slim and rocking a low cut with a sharp edge up. We both had our hair cut short. Mine just had waves all in it.

"Well, you know, li'l some-somethin'," Hammer popped his collar and walked directly over to me with thug swag. "Peep this before you get ready to bounce."

"What's up?" I leaned my ear toward his mouth as if he was about to tell a secret.

"My nigga, you done fucked Keisha's head all up!"

"What make you say that, dawg?"

"The gift you brought her. She's in my bedroom now, showing it to my wife, cheesing from ear to ear! Her ass love surprises! The good ones."

"Word, yo?" I smiled, glad that I had made her day with the gift I purchased for her.

"Hell yeah! That's what I'm talking about, Korey! Man, listen, since Keisha's ex-boyfriend broke her heart, she hasn't been herself. So to see her smiling makes me feel good."

"What do you mean by she hasn't been the same? Dude messed her up like that, yo?"

"She just be doing a lot of crazy stuff with me when her and my wife aren't working on cases and shit."

"Like what?"

"Drinking and even blowing blunts with a nigga. She's not really the drinking and smoking type."

"Shorty probably depressed, that's all. She'll snap out of it."

"It's crazy because every time she gets drunk, she get into her feelings and start crying over what that cracka did to her! And between you and me, my nigga . . ." Hammer paused and got real close to me. He lowered his voice and said, "She wants me to fuck this cat up, K."

"Damn, her heart ain't nothing to play with," I said in response, shaking my head.

"Nah, it isn't."

"So you're gonna see this cat?"

"In due time I will. Besides that, Keisha is just like her sister. One of the best chicks you'll ever meet. That's why, Korey, I couldn't wait for you to come home so that the two of you could click up! I mean, that's if you're not planning on getting back with your daughter's mom. I know that was your heart and shit before we left the streets. You were crazy in love with her. You two still in love, K?"

I shook my head. "Man, believe it or not, I haven't heard from Shamika in a while."

"You kidding." Hammer looked at me, surprised. He knew the love Shamika and I had was strong. She and I were together every single day and night when I wasn't in the streets hustling. She and I grew up in the same neighborhood and were dating way before I thought about putting drugs in my hands and getting all into the streets. She was the one person who always told me she didn't like what I was doing, but I continued hustling anyway.

"She just stopped writing me, bruh," I carried on, but not really wanting to talk about it. "I guess she found another cat to treat her right. You know how it is. When the cat's away, the mice will play."

"It is what it is. Life goes on. You were good to Shamika, though. I just knew if no one else would be down with you through thick and thin, she would! Man, you spoiled that girl!"

"I just charge it to the game, bruh." I waved off continuing to discuss her. I walked over to my dresser and retrieved what I had brought my daughter. "How you like this, bruh?" I removed the sparkling sky blue tennis bracelet from the box.

"Yo, my nigga, this is nice!" Hammer said after I handed it to him to check out.

"I know, right? Keisha helped me pick it out. You know when I see my baby girl, I can't come empty-handed!"

"Man, I know that's right." Hammer handed it back to me. "How much that joint run you?"

"Almost eight hun'."

"Now how many niggas you know fresh out the joint spending eight of them thangs on their kid, K? That's why I say we gotta make as much money as we can. There's no way you can look out for your daughter like I know you want to without them DPs."

I nodded in agreement.

"Aren't you glad you got a brother in high places?" Hammer placed his arm over my shoulder and said while looking me in the eyes. "Man, we kings. Partnerz in Crime kings. We supposed to have it all!"

Hammer and I wrapped up our convo and stepped downstairs where Keisha and his wife were in the living room, kicking it.

"Dayum, it took the two of you long enough," Keisha said, ready to go. "I'm starving!" She was wearing a green and white Boston Celtics jersey skirt with matching Air Nikes. Hammer's wife had on a black-and-white Brooklyn Nets jersey skirt with the matching Air Nikes. They both had their hair pulled back in ponytails, looking like don divas. Boss chicks, if you will.

"Y'all look good!" I told the both of them, looking at Keisha first, then over at Kolanda.

They both blushed and replied in unison, "Thank you."

"Now, where are we going out to eat, Ham, babe?" his wife asked, sliding into a white quarter-length mink. Keisha was putting on a black one. *These girls got style for real,* I silently acknowledged. I couldn't believe I was actually fresh out the joint and in such wonderful company. Being with my brother and two hotties was a dream come true!

"Geneva's Chicken and Waffles. My nigga love fried chicken. Right, Korey?" Hammer said.

But Keisha cut in before I could say yes. "Why you always gotta use the N-word so much, Hammer? Dayum! It's N this, and N that!"

"'Cause I can do that." Hammer slightly pushed Keisha in her back as we were going out the door. "Now what?" he playfully provoked her to do something about it.

"I'm just saying. Stop using that word so much. It's negative."

"'Stop using that word so much, it's negative,'" Hammer repeated her, being sarcastic. We all got inside the Range Rover. Hammer's wife drove while he sat on the passenger side. Keisha and I sat in the back.

"I swear, you look so beautiful," I leaned over and whispered in Keisha's ear.

"Thank you. You're looking very handsome yourself, Korey."

"'Preciate it. By the way, thank you for being there for me earlier, coming to pick me up and all and taking me shopping. I really thank you for that."

"No problem."

"And, if you don't mind, or you're not too busy tomorrow, I would like for you to take me to see my daughter."

"We can do that," she said with a nod before Hammer drowned out anything else I may have wanted to say to her by turning up the volume on 50 Cent's "21 Questions." I rested my head back on the seat's headrest and silently thanked God that I was finally out of the joint. And, although I learned a helluva lot in that place of solitude about myself and others, it's a place that dehumanizes you and fucks with your head. If you're not strong, you'll come out of that place of torture and horror like an animal! Thank God I kept my sanity.

# Chapter 7

## *Crazy*

### Keisha

I had to be a crazy bitch to come out of my comfort zone and "well-behaved girl" demeanor to please my brother-in-law, Hammer. But since it was his boy Korey's first day home, I did something I knew my father would not have approved of. I compromised my womanhood by fucking exposing my goods to a stranger! My father would have beaten my ass for that. Where was my integrity? Where was my respect for myself and this precious body of mine?

Speaking of my father, God rest his soul in peace, he wouldn't dare allow my sister and me to think about dating until we first graduated college and scored good jobs that would allow us to hold our own in the event something happened to him. He wasn't the average Joe Blow father. He was a gentle soul, but a gangster, who did everything in his power to see to it that my sister and I had everything we could ever want, except boyfriends too early in life. Guys would beg for my name and number on a regular growing up. I would lie and say I was a Catholic who was studying to be a nun! Oh, the lies a good girl will tell to please her loving father. With my dad having eyes all over the little town of Matthews, North Carolina, where my sister and I were raised, there was no way I could get caught slipping, trying to be grown up before my time with guys. My dad would have beat the hell out of me and dared me to call the police! Half of the police force in Matthews was on his payroll! So my sister and I kept our legs shut, tight if I may add.

I was thirty-eight years old now. I was thirty-four years old when I got my cherry popped. Oh, how I was in love with Joshua Freeman. By the way, Josh was a tax attorney who worked for my father. I thought he was cute for a white guy. He thought I was the sexiest thing walking in Matthews. When he would be at our home discussing business with my dad, and I would be around, I would catch Josh sneaking peeps at my voluptuous ass in one of my short, tight dresses or skirts. But Josh wasn't stupid. He knew if he showed any sign of liking me around my dad, the chances of him continuing to be my dad's tax attorney would be terminated. Immediately! So Josh kept his hots for me on the low. And I kept my secret fantasy of him making love to me to myself. But when the Feds indicted my father for being one of the most feared and biggest drug dealers in Matthews and convicted him of the same after a nearly two-month jury trial, that's when Josh made his move.

My sister and I couldn't stomach our father receiving a life sentence! Josh was at the trial to offer his support. He was there to comfort my sister and me, which we needed after seeing our father escorted by marshals to federal prison. I had no idea that him comforting me would lead to us making love that very night. It was the first time I had ever had an orgasm. Josh made me feel good that night. I instantly fell in love. For nearly three years, he and I were in a serious relationship. Then I showed up at his job one day unannounced and caught him in his office, hugging and kissing his secretary!

That was the day I acted the fool. I took my keys and scratched up his brand spanking new Benz. I busted out all his windows and flattened all of his tires!

"Keisha, sis, I can't wait 'til my brother Korey comes home. I'm telling you he will make a good-ass man for you," my brother-in-law Hammer kept reminding me after seeing me day in and night out, stressed over my failed relationship with Josh.

Then that phone call came. Korey was out and at the bus station. Hammer asked me to do him a big favor. He wanted me to go scoop Korey up and treat him right. "Treat him right?" I repeated my brother-in-law, looking for clarity on what he meant by that.

"What I mean is wear a little somethin' somethin' that will make him feel good his first day home."

"Like what, Ham?"

"Like put on that leather Chanel trench coat with no bra and panties underneath. I swear my brother will get a kick out of that!"

"What I look like, Hammer? A fuckin' tramp? I ain't doing that!" I told him, especially since I had just come out of a relationship that had gone sour.

"Keisha, no one's saying you're a tramp. C'mon, you know I know you better than that. I'm just asking you to show my brother a good time. Shit, he's been in the joint twelve years! It will do him dayum good to touch a titty and play in a good pussy! Do that for me. Besides, you know you need some dick to cheer your ass up from what that punk-ass white boy did to you."

I didn't need Hammer going there, but he was so right. A girl was yearning for some much-needed affection. But I needed my brother-in-law to do something for me if I did what he was asking me to do for Korey.

"Okay, but I'ma need you to do me a favor as well when you think the time is right."

"Anything, you know that."

"I want you to catch up with Josh and fuck him up!"

"Dayum, why we gotta go there, though, Keisha? Let that cat be. He done went on. You gotta do the same, baby girl."

"I'm not saying kill him. But I want you to beat his ass real good for cheating on me."

"Look, Keisha, you know I'll do anything for you. But if I go and bust that cracka's bubble, it could cause all types of problems. Then guess what? My ass gon' be right back in prison and your sister will never forgive me for it!"

"You smart enough to handle business without leaving a trace of evidence. C'mon now. You know how to cover your tracks. My sister ain't got to know about this. I won't say shit to her about it, and that's my word of honor. So there you have it."

He looked at me like I was insane. "A'ight. Go handle your business with my brother, Killa Korey, and I'll let you know what I can do for you on that issue later."

"Oh, nooooo," I said. "Let me know if you gon' handle that for sure or not. We gotta lock that in right now! Don't even play me like that."

"No one is trying to play you."

"A'ight, then. Lock it in. Give a girl your word."

"I got'chu. Have I ever told you I would do something and didn't do it?"

"Never."

"Then don't trip over that cat who hurt you. But, Keisha, I really want you to think about what you're asking me to do."

"I know what I'm asking you to do, Hammer. Just get it done!"

Hammer was the brother I never had and the man my sister quickly fell head over heels for, surprisingly with our father's blessing. My father loved Hammer. He told my sister and me that Hammer was like a son to him and for us to embrace him like family. Kolanda did just that. So did I. But she fell in love and married his ass. I discovered from being around my brother-in-law that he was very loyal, loving, and protective, just like our father. And just like our father, he all about that G life. The way he talked about Killa Korey and how they used to go hard in the streets made me believe that Killa Korey had the same thug edge as my brother-in-law, which secretly I liked. That was one thing my sister and I had in common. We had a lot in common, but we both desired a man like our father. A G, hardworking, loving, rough around the edges, thuggish!

I made myself look as good as I could. My body was identical to Melyssa Ford's, curvy in all the right places. But not even a body like mine made Killa Korey rise to the occasion. But after a wonderful time together with him, absent a sexual encounter, he had me wanting to know more about his intriguing, handsome ass.

# Chapter 8

## *I Need a Man*

It was a little after 11:00 a.m. when I twisted and stretched my way out of my beauty sleep, thanks to my brother-in-law's high-amped speakers blasting. The bass from his speakers literally sent vibrations through my bed, interrupting a dream I was having where I was getting my pussy fingered.

> *You can find me in the club*
> *pocket full of bud*
> *Mommy, I got what'cha need*
> *Come give me a hug*

That's all I could hear my brother-in-law shouting. He was pumpin' and reciting the hell out of 50 Cent's "In Da Club" like his ass was having an early morning house party! He knew I didn't like it when he blasted his music like that, but still, he did it every weekend, saying that the reason he did it was to remind himself that he was no longer incarcerated and restricted from listening to his music at a volume he desired. He knew I liked sleeping late on the weekends because I worked like crazy five days a week. I swear, if I didn't have mad love for him, I would have rushed into his and my sister's bedroom and slapped his face as hard as I could and hauled ass!

I slipped into my leopard satin bedroom slippers that matched my leopard satin V-string panties and bra, and I walked over to my dresser where I viewed my reflection in the huge mirror attached to it. My hair was all over the place. I picked through it and fingered cold from my eyes, which had bags underneath them like I hadn't gotten any sleep. Well, I did, but I didn't.

I spent a great deal of time lying in bed thinking about what I wanted out of life. For some reason, hanging out and kicking it with Korey at the mall and at dinner made me focus more on my life. I had money. My dad made sure that my sister and I had enough of that to live on for a long time. My sister and I were civil law attorneys. We had clients up the ass! So money wasn't one of my issues. Neither was having a nice car. I had a BMW and a Mercedes. I stayed with my sister and her husband in this big house my father left us, but I had a condo uptown near my office on Fifth Street. What I didn't have was a real man! I didn't actually know how bad I really needed one until I drifted off to sleep shortly after coming in from dinner with Korey, my sister, and my brother-in-law.

I drifted off into a dream. In it, Korey had entered my bedroom and slid into my bed where I was lying on my side, enjoying the soothing air from my ceiling fan that put my body and mind in an extremely relaxed state.

*The central heat was at that "just right" temperature where it wasn't too hot. Just nice and cozy enough for me to sleep as I did nightly, in only panties and a bra. Korey slid into bed with me and, without saying a word, began softly kissing the back of my neck. While pecking my neck, he took and lifted my bra, freeing my tits that sprang forth like a jack-in-the-box. He gently caressed them one at a time until the nipples on both of them were hard as stone pebbles. I could feel his bare*

*chest touching the flesh of my back, while his muscular
arm that rested on top of my waist permitted him easy
access to play with areas of my body that my father
taught my sister and me were holy ground.*

*He reached for my hand and placed it on his manhood.
It was every bit of nine inches, thick, hard, and throbbing. I placed my mouth over it and began sucking him
off from the side. While I was bent over sucking Korey's
sweet lollipop from the side, he fingered me with my ass
up, doggie style.*

*I never had a dick the size of his in my mouth before. I
wanted to feel it inside me. "Fuck me. Please, fuck me,"
I told him after letting off his strongly erect dick. He told
me to turn around because he wanted to put his dick
inside me doggie style. I positioned myself in the position he so desired. He eased behind me, about to place
his manhood where I so desperately needed it to be.*

That was, until my brother-in-law's loud music awoke
me! "I need a man bad," was all I could say!

Now can you see why I wanted to slap the hell out of
my brother-in-law? I knew one thing: with me going
through with my end of the deal he and I made, he better
beat Josh's ass for me! For now, I couldn't wait to fulfill
Korey's wish of taking him to see his daughter, Olivia.

# Chapter 9

## *The Game Chose Me*

### Korey

That night, after having a very wonderful time out at dinner with my brother, his wife, and Keisha, I came in and crashed. I slept like a baby on that queen-sized soft mattress. It was far from the hard mattress the prison issued you to sleep on. Those mattresses make your whole body hurt.

Hammer woke me up at about 9:00 a.m. His wife had breakfast made. She fixed turkey sausage, scrambled eggs mixed with cheese, buttered toast with strawberry jam, and milk. Keisha was still in bed. Hammer rolled a blunt, fired it up after we ate, and asked me if I wanted to hit it.

"I'm cool," I told him.

He passed it to his wife. She hit it, passed it back to him, and left us alone. Hammer told me that he needed me to ride somewhere with him after he took a shower and got dressed.

I told him, "A'ight," and headed to the shower.

I peeped in Keisha's room before hopping in the shower. She was lying in bed on her stomach with the covers over her head, knocked out. I went and took my shower and threw on black and red Jordan sweats, with the matching Air Jordans.

By now, Keisha was up and moving about. I told her that Hammer and I were about to go somewhere and that I would call her phone later because I still wanted her to take me to see my daughter. Without saying anything, she placed her thumb up and nodded her head. I got the impression that she was not really a morning person. She was moving around slowly in her house robe and slippers and with her toothbrush in her mouth.

A little after twelve, Hammer and I stepped outside. We hopped into his milky white Corvette. The windows on it had heavy dark tint, and the rims were shiny chrome. It was the latest on the market. Hammer had it looking like a spaceship! Being that the sun was out and shining bright, the candy paint that reflected the sun's rays made his car sparkle that much harder.

"This joint fly, yo. No bullshit!" I highly admired it. Not to mention, Corvettes were my favorite type of car.

"You like it, K?"

"Man, Ham, I love this joint."

Before we could hop inside to take a seat, Keisha walked past us with tight lips. She rolled her eyes at Hammer. "You need to learn to play your music at a low volume when I'm trying to sleep!" she said, pushing Hammer on his shoulder as she walked past.

"Shut up before I put my brother on you."

"Whateva." She got into her BMW, shut the door hard, and burned rubber.

"Man, y'all a mess," I told Hammer. "Why is she upset, though, Ham?"

"She just need some dick, K. That's why you shoulda put that dick fresh out of prison on her last night!"

"You a mess, yo."

"Real talk, my nigga. I love my sister-in-law, don't get me wrong. But her ass need to be fucked! She hear me and her sister getting it in all the damn time. Shit, I keep this dick up in Kolanda! That's why I have to turn my music up loud in the house sometimes. Kolanda's a screamer!"

"So you actually think that's what she needs, huh, Ham?"

"Know so. Listen, man. Imagine how it was for us when we were in the joint and couldn't get no pussy. We were miserable as a mu'fucka. Women are the same way."

"You got a point," I agreed. God knows doing time was killing me, not being able to touch, kiss, and put this dick up in one.

We took a seat inside the car. That's when it hit me to ask my brother something I'd been wanting to ask him since he showed me his narcotics stash. "Hammer, I got something I wanna ask you. I have to."

"Then ask, Korey. What's up?" He gave me his undivided attention.

"I think I know the answer already, but until I hear it directly from your mouth, I won't know for sure."

"What's up?"

"The question is, are you back like knee-deep in the game? 'Cause, dawg, I mean, you haven't been out a whole year and you rolling like a mutha!"

Hammer started laughing when I asked that question. "K, man, your boy ain't faking. I'm trying to get filthy rich or, like my man 50 Cent say, 'die trying!'"

"So you knee-deep in this shit, huh?"

"I am. But, K. This time I didn't choose the game. It chose me. And, bruh, that's on my solid." Whenever Hammer and I said that something we said was on our "solid" that meant it could be supremely trusted. No exception.

"How so?" I asked, wanting to know. I had to know.

"It's sort of a long story. But when the Feds had me in Edgefield, South Carolina, I met an old man from

Matthews, North Carolina. He didn't have any homies on the compound, so I used to go up to his cell and kick it with him. You know how we do the older cats. We make sure they okay. Well, I used to help the old man out a lot. Like I would carry his commissary bags for him. I would help with his laundry and all that. Whenever the old man needed me, basically I was there. He told me that I was like the son he never had. He began sharing personal shit with me, like how he lost his beautiful wife giving birth to their twins. When he showed me his girls, man, I was in love! He ended up letting me write Kolanda. She and I hit it off immediately like it was meant to be. When she and Keisha would come see their father, Kolanda would call me out. Their father used to speak highly of me in their presence. He was good people, my nigga. I didn't know until later that he was one of the biggest drug dealers in Matthews! Pops was stacked like that, yo!"

"Word?" I interrupted.

"Dawg, that's on everything. Pops was knee-deep in this shit! The Feds gave him life! All type of niggas he helped out and shit snitched on him."

"Dayum!"

"Yeah, he was that dude," Hammer carried on. "He was also bad off sick, Korey. One night, he and I were just kicking it in his cell, and he started coughing and wouldn't stop. I went and told the dorm officer, who checked him out, then called medical. They took him out and, dawg"—Hammer paused and looked somewhere left of me with tears in his eyes—"that was the last I saw of him. He passed away from lung cancer. That man was like my father, K. And you know I never knew my real father and mother. I fucking grew up in foster homes and shit. So, to be honest, I clung to the old man. He was my fam, like you. His death hurt me."

"Man, I'm sorry to hear that, bruh," I told him as he wiped a tear from his eye. I knew this guy meant a lot to him because I'd never seen him get emotional like this.

"It is what it is, Korey. Shortly after his death, I was released. When Kolanda and Keisha came to get me, me and Kolanda locked it in. We got married. Later that same day, she told me that her father knew that I would come home sooner than I thought I would. He always kept up with the crack law and shit. That's when she took me in that same room I took you in. The one with the safe. She handed me a piece of paper with the combination to the safe and told me that whatever was in it, her father wanted me to have. It was full of heroin and two hundred thousand!"

"Wow!"

"That's why I said the game chose me. I wasn't expecting this, Korey. I actually thought I was gonna faint when I saw all that shit! I couldn't keep the money and flush the drugs, my nigga. So, I did what any hustler would do and started grinding!"

I sat looking at my brother, who looked me in the eyes the whole time. How could he have known that the game would come to sit on his lap like a very beautiful woman and flirt with him beyond what he could fathom? Again, I didn't know how to respond to this.

"Everything I just shared with you is the truth, Korey. And, dawg, I'm not trying to pull you into my newfound world. But, at the same time, I trust you more than anyone. You're my dawg. Ride with me on this shit if you'd like. But if you don't wanna roll, hey, I can't make you do what you don't want to do."

"Just tell me what you plan to do once you get rid of all of that dope. Are you done? What's your plan?" I asked.

"The plan is to stack the dough until we can't stack no more, my nigga. 'Cause you can never have enough money in this world. It's what makes the world turn.

After we hustle off everything, though, we'll invest in some legitimate shit. You got any ideas?"

"I've got plenty."

"Well, don't lose them. For now, I need you to ride with me to go pick something up." Hammer ignited his engine. 50 Cent's "Hustler's Ambition" began playing.

"Something like what, yo?"

"You'll see." He backed out of the lot and hit the road.

"I got this whole little area over here sewn up, K," Hammer said to me after we rode about thirty-five minutes out to Lake Norman. We had pulled into a nice, seemingly quiet trailer park. I saw sprinkles of whites throughout this huge trailer park.

"By that, you mean—"

"Got a chick over here running things for me. Man, K, heroin move over here like a muthafucka! Cats over this way can't get enough of that good-good I got. Right now, though, I need to step inside that trailer over there," Hammer said, pointing at it. "Gotta pick up some loot as well as make this here drop."

"A drop?" I shot back. I had no idea he had dope in the car.

He retrieved a brown paper bag from under his seat and tucked it under his arm. "Also, my nigga, hear me good. If I'm not out of that trailer in five minutes, you come in the muthafucka to see what's up. Now, here." Hammer again reached under his seat. This time he pulled a Mac 10 from it. He placed it in my lap. "Five minutes, my nigga."

"Yo, what's this?"

"You know what it is, K."

"What you want me to do with this?" I gripped it to give it back. Before I could, he was getting out of the car.

"You know what to do with it. Have my fuckin' back!" He exited the car and walked to the trailer he pointed at. He was looking both to his left and right as if checking for the cops, just like we used to do back in the day while hustling hard on the corner. I couldn't believe he had put me in this position so damn soon. But what the fuck was I supposed to do? I had to back his play.

# Chapter 10

## *Don't Test Me*

I cocked the Mac to make sure it was ready to fire in the event I needed to handle business. I checked my watch. Hammer had been inside now a little over two minutes. My phone vibrated. I checked it. It was Keisha. I sent her to voice mail when I saw this middle-aged white man approach the same trailer Hammer entered. The guy entered with the butt of a revolver sticking out of his back pocket. My heart rate began to increase, and my hands began to perspire. They always did whenever I was faced with involving myself in dangerous situations.

Figuring something might not be going right with my brother inside this trailer, as well as seeing that he'd been in there for five minutes now, I exited the car with the Mac under my armpit. I stepped to the door and knocked on it.

The guy I saw enter cracked the door open. "Can I help you with something?"

"Sure you can." I yanked the door open and aimed the Mac at his face. "You can take me to where Hammer is inside this trailer," I spat, looking around. I didn't see him anywhere. The guy quickly threw his hands up. "Where is he?" I shouted, before reaching for the pistol in his back pocket.

"He's in the back, man," he stuttered.

"All is well, K," Hammer said, walking out of a room carrying a small garbage bag. An older petite blonde was following him. "I was just on my way out."

"Hammer, what's going on here?" the man I had the gun on looked over at Hammer and asked.

"It's cool, K. You can let him go. Larry works for Sheila here."

I pushed him over toward Hammer and the white bitch next to him. Hammer reached inside the front pocket of his jeans and put a wad of cash in this cat Larry's hand. "Sorry for your troubles," he told him. "C'mon, K. Let's get out of here."

I dumped the bullets from Larry's revolver onto the floor, then tossed him his pistol.

"Sheila, call me when you run out. And, by the way, no need for y'all to be alarmed. This here is my brother. He was just looking out for my best interests."

We rolled up out of that trailer. The moment we got inside Hammer's car, he looked over at me and said, "Nigga, you still on point just like you used to be in the old days!"

"Man, why the fuck you put me in that position? You could have gotten that cat Larry shot."

"He'll be all right." Hammer burned rubber out of that trailer park. "My nigga, I'm glad your ass home!"

When he said that, my phone vibrated. I retrieved it from my pocket. It was Keisha. She was calling, wanting to know what time I planned on seeing my daughter. I told her after six. At the moment, it was a little after one. When I got off the phone with Keisha, I told Hammer to pull over and stop the car. I had something to say. He reluctantly pulled over in spite of us being dirty with guns and a car full of money.

"Yo," I said to him. "Look at me." He gave me his undivided attention. "I just got home from giving the fucking Feds twelve long years of my life. I wanna see my daughter, and I want to take shit slow. I told you this already. Don't fuckin' put me in a situation like that again, dawg. Besides, you know me. You know I'll be there for you through thick and thin. I'll never leave you hanging if I can help it. But you also know that I'm not the type who likes exposing my hand before it's time."

"I know, K. And, yo, my apology. Real talk, dawg. My apology," he looked me in the eye and said to show that his apology was genuine. "I just needed to see if you still had it, my nig. That's all."

"Don't test me. Never. 'Cause you already know how I get down. In the future, tell me what's up your sleeve. And, if I choose to take part, respect that. If I don't, respect that too, yo. We're men, Partnerz in Crime kings, remember? Not peewees. Peewees slip out here and end up in prison or fucking laid out for a coroner to come pick 'em up. That's not for us."

"I got you, K. One love, my nigga. That'll never happen again." Hammer locked trigger fingers with mine, Partnerz in Crime style. "I love you, K, man. Boy, I love you to death!" he said the thug way.

"The feeling is mutual. That much we should never get twisted or misunderstood."

# Chapter 11

## *Visiting My Daughter*

"That's where my li'l daughter and her mother live, right there, Keisha." I pointed to their place as we were going through Double Oaks Apartments neighborhood. Being in this area on the west side of Charlotte brought back so many memories. Mainly because just a few blocks away from Double Oaks Apartments was a neighborhood Hammer and I both hustled in day and night: Fairview Homes. Hammer and I both gained street reps on Kenny Street as being young, ruthless drug dealers who cats didn't play around with when it came to paying up money owed to us.

However, no matter how bad you may be in the streets, someone will always try you. One cat snatched an ounce of powder coke from me one day and ran. When I caught up to him, I shot him in the face three times, poured some coke over him, and left his ass laid out like a rug next to an abandoned school building. His death was seen as drug related by authorities. Luckily for me, no one was around to witness the shooting. No one but my partner in crime, Hammer. That's how I got the aka Killa Korey. Hammer gave it to me.

Back in those days, it was nothing for someone to come out the house and step on an addict's thrown-away dirty needle if not careful. It was a common sight to witness crackheads ripping and running up and down the street and throughout the neighborhood in search of their next fix, like zombies!

I suddenly felt bad thinking about how it used to be and how my thug associates and me kept the elderly up all times of the night with our around-the-clock drug dealing and with the reckless shooting of guns. We were all just a bad influence on the kids and our whole community. One thing I was glad to see, though, was this whole area over here now had been cleaned up and remodeled for the better. The apartments and houses had been upgraded. No one was on the corners like back in the day, selling drugs.

"That apartment right there, with the MERRY CHRISTMAS written in different-color Christmas lights. That's where my daughter and her mother live," I reiterated after briefly reminiscing over how it used to be over here.

Keisha pulled up directly in front of my daughter's mother's apartment. "Okay, then," she said. "Are you ready?"

"Not really."

"Why? What's wrong?" She looked over at me with concern.

"I haven't seen my daughter in years, Ke. Her mother stopped bringing her to see me. Just stopped everything. Olivia was about to be eight the last time I saw her."

"Why did her mother stop bringing her to see you? What did you do, Korey?"

"I don't know." I ran my hand over my head, wanting to know the answer to that one myself. "I guess she just wanted to move on. After all, I had a lot of time to do in the fed."

"Yeah, but—"

"I know, Ke. She should have still kept in touch for our daughter's sake, right?" I cut in.

"Yeah."

"Shit happens. I know that it hurt me not hearing from them. At least the number and address hasn't changed, though. Matter fact, after we got back from Geneva's last night, I went to my room and called my daughter's mother. She answered, but I hung up."

"Why you do that, Korey?" Keisha asked with a chuckle.

"Fear, I guess. I don't know." I shrugged.

"What is there to fear?"

"The unknown. Rejection after all these years. For all I know, Shamika, my daughter's mother, might be married with another child!"

"Look. The fact of the matter is, Korey, the two of you have a daughter together. You're home and want to be a part of her life. There's nothing to fear. If your daughter's mother has moved on, hey, wish her the best and do what you can to be a good father to your daughter. That's all you can do, Korey. That's all you can do."

I nodded in agreement with Keisha's advice. And seeing that it was after 6:00 p.m., I reached into my pocket and retrieved my address book to double-check my daughter's mother's address so that we could be perfectly sure we had arrived at the right apartment. It was the correct address.

"Would you prefer I wait here in the car?"

"I don't know yet. Hold on." I whipped my phone out and dialed my daughter's mother's number.

The phone rang four times before I heard a soft female's voice. "Hello?"

"May I please speak to Olivia?"

"Speaking."

"Hey, baby girl. You know who this is?"

"Voice sounds familiar, but no, I don't. Who is this?"

I didn't know whether to say "Korey" or "your daddy," being that I hadn't been physically in my daughter's life for a long time. Since she had my blood running through her veins, though, and she dayum near looked just like me, she was mine and, like Keisha told me, I had nothing to fear.

"This . . . this your dad."

"Yeah, right! My father's in prison, and I haven't heard from him in five years. So whoever this is," my daughter said, stretching the word, "find someone else to play with, please!"

"No joke, Olivia, babe. This is your dad. I'm home."

"Dad, is this really you? Or is this somebody playing with me? Mama, I think one of your friends playing games on the phone, talking about they my daddy! Isn't Daddy still in prison?" I heard her say to her mom.

"With all the time the judge gave him, the last I looked, yes, he's still in prison. Give me the phone," her mother replied. She grabbed the phone from Olivia. "Hello, who is this?" she said.

"The man you left hanging in the joint."

"Korey, is this you?"

"Unless you got a baby by another cat under the same name, it is."

"Where you calling from, Korey?"

"My cell."

"Jail?"

"No, my cell phone. I'm in your driveway."

Seconds later, she was opening her living room door and stepping out on her porch. I stepped out of Keisha's BMW and stood in her driveway with my hands lifted skyward.

"Oh, my Godddd!" I read her lips as she stretched her neck forward. She looked back into her crib and motioned for our daughter. Olivia ran to me with her mother following.

"Daddy, I thought someone was playing with me!" She smiled, wrapping her arms around me. "I didn't know it was you, for real!" She hugged me tight.

"It's me, baby girl. Gosh, you've gotten big! And you so pretty!"

"Thank you." She looked up at me while in my embrace, blushing hard. "I swear I thought someone was playing with me!" she repeated.

"Boy, how long you been out?" her mother interrupted and playfully hit me on my shoulder while smiling.

"Not long," I said, kissing my daughter on her forehead. Her embracing me like I had been in her life and never left made me feel so good.

"Well, come inside. It's cold out here." She led the way, with Olivia holding my hand.

"Damn, look like Santa gon' be good to somebody!" I said, checking out the many gift-wrapped presents underneath the well-decorated tree in their living room.

"Santa? Yeah, right! Olivia knows who Santa is. Her hardworking mother!"

I looked at our daughter who was standing next to me, with her arm still wrapped around me and mine gently around her neck. "My mom out of it, Daddy," she whispered, shaking her head and pursing her lips. "Completely out of it." She then twirled her index finger around her ear as if to indicate her mother was cuckoo.

"Korey Taylor is finally out. Lord, I can't believe this!" Shamika said, putting her hands together and making a loud clap. "Oh, my God!" She smiled harder than I saw Hammer smile when he first saw me. "Well, y'all sit down while I get some hot chocolate," she said, about to walk to her kitchen.

"Oh, I got someone out in the car waiting on me. So . . ."

"Who? One of your boys? Tell him he can come in."

"A'ight, cool. I'll be back." I released my daughter's hand and headed toward the door.

"Olivia, come help me with this hot chocolate."

"I'll be back, Daddy." She looked at me and smiled before following her mother into their kitchen.

It didn't take me having two eyes to see that my daughter's happy demeanor let me know that she was extremely excited about me being home. Her and her mother both were, which made my fear instantly go away. For some reason, though, I assumed that my daughter's mother would be looking stressed out, out of shape, and all that type of stuff that comes with having to raise a child alone with little education and little financial support. Since she only sent a few pictures of our daughter and none of herself while I was incarcerated, I honestly had no real idea of how she was looking. To my surprise, though, not much had changed. She still had that chocolate skin tone, she was petite, and she was still the pretty black-haired girl I fell in love with at first sight years ago. She had her pretty silk black hair in a French wrap; and she was wearing a red turtleneck sweater that came down past her buttocks, with some black tight leggings that were hugging her nice little thick thighs wonderfully. She never was the type who dressed up her face with makeup. She didn't have to. God had done a great job blessing her to be naturally beautiful.

I stepped outside. Keisha was in the car, bobbing her head and singing to the melody and lyrics of Stevie Wonder's "All I Do."

"KeKe, would you like to come inside with me?" I asked. I wanted her to meet my daughter and her mother.

"Sure."

KeKe followed me inside. The moment we stepped inside, my daughter's mother was coming out of the kitchen, carrying two cups of hot chocolate. She literally stopped in her tracks when she saw KeKe behind me. She gave me a crazy look like, "No, you didn't bring a bitch over to my house!"

I downplayed how she looked at me. If she could have a man, certainly I could have a woman, I figured. "KeKe, this is my daughter's mother, Shamika. Shamika, this a friend of mine, KeKe."

"Nice to meet you, Shamika." KeKe gave a friendly wave with a toothy smile.

"You, too," Shamika shot back while handing me one of the hot chocolates that she was carrying. She kept the other one for herself, being funny. She wasn't about to serve another woman. That's just how she was.

"Livia, bring your daddy's friend a cup of hot chocolate," she yelled before sitting in a chair across from the black leather sofa we were sitting on. She was evil-eyeing me the whole time while sipping her hot chocolate. "So, how long have y'all known each other, Korey?" she asked. I got the impression that she couldn't wait to ask that question.

"Not long."

"What's not long? A year? Two years? Three?" she asked, wanting me to be precise.

Before I could respond, my daughter emerged from the kitchen carrying two cups of hot chocolate. "Sorry it took me so long, Daddy. But here you go." She handed me the cup of hot chocolate for me to hand Keisha and she kept one.

"Thank you, cutie," I said to her. Keisha smiled and followed with a thank-you of her own for my daughter. "Olivia, this is my friend, Keisha. Keisha, this is my li'l princess, Olivia."

"How are you doing, Ms. Keisha?" my daughter greeted her with a wave and a polite smile.

"Not bad. Nice meeting you. You look just like your dad!" Like me, Olivia had light skin with hazel-green eyes and pretty black wavy hair like she was mixed with a race other than that of color. She was. My mother was half Cherokee.

"That's what everybody says. Don't they, Mama?" she said, looking over at her mother.

"That's what they say," her mother replied, still giving me that "how dare you" look.

"Is that a good thing or a bad thing, Ms. Keisha?" My daughter turned to KeKe, eager to hear the answer.

"Why, it's a good thing. You're very pretty!" She reached and playfully tapped Olivia's nose then sipped on her hot chocolate.

"Oh, my God, puhleeze don't tell her that! She already stays in the mirror for hours!" Shamika interjected.

"Yo, I can't count the days I spent in prison thinking about you, Olivia. We've got a lot to catch up on, baby girl."

"Like what, Daddy?" She sipped on her hot chocolate, looking up at me.

"Like how you doing in school, first of all."

She looked over at her mother and smiled. "Mama, my daddy doesn't know, does he? I'm hopefully graduating this year a straight A honor roll student! So far, that's all I been getting on my report card. I'm a straight A student."

"It's true. She's very focused. But she knows I wouldn't have her no other way. She can't talk to boys at all, and I definitely don't allow her to go to parties and sleepovers! That's where girls sneak around and get pregnant. And she knows I better never hear that she has taken a drink or put a cigarette or a joint of weed in her mouth! 'Cause I work too hard to make sure she doesn't want for anything to have her jive around with her education and life. It's not happening on my watch!"

"Sometimes you are a little too strict," my daughter said, shaking her head.

"Maybe so, but I promise you this: you won't end up pregnant and having to drop out of school and struggle just to make ends meet!" Shamika said sternly, no doubt having in mind her own experience of getting pregnant young. She dropped out of school when she was sixteen all because she wanted to have her independence, party, and have what she called fun with her friends.

Her parents were in the military most of her teenage years, so her grandmother raised her. Her grandmother did the very best by giving her right guidance, but when she got with me, it was a wrap!

Like most chicks I had back in the day, Shamika loved my thug swag, my hazel-green eyes, and the way I took my time with her in that bedroom. And since I was making a lot of loot in the streets in those days, I made it my business to have her looking nice at all times. I knew it's not all about material things, but a week didn't go by that her hair and nails didn't get done. Shamika was no stranger to Gucci, Prada, and Dolce & Gabbana. All her little girlfriends were jealous of her. Then she popped up pregnant. Shortly after having Olivia, I was on my way to jail.

"Your mother certainly has her reasons, Olivia, for being strict," I said to her because I could discern that our daughter wanted to do some of the things that other young teens were doing. "There's a time and place for everything, though, sweetheart." I kissed her cheek. There was no way I was going to go against Shamika and how she was raising our daughter. She was doing a helluva good job and, deep inside, I was proud of her. Now it was my turn to do what I hadn't been allowed to do, and that was be her father.

"So, tell me, Olivia, what do you hope to major in when you go to college in a couple years?"

"I want to be a lawyer." She wasted no time answering me like this was something she had thought about over and over again.

Keisha looked at me and lifted her eyebrows when my daughter said she wanted to be a lawyer.

"Okay, that's what's up." I nodded. "Keisha here is an attorney."

"Really, Ms. Keisha?" My daughter's eyes widened. "You're a real lawyer?"

"Mm-hmm," Keisha affirmed. "I handle civil cases."

"As in winning lawsuits for people?"

"Yeah, I guess you can say it like that. What type of attorney would you like to be?"

"Criminal attorney."

"Oh, okay. Why criminal law, Olivia?"

Olivia looked over at her mother, who spoke up for her. "When her father was in prison, she would always ask me why he had to be incarcerated so long and if there was a way to get him out early. I would respond by saying that if she wanted her father out of prison, she should consider becoming an attorney so she could fight for his freedom. She's been wanting to be an attorney ever since."

"Wow. You love your dad just that much that you would focus your attention on becoming an attorney someday? That's a beautiful, unselfish thing, Olivia. What a good heart you have," Keisha said to her.

"Yep." Olivia looked at me and nodded.

Tears came to my eyes to know that my daughter thought of me and wanted me home so that I could be in her life. All while I was in prison, I thought of her and hoped that I was on her mind a time or two. I sent many pictures and wrote many letters so that she would know what her daddy looked like and how her daddy felt about her. Being in her presence at this moment made me feel like I was in heaven.

Shamika's phone started ringing, snapping me out of my thoughts. "Korey, y'all, excuse me a minute," she said, getting up to answer it. It was probably her man, I figured.

While Shamika was in her bedroom talking on the phone, Keisha and my daughter and I continued to chat about this, that, and a third. My daughter wanted to know everything! She wanted to know if Keisha and I were a couple. Where was I staying? How did I get out of prison so early? And what was I getting her for Christmas? While she and I conversed, Keisha's cell started lighting up. She answered it. It was Kolanda, wanting to know how much longer she and I were gonna be because she had cooked, and she and Hammer were waiting for Keisha and me to arrive before they sat at the table to eat. Keisha told them to go ahead and eat because it was already late.

Shortly after Keisha hung up the phone and told me who it was and what was up, I kissed my daughter and hugged her tight. "I'ma call you tomorrow, princess, so that we can talk some more. But Daddy will never leave you again to go off to prison. That's a promise, you hear me?"

"Yes, sir." She nodded.

Her mother stepped back into the living room right about the time Keisha and I were about to bounce.

"Korey, I'll be out in the car. It was nice meeting you, Olivia."

"Nice meeting you too, Ms. Keisha." They hugged.

"Nice meeting you too, Shamika." Keisha waved at my daughter's mother on her way out.

"Have a good one," Shamika replied, waving her good-bye.

The moment Keisha went outside, Shamika looked at our daughter. "Give your daddy another hug, Olivia, and let me speak with him a moment in private."

"Daddy, I love you, and I'm glad you're home. Don't forget to call me, okay?" She hugged me tight.

"I won't, sweetheart. I promise."

My daughter obeyed her mother and went straight to her room. When she did, Shamika walked up to me and held her arms out to hug me. "Korey, God does answer prayers," she said, embracing me. "I'm so glad that you are home because Olivia really needs you. All she does is talk about her daddy."

"So why did you stop writing me and bringing her to see me?" I wanted to know immediately.

"Now isn't the time to talk about that, Korey. I had my reasons. What's up with you and that lawyer girl? Is she your lady?" She looked me in the eyes for the truth.

"Doesn't matter, Shamika." I waved it off, turning my head.

"Since when did it stop mattering, Korey?" She cupped my chin, directing my face back to hers for eye contact. She looked like she was about to cry.

"When you left me hanging to do twenty dayum years by myself!" I stared into her eyes and made tight my lips. I just couldn't believe she abandoned me like she never loved me at all.

"I told you I had my reasons, Korey."

"You always got your reasons, Shamika!" My voiced raised a little for her to know that I was hurt by what she did.

I then walked out of her crib without looking back, leaving her there to think about her leaving me hanging while in the joint. Words couldn't express how I felt thinking about her and not being by my side. For years, I didn't even get a card for my birthday from her. And for years, when I wrote to her, she wouldn't even respond. I loved this woman. Woulda married her had I not gone off to prison. I couldn't count the times we lay up in bed after good sex and I heard her whisper in my ear, "Korey, I love you very much," only to discover later, while I did hard time in the fed, that her love was the type of love that would leave a brother hanging. What I really wanted to ask her was, "What did I do to deserve you leaving me?"

# Chapter 12

## *What's Wrong?*

### Keisha

"A'ight, we can roll out now," Korey said, having come out of his daughter's mother's place and slamming my car door once he was inside. His face was flushed with anger.

"Are you okay?"

"I'm fine."

"Not slamming my door like that, you aren't. What's wrong?"

"Let's just get from over here," he said, nose flared and lips tight. He wouldn't even make eye contact with me.

"Well, we're leaving. Don't worry. But why the sudden change, Korey? Just moments ago, you were all smiles hugging on your daughter. What happened?"

"My daughter and I are fine."

"Then what is it?"

"It's my issue with Shamika."

"What about her?"

"Told you. She bounced on me while I was in the joint. I want answers as to why."

"Okay, but, Korey, you're home now and—"

"True, but that doesn't change the reality of what she did. When I went to the fed, I didn't leave her on bad terms. We were in love. Hell, I thought that she was going to be the woman I married. She was the person I least expected to not ride with me."

"People change, Korey. You were gone twelve years! But, again, you're home now. Put that behind you and move on. You have to, or it's going to eat you up!"

"Some things you can't move on from until you get answers. That's where I am with that. Bottom line."

"Never say what you can't do, Korey."

"That one I can't move on from without answers, Ke. I just can't." He shrugged.

I hit the highway but continued to talk to him about the issue. "Did you ask her why she left you?"

"I did, but she doesn't want to talk about it. Says she had her reasons, though, and that now was not the time to go into it."

"Then give her some time if that's what she needs."

He looked over at me like, "Are you serious?" and then said, "I been gone twelve years, Ke. Five of which she was not in my life. How much damn time does a woman need before she's able to give an explanation for her disloyalty?"

"I can't speak for her. But don't get impatient is all I'm saying. You've waited this long. Waiting a little longer, I'm sure, won't hurt you, Korey."

"Psss." He blew air through his lips and gave me a dismissive wave of his hand. That made me feel like shutting my mouth because apparently, I wasn't telling him what he wanted to hear. He faced the window and began stroking the hairs on his faint goatee as if in deep thought on the matter.

I turned up the volume on my *Stevie Wonder's Greatest Hits* CD. "All In Love Is Fair" was playing. I couldn't imagine being in prison and having someone I love mistreating me. That would break more than my heart.

It would totally crush my spirit. It would cause me to have trust issues and diminish my wanting to fall in love again. Baby boy needed answers that only his daughter's mother could give, not Keisha Monica Harris.

But I did want to tell him that, although I had never been to prison where a loved one left me hanging, I had been hurt. Hurt by a man I thought loved me very much. That hurt made me angry and bitter inside toward the man who hurt me. I'd become somewhat reclusive since, isolating myself from the thought of falling in love ever again. That hurt was why I wanted my brother-in-law to fuck Josh up! I wanted him to scar that bastard's face up like he scarred my heart. And, yeah, I knew I told Korey to put the issue of his daughter's mother leaving him behind him and move on. It would seem a girl would take her own advice and do the same. Well, you could call me a hypocrite. I didn't always practice what I preached. I'd move on after Josh got his ass kicked!

"You going to be all right or what, baby boy?" I looked over and asked Korey, who was now resting his head back on the seat's headrest with his eyes closed. I turned the music down.

"I'll be a'ight. Thanks for asking," he replied softly. I could see he had calmed down.

"You hungry? I know I am," I said, having pulled into a KFC drive-through.

"Yeah. Hell, order me whatever you're having."

"I'm ordering the Cajun chicken wings, coleslaw, mashed potatoes with gravy, and a large Coke."

"I'm cool with that." He nodded.

As I was ordering us food, Korey's phone lit up. He put it to his ear and began talking. It was Hammer. They kicked it briefly. I forgot my sister had cooked dinner. I didn't know if that was what Hammer was calling for. I could see Korey was really hungry because he tore into his wings the moment he got off the phone. He looked so cute eating and wiping off the chicken grease residue that covered his sexy pink lips. I wanted to kiss his lips, and a little something else, too. Instead, I wrapped my lips around my chicken wings and kept my lustful thoughts to myself.

A week passed, and every time I saw Korey around the house, his ear would be glued to his phone. He and his daughter talked morning, noon, and night. He would come into my bedroom, while I was working at my computer, just to tell me how he and his baby girl couldn't get enough of each other. She wanted to know everything about her dad. What made him happy? What made him sad? Where was he working? When was he going to come and take her shopping and to his house to spend the night? He was so excited about catching up for lost time with his daughter.

I asked him if he had been talking much with Shamika, because he didn't mention her at all, not since that night I took him to visit his daughter. He told me not really. He would call, ask how she was doing, she'd say, "Fine," and then she would hand the phone to their daughter. He told me that he was taking my advice and being patient about them discussing what she did to hurt him. He didn't ask me to take him back over to her apartment. I figured she didn't care for seeing me over there with him in the first place. Women's intuition. I think she still loved Korey.

One thing Korey was doing for sure, however, was spending a helluva lot of time with Hammer. When I wasn't at work at my office uptown, I would come in, and he and my brother-in-law would be at the bar in his and Kolanda's bedroom, discussing business and counting money. Lots of money. I knew what their business was. It was in narcotics. My brother-in-law couldn't wait to have Korey assist him in his business. I stayed away from my brother-in-law's narcotics endeavors. My dad always told my sister and me that our business was in the courtroom as it related to our profession as attorneys-at-law. I had a few investments in real estate, but that's where I drew the line.

My dad would say that if he were to ever find out that my sister and I were participating in anything illegal, it would be the end of our careers. He'd kill us! He had to be turning in his grave right now because my sister helped Hammer all the time, carrying narcotics here and there. I didn't say anything because she was grown and Hammer was her husband. If something were to go wrong, Hammer would have never let her taken the fall. He loved my sister tremendously. He'd have died for her. He told me that he'd die for me as well. But I didn't want a man dying for me. I wanted a man to live for me. What good are you if you're dead?

Hammer used my sister's connections with a friend who worked at the DMV to help Korey renew his license with no problems. After Korey got his license renewed, my brother-in-law brought him a brand new dark blue Corvette like his white one, with dark-tinted windows and factory chrome rims.

The day Korey got his new car, he called me at my office and told me that he was on his way to pick me up for lunch. I told him, "Okay."

I ate a turkey salad with heavy tomatoes and cucumbers. He ate a chicken breast sandwich with some French fries. I had an extra hour, so he drove out to Hornet's Nest Park, where we talked about him wanting to put some money in a savings account for his daughter, and him enrolling in barber school. He said he loved cutting hair and he wanted his own barber shop. I told him that I wanted a husband and one child, maybe two. Then, while looking me in my eyes, he reached and gently caressed my cheek.

"Baby girl, you've got a bright future ahead of you," he said as if he were psychic. "You're the type of beautiful woman who would make a good wife and a good mother."

"You really think so?" I asked softly, looking into his hazel-green eyes. They were pretty. They revealed a gentle soul behind him being what my brother-in-law told me he was: a gangster.

"I know so."

"Thank you." I twisted my body and smiled with his hand still gently caressing my cheek.

"Can I kiss you?" he asked, surprising me.

"Yes, please," I quickly responded without hesitation.

He leaned in and touched my lips with his. His lips were soft. His eyes were closed. "Mmmm," I moaned between us tongue dancing. Then his phone vibrated, bringing our intimate moment to a halt.

It was his daughter calling. He told me that she was at her grandmother's and wanted to know if there was a problem with him and her mother because she said her mother had been in her room crying a lot and looking stressed.

Korey took me back to my office and told me he'd call me later. I told him that was okay, and that I hoped all was well with Shamika. I got back to work happy, for his kiss had me on cloud nine!

# Chapter 13

## *We Need to Talk*

**Korey**

I listened to Brian McKnight's "Do I Ever Cross Your Mind" over and over and over until I pulled up at Shamika's crib. That song made me wonder if Shamika thought about me like I thought about her while I was away. I thought about her and my daughter more than I thought about regaining my freedom.

My daughter had called me and asked if I could check up on her mother. She was concerned that something was wrong, stating that she had somewhat of a sad demeanor lately. Since I'd been home, Shamika and I hadn't talked much. She was always working or about to go to sleep when I called to talk with Olivia. I still wanted answers to why she left me. But since Hammer and I had been getting that paper and I'd been busy putting mine to the side and thinking about what I wanted to do with it, I hadn't been pressing the issue with Shamika to give me an explanation. Not to mention I'd been finding myself falling for KeKe. She'd been there for me, offering me good advice and a shoulder to lean on.

I killed my car's engine, removed the key from the ignition, and pulled my phone from my pocket. I dialed Shamika's number while looking at her front door through the windshield of my new Vette that my brother bought me as a welcome home gift. Her phone rang six times. I knew she was home because her car was in the driveway. She had a nice little red Honda Civic.

"Hello?" she finally answered groggily, like she'd been asleep.

"Shamika?"

"What?"

"This Korey."

"I know."

"I'm outside your apartment and would like to come inside."

"For what, Korey?"

"What'chu mean, for what? We need to talk."

"We needed to talk before, but you walked away acting like a little boy! Guess you had to get back to your lawyer girl!"

"Look, I'm getting out the car. Meet me at'cha door." Seconds later, I was at her door.

"What'chu want?" She stood with the door open. Her hair was all in disarray like she was stressed about something.

"You know exactly what I want." I stepped inside and walked past her.

"No, I don't." She shut the door, then turned to face me.

"I want answers. That's what I want, Shamika." I got straight to it. I couldn't help it. I'd waited for this moment long enough. It was time.

"You think you're the only one who wants answers, Korey? Well, you're not. I want answers too!"

"Why you leave me? Was I not a good man to you, Shamika, before I went off to the joint?"

"I don't know. You tell me. You're the one who left me to raise our daughter alone!"

"I shouldn't have to tell you jack! You didn't want for anything when I was home. I provided for you and our daughter. Yeah, I was in the streets, but that was the hand I was dealt, and I played it! You knew all of that before I went to prison, and guess what? You didn't leave me then, so why would you leave me when I need you most, Shamika? Huh?" I lifted my voice a little to let her know beyond a doubt that I was dead serious and deeply hurt by her leaving me. It was cold in the joint without the warmth of her loving presence.

She made her lips tight and shook her head slowly with anger surfacing that I could clearly see in her face and eyes. Tears were in her eyes.

"And I don't care nothing about you about to cry, 'cause I did a lot of that in the joint from missing you and our daughter."

Smack! She slapped the hell out of my face while I was talking. She was upset. "You act like I didn't ride with you at all!" she snapped with venom. She was upset, but hell, that made two of us. "I stuck by you for seven years straight! Came to see you and everything," she continued.

"Don't matter! You didn't endure to the end! And don't smack me like that again."

"Or what?" she challenged, pointing her finger in my face and touching my forehead with it. She always got aggressive when she was mad. She knew I could never hit her, though. She's a woman. No man should ever hit a woman.

"You need to control your emotions. Now get'cha finger out my face." I lightly swiped it down.

"And you need to get your facts straight!" she shot back, continuing to point her finger. "You come over here the other night with your li'l lawyer chick, giving me the cold shoulder like I just utterly abandoned you while you were on lockdown. I held you down. It was temporary, but I was there. Was your lawyer chick there?" She continued pointing her finger in my face, touching my nose with it.

"Never mind that. The point is you didn't stay!"

"I had my reasons. I told you that when you were over here the other night."

"Which was what? You found another fucking man?"

"You always hollering, 'You found another man.' You used to ask that in your letters to me. But do you actually think I would do you like that? I don't open my door to every guy who comes knocking. So it had nothing to do with me having another man. That was how *you* perceived it!"

"How else was I to perceive it? You stop writing me out of the blue, you stop sending me pictures of our daughter, you stop visiting me."

"But you've always had our address and phone number. That never changed. So what does that tell you, Korey? Matter of fact, let me show you something. Follow me."

She quickly walked into her bedroom with me behind. "Do you see that, right there?" She pointed above the head of her queen-sized bed. There, on the wall, was an enlarged twenty-four-inch picture of me. It was a picture that I had taken solo while in prison with my shirt off, muscles everywhere. "Do you see who that is and what's written underneath it?"

I had to step closer to see what was written underneath it. THE LOVE OF MY LIFE, FOREVER! it read.

"Now, do you actually think that I would bring a man into this house with my daughter's father, and the love of my life, on my wall? I would never do that, Korey! And do you think that I would bring a man around our daughter, knowing how crazy you is? If something were to happen to your daughter under my watch while you were doing your time, I would never hear the end of it once you returned to society. I'm not stupid, Korey! And, I'm not a whore. I belong to one man. But while he was in the joint,

I took that time to grow up. It took a lot of prayer and faith in God. But I grew up. So, I didn't leave you for no man, as you supposed."

"Then why did you leave, Shamika?" I needed to know for my own inner resolution. "I needed you," I told her.

"So that you could become a man! That's why I stepped away."

"So that I could become a man?" I repeated her. "What the hell is that supposed to mean?"

She looked me in my eyes and took a deep breath. "Korey, you and I been together since we were in our late teens. You are the only guy I have ever loved. So you know I'm not going to stand here in your face, look you in the eyes, and lie to you. You grew up without your father, and you always told me that was one of the reasons it was easy for you to get out in them crazy streets, right?"

"That's true," I said with a nod.

"God bless the dead, but you hurt your dear mother by being in and a part of that street life. The streets made you a menace, Korey. And a drug dealer. The streets took you from your mother. You never gave yourself a chance to grow up so that you could really enjoy life and family! The streets wouldn't let you."

I continued nodding my head in agreement with what was coming out of her mouth. She was dead on point. She was speaking truth. And my heart was bearing witness. For no man can fight with the undisputed hands of truth and prevail. Only a fool would think he can.

"You were doing manly things while hustling in the streets. You took good care of Olivia and me, but inside you were crying out for that real father figure you never had to help you navigate in the right direction."

Tears fell from my face without me being able to control them at the truth Shamika was delivering like a mailman. She placed her arms around me and held me tight. I swear no girl in this world knew me like she did.

"It's okay, though, Korey. It's okay," she consoled me. Then she stepped back a little and placed her hands on my shoulders while looking me squarely in the eyes. Tears were coming from her eyes as well. "The reason I stepped away from you while you were in the joint was because there was no way you would have been able to completely focus on healing and getting your mind right with me in the way. I know you, Korey. Sometimes those we love and put above everything have to step out of our life so that God can step in. Every day, I prayed for you. See, Korey, I'm in the church now. I gave God my life. I don't go clubbing. I don't hang out with women who do all those worldly things. Bad company corrupts good character. All I do is work, spend that quality time with Olivia, and go to church and read my Bible."

"I miss you." I pulled her close and held her like she just held me.

"I missed you too. And I love you."

"I love you too, Shamika. I was just mad and needed answers."

"Well, now you have them." She walked over to her mirror and brushed her hair into a ponytail, pinning it upward. "Now," she said, facing me and pointing her finger, "is this lawyer girl your new sweetheart?"

"She's a friend. Hammer introduced us."

"Hammer? Your ace from back in the day? He home too?"

"Yeah. I been staying at his and his wife's house."

"He's married?"

"Yep. Keisha and I are only friends, though. For real, I have never been able to shake my love for you. It's deep in here," I said, my thumb pointing to my heart. "I really love you, Shamika." I stepped to her and placed my arms gently around her waist. I kissed her on her forehead.

"So where are you working?" She avoided intimacy.

"Nowhere right now. I'm going to enroll in barber college soon, though."

"Is that Hammer's Corvette you're driving out there?" She removed my hands from around her waist and began walking toward her living room. Something just hit her mind. Like she could sense I was doing something I didn't have any business doing.

"No, it's mine." I followed closely behind her. "What's up?"

"So you back in the game already, huh, Korey?" She opened her front door.

"That's neither here nor there."

She slapped me, then pointed her index finger in my face again. "Are you kidding me?" She stared in my eyes with one hand on her hip. "You just got out of prison. Are you trying to go back and be out of your daughter's life again? Get out of my house!" She pointed to the door. "Because apparently, you didn't learn anything good while you were away! Bye!"

"Shamika, calm down, will you? You get pissed too fast, baby girl, dayum. Calm down. It's not what you think, a'ight?" I said, lying. I was barely able to look her in the eyes at this point.

Hammer and I were full throttle in the pharmaceutical business. I knew that I was in danger of once again throwing rocks at the penitentiary. But Hammer and I were both playing it low key. We were extra selective and careful with who we chose to deal with. Our only friends and hang-out partners were each other, his wife, and Keisha. He and I were hustling hard, but we were not in the streets. All the major problems occur when cats are all out there in the streets, where someone is always looking at you and what you have with that jealous-envious eye, wanting to either rob you or simply test your street muscle.

"It's not what you think it is, Shamika," I reiterated and reached for her hand.

"Tell that lie to someone who will believe it. And don't touch me!" She swiped my hand to avoid me touching her.

"There you go trippin'!"

"Bye, Korey Taylor."

"You think I wanna be in a position out here in this world where I can't take care of myself and our daughter?"

"Do you think that our daughter wants to be in a position to continue to have to grow up in this world without her father? All she did while you were away was talk about you. She missed you, Korey. I missed you! Why can't you just work an honest nine to five? That's what I do."

"Shamika, babe, with all due respect, we're two different people. You—"

"Only by choice, Korey!" she cut me off. "Now, when are you going to stop making bad choices? What if you die in them streets, hustling? That would kill Olivia. She would have to live with that her whole life, seeing her father, who she loves, in a casket!"

I inhaled and exhaled hard, causing my jaws to inflate, while turning away from Shamika, looking over at my car. "Look, Shamika. I love you. And, I'll just have to see you later," I said and then began walking to my car.

"You don't love me. And you don't love Olivia! You love making bad decisions!" she shouted; then she went back inside her place, slamming the door behind her.

# Chapter 14

## *Discussing Biz with Hammer*

"Korey, what up, yo? Where you at?" Hammer asked. He called while I was mobilizing.

"I'm on the highway. Just left from Shamika's crib. What up?"

"I was trying to reach you earlier, but—"

"My phone was off. She and I had a lot to catch up on. Feel me?" I cut in.

"You know I do. You didn't go over there to make another Olivia, did you?" Hammer said, laughing.

"Nah. We got plenty time to do that. We just kicked it about her not being there like I would have liked for her to be while I was away. She gave me an explanation, though. I ain't mad at her."

"What she say, yo? 'Cause not being there for you is no small oversight."

"She's into God now and just wanted me to get my head right, absent any distractions from her. It's all good, Ham. I ain't tripping. She grew a lot and, for real, put some heavy shit on my head."

"You still love her, huh?"

"Man, I never stopped."

"Nothing wrong with that. That's your daughter's mother. If anybody deserves a pass for any offense toward you, it's her. Shamika was always a good girl, though, K. A little crazy, but good people."

"She's still crazy. Smacked me twice while I was at her place."

"What?"

"Hell, yeah. I made her upset by insinuating that she'd been disloyal to me while I was locked up. Not to mention, her ass didn't like me having Keisha with me the other night."

"Shit, man. It is what it is. Look, though, K. Meet me at Bojangles, off West Trade. I gotta discuss something important with you. Something real, real important."

"A'ight. I'll be over there in a li'l bit."

"Bet."


"K, peep this." Hammer, having met me over at Bojangles, leaned forward at a table he and I sat at across from one another, eating fried chicken. "My nigga, look at this." He slid a large manila envelope across the table to me.

"What's this?" I asked, wiping my greasy fingers with a napkin before I went to check out what was inside.

"You'll see," Hammer replied, watching me and biting into his chicken at the same time.

Inside was an enlarged eight-by-ten picture of some Middle Eastern–looking fat guy who looked to be in his mid-fifties. "Who this, yo?" I stared at the pic, then at Hammer.

He looked to his left and to his right, then wiped his mouth with a napkin and spoke with his voice low. "That's Raheem. In the streets, they call him Fat Rah."

"A'ight, what up with him?"

"Got out the joint two years ago. That mu'fucka helped the Feds bury my wife and Keisha's father."

"He snitched on the old man?"

"Like Sammy the Bull did John Gotti. He was the government's star witness."

"Damn, that's fucked up. Where is he now?"

"Mu'fucka living quietly in Monroe. They had him in the witness protection program, but our sources say he walked away from it."

"Who hipped you to his whereabouts?"

"My wife got all type of connections, K. She know by lawyers and mu'fuckas who work for the FBI. Her people looked into it. You know money talks. Feel me?"

"So what you got in mind?" I asked, sliding the envelope back to him.

"I wanna pay him a visit. Source says this rat still getting loot on the low."

"Word?"

"The old man was good to this nigga, K. I know because he told me from his own mouth while we were locked up together. He was hitting him off with two bricks of heroin a month. Made him a millionaire for real, only to have this mu'fucka take the stand on him and tell the court about their business endeavors. Now he's out eating and living good, while the old man died in the joint with a life sentence that his ass contributed to him getting. I wanna see this nigga personally, K."

"How soon?"

"ASAP. I got his address. We'll discuss the plan later. You in?"

"Definitely," I replied. Like Hammer, I hated a rat. The government used one to convict us. The cat who ratted on us didn't live in the Queen City anymore. After the government gave him immunity for testifying, he moved to the West Coast and hadn't been heard from since. As far as I was concerned, if a cat is going to be in the game, then playing by the rules is essential. Or else you face the fury of what comes with being disloyal. Usually the price for unfaithfulness is death. Feeling where my ace was coming from, I was all in on this one.

# Chapter 15

## *What'chu Want*

After discussing business with Hammer, we both left Bojangles. He had to take care of something with his wife. Keisha was at the office working overtime on this lawsuit she and Kolanda were near settling. Some unarmed Spanish cat got his ass beat by two cops: one black, the other white. Someone recorded the beat down on their phone. According to Keisha, the cops used excessive force. She was certain that after a year of fighting this case, she and her sister could get a settlement.

I couldn't get over seeing Shamika and having her chew me out. So I called her and told her I was back on my way to her place. Fortunately, she didn't tell me I couldn't come back over.

By now, it was after seven. Darkness had blanketed the atmosphere, and the temperature was at like forty degrees.

"You just got out the bathtub or something?" I asked, seeing her answering the door in her bathrobe and her hair all wrapped in a towel.

"Yeah. Now, what'chu want?" she said, shutting the door behind me, then walking in front of me to her bedroom. Her bathrobe was barely covering her buttocks, and when she walked, they were wiggling nicely underneath it.

"I want you to know that you mean the world to me. Always have and you always will."

"I hear you." She sat on the edge of her bed and began putting lotion on her legs.

"And I want to apologize to you for being angry with you over the years for thinking that you utterly abandoned me."

"I accept your apology. I know when I backed up you wouldn't understand why I was doing what I was doing at the time."

"No, I wouldn't have." I sat next to her. I didn't challenge her method of doing what she felt was right. But deep inside, still, I knew that a man needed his woman's presence beside him when he was down or at any other hard time in his life. "I'm home now, and I'm doing what I have to do to make sure I ain't gotta beg a mutha for nothing. I'ma take care of mine by all means."

"You got a problem, though, with taking the easy way out, Korey. That needs to change. I just pray that you come to your senses. I thought prison would have helped. I see that it didn't." She continued putting lotion on her pretty chocolate legs.

I removed my coat and sweat jacket, exposing my muscular biceps and triceps in my white tank top. I sat back down next to her on the edge of the bed.

"What are you getting all comfortable for?" she stopped putting lotion on her leg, which was lifted enough for me to see her zebra-striped panties; and she looked at me with somewhat of a sideways smile, then went back to putting lotion on her leg.

"I'm getting comfortable because I'm next to the woman I love. And it feels good." I tenderly placed my arm around her waist and slightly pulled her to me.

"Mm-hmm. Whatever. Did you run that same line on your lawyer girl?"

"Why bring up a woman who is not you, Shamika? I'm not here to talk about Keisha. Now, let me have this." I reached for her foot and lotion.

"What are you doing, Korey?" she asked, shaking her head, but yielding it to me.

"About to give my baby a foot massage. You still like those, don't you?" I said, covering her foot with lotion.

"You didn't get my permission."

"Do I have to? Now relax."

I stood up. She rested back on her elbows, looking up at me, slowly shaking her head. She knew what time it was. I began caressing her well-manicured pretty little foot gently and massaging her sole with my thumbs. "You like how this feels?" I asked, massaging up and down and in a circular motion.

"Mm-hmm. You know I do," she softly replied with a nod.

"Then just relax, baby girl," I told her, feeling that she was a little nervous and tense. After all, we hadn't been together intimately in years. I was a little nervous myself.

She took in a deep breath as I placed her big toe in my mouth and sucked on it seductively. I licked, sucked, and maneuvered my tongue on, over, and in between her little toes while continuing to massage her sole with my thumb.

"I like that, Korey."

"I know you do."

She lay on her back, taking in air between her teeth, looking up at the ceiling while I worked my mouth magic. By the time I got to her other foot and did the same, my dick was solid, rock hard! It was literally bulging through my sweats. I took her foot and placed it on my hard-on to assure her that I wanted to do more than massage and suck on her toes. She raised her head and stared at my hard dick that was now throbbing inside my briefs and sweats as I guided her foot over it. It had grown since our last encounter from seven inches to nine.

I put her foot down and got on top of her. She tenderly wrapped her arm around my neck and met my lips for a passionate kiss. "What was so funny?" I asked her with my hard-on touching her juicy pussy print through her black-and-white zebra-striped panties.

"Nothin'. I just see that it still doesn't take much for you to get an arousal," she softly shot back in between our lips and tongue reintroducing themselves after such a long hiatus.

"What are you going to do about it?"

"What do you want me to do?"

"I want you to take your robe and panties off," I told her. I then let up only to get completely naked myself.

"You haven't had any since you been home, have you?" she asked while coming slap dead up out of her robe and panties like I desired her to.

"No, I haven't. Been saving it for you."

Her body was petite and flawless from head to toe. She always loved for me to suck her breasts, so since she sat back on the bed, I got down on her level and kissed her at her titties. Her titties were a nice handful with perky nipples. I targeted the left one with my mouth, licking and gently sucking on it while gripping and gently squeezing the other at its nipple with my fingertips.

"Oooo," she moaned, cocking her head and closing her eyes. "You still know how to suck my tits. It feels good. Suck my pussy like you did the night before you got arrested." She began to completely relax and turn into that girl I loved sexually.

She lay back and put her legs up a little higher than one would being in a missionary position. Baby girl couldn't help herself at this point, with me naked in front of her and touching her the way she was supposed to be touched. She was always weak for me sexually, and I was for her. We both were freaks for each other. I knew that part of her being stressed all out lately and all aggressive with me earlier had a lot to do with her missing the thug loving I used to put on her ass daily prior to me going off to the joint.

I put my face between her legs that were lifted and opened wide. I kissed the lips of her juicy fruit. "I missed you while I was away," I spoke to it, licking her moist slit. "But daddy home now and gonna give you what you've been being neglected of." I continued talking with what I believed belonged to me, Korey Taylor, and only me.

Slowly, I licked her clit, causing her body to tense from pleasure. A soft, "Uhhh," escaped her lips as I sucked her sweet pussy. I simultaneously gripped her tits and gently squeezed her nipples with my fingertips. This was enough to drive her crazy. My sucking her hot cherry button and pussy always did. She gripped my head, pulling me closer to her. I licked up and down her clit with the tip of my tongue faster and sucked on it more aggressively. Her breathing got heavy and her moans louder and deeper. She began slowly twirling her hips. This tongue was feeling tremendously good to her. She was cumming like a muthafucka! She lay there on the bed a moment, unable to move.

I got over her and kissed her lips.

"What did you just do to me, Korey?" she said softly with a slight tremble in her voice.

"I made you feel good, baby girl. That's what you needed, isn't it?"

"But I'm saved now. A Christian woman. You're not supposed to do that to me. Move." She playfully pushed me.

"God made us for each other. I love you, Shamika." I placed her legs around my waist. She wrapped her arms around my neck.

"Can I make love to you now?"

"You already started." She kissed me.

I gripped my solid dick, hard as a rock, and placed it at her moist pussy lips. I eased inside her slowly. "Uhhh, sss," she moaned and tightened her arms around my neck.

"Don't worry, baby girl. You know I'll be gentle." I began slowly stroking her pussy. I could tell by its tightness that it had been locked to the public. This was my pussy. "You miss this lovin', don't you, Shamika?"

"Uhh, huh. Ssss."

"Next time I come over here, I don't wanna see you all stressed out with your hair all over the place. You hear me?" I said while stroking her middle and hitting her bottom with pinpoint accuracy.

"Yessss," she softly answered me.

"I want to see you looking pretty. And I want you welcoming me with open arms like you used to do before I went off to do time. You hear me?"

"I hear you, Korey," she moaned. Tears were coming down her eyes. She always started crying when I hit that pussy off like she liked it. Nice, slow, and hard.

"You love me?" I continued to tease.

"Yesss. You know I love you, Korey."

When she told me that, I felt myself about to cum. I pulled out. "Show me how much you love me." She knew what I meant because she sat up with me standing in front of her with my dick solid, hard. She gripped it and began sucking the hell out of my dick. The last time she sucked my dick like she was now doing was the night before I was arrested. Back and forward she went with her hands gripping my hips. No woman had ever sucked my dick like Shamika. She got me off, then got me back hard again, bent over doggie style, where I hit her off until we both were burnt out and crashed. When I awoke, she was serving me breakfast in the nude. After eating, we went at it again.

# Chapter 16

## *I Don't Play Games*

Having worked things out with Shamika and hitting her off sexually, I had to leave to go handle business with Hammer. I saw that he and Keisha had been trying to reach me like all night and all morning. I left Shamika's at 1:00 p.m., but not before placing five grand on her dresser while she was in the bathtub getting herself ready to go pick up our daughter from her grandmother's house. "Take that money I left on your dresser in your bedroom and go Christmas shopping for you and Olivia," I told her, giving her a kiss before finally rolling out.

When I got to Hammer's place, I saw Keisha coming down the stairs as I was about to up to my bedroom. "What up, Ke?" I greeted her.

She didn't look happy to see me. In fact, she blew air through her nostrils and poked her lips. "I don't know. You tell me."

"I saw you had tried reaching me last night and this morning."

"Apparently you were too busy to respond," she cut in, snaking her neck like the chicks in the hood do when they are mad at something their man did.

"Nah, I was with Shamika. We had a few things, issues, to resolve. It's all good now."

"I bet it is, Korey," she said, rolling her eyes and walking away toward the kitchen.

"What's that supposed to mean, Ke?" She didn't look back to respond. "So it's like that?" Again, without looking back, she gave me a dismissive wave of her hand.

I went to my bedroom, shaking my head at her tripping. I picked out some gear, which was my black-and-white Adidas sweat suit with my matching black-and-white shell-toe Adidas; then I prepared to shower. I didn't see Hammer's car in the driveway, nor did I see his wife, so I assumed they weren't present inside the house.

I showered real good, thinking the whole time while washing my body about how happy I felt knowing that Shamika and I were on good terms and that I left her smiling and not stressed. My daughter didn't like seeing her mother all stressed out. She shouldn't have had to. It worried her. No teenager should have to worry about their parents' mental and emotional state of being. I felt Shamika just needed to know that I loved her still and could still make her day with this dick! She was always concerned about me being in the game. What woman who truly loves her man wouldn't be?

I got out of the shower, dried off, and wrapped the towel around my waist. I walked back to my room only to discover a surprise. Keisha was sitting on the edge of my bed with the briefs I had on last night, which I had taken off before going to the shower. She had them in her hand, twirling them around her index finger.

I saw also that she had changed into the purple nightie that I had bought for her. The one that read SPECIAL across the breast area. Her nose was flared. She was slowly shaking her head from left to right and chewing on her bottom lip while staring in my direction.

"Keisha, what's up, baby?" I asked, looking at her strangely too. I was tripping inside to see her in my room with my dirty briefs in her hand, twirling them around and around her index finger, looking all mad.

"You know exactly what's up, Korey." She stood up.

"Then why would I ask?" I reached for my briefs. She threw them across my bedroom.

"Looks to me like you and Shamika did more than resolve that little issue that you needed answers on. You fucked her, didn't you?" she asked, looking me squarely in the eyes with her arms crossed.

"That's neither here nor there, Ke. Whatever I do with Shamika ain't got nothing to do with what you and I share," I told her while walking over to grab my dirty briefs to put them in my dirty clothes basket. She quickly walked over to them, beating me to them. "What are you doing, Ke?" I said, seeing her grabbing them. She then stood back in front of me with her arms crossed.

"Answer my question." She raised her voice and snatched the towel I had wrapped around my waist, leaving me before her in the nude.

"Keisha, are you kidding me right now?" I reached for the towel. She tossed it across the room.

"Does it look like I'm joking around?" She tossed my briefs to the floor again as well.

"No, but you are trippin'. And I don't like you being this way." I retrieved my towel and wrapped it around my waist.

"I just want to know if you—"

"Keisha," Kolanda interrupted, peeping into my bedroom. "Do you have a minute?"

"No. I'm busy right now!" she told her sister. Then she walked over to the door and closed it. I looked at her and how she was carrying on all mad and marching back over to get in my face. I laughed because her trippin' was funny to me.

"Did you or did you not fuck her, Korey?" she asked again, looking me in my eyes with her arms crossed.

"Yes. Yes, I fucked her. You happy now?" I stood looking at her with my arms and hands out as if about to receive something into them.

"So us kissing in your Corvette when you picked me up for lunch, what was that, Korey? You playing with me?"

"I don't play games, Ke."

"What was it, then?" she asked, poking my chest with her index finger with every word she spoke.

"It was me showing my affection for you."

"Affection?"

"Baby girl, I like you," I said, gently reaching to take her hand into mine. "I wouldn't fucking play with your heart if I didn't. So stop all this tripping." I pulled her close because I saw in her pretty brown eyes that all she wanted was for me to show her that I cared for her, that she meant something special to me. *No wonder she went and threw on the nightie I bought her.*

"Don't be letting that pretty face of yours look all mad and shit for nothing. You all mad for nothing, for real." I wrapped my arms around her passionately and pecked a soft kiss on her neck.

"Then kiss me. Kiss me like you kissed me when you took me out for lunch in your Corvette," she said softly. She wrapped her arms around my neck and jumped up in my arms with her legs locked around my waist.

"You're something, girl. But is this what you want?" I tenderly pecked a kiss to her lips. The top first, then the bottom.

"Mmm," she softly moaned through her throat, letting me taste her sweet tongue. She was a great kisser. We tongue-danced for a whole two minutes.

"I want to be your lady, Korey," she muttered in between us passionately kissing.

"You already are, Keisha."

"I am?"

"As far as I'm concerned, you are, cutie. You been here for me since the day I got out. Just don't trip off me seeing my baby mom. I gotta be there for her and our daughter."

"Does she do this?" She unwrapped her legs from my waist, got down on her knees, and removed the towel from my waist. She took my semi-erect dick in her soft, warm, gentle hand and inserted it into her warm, moist mouth. She placed her hands behind her back and began slowly sucking my dick forward and back while looking up into my eyes. She sucked me wonderfully. I noticed that while she was looking me in my eyes while doing so, I felt shivers up and down my spine. Shamika knew how to suck my dick real good too. She was the best I ever had. But Shamika never gave me head while simultaneously looking me directly in my eyes as Keisha was doing. I felt Keisha was looking into my soul and making an emotional connection. Her pretty brown eyes and mouth magic working in harmony was telling me in no uncertain terms that she wanted more intimacy with me. She wanted a connection in our souls that would never be broken sexually.

*This girl damn good!* I silently gave her props. I wasn't in church, but she was blessing me with this wonderful, magnificent blowjob that had me trembling with pleasure. I felt myself about to cum, so I pulled out of her mouth.

"What's wrong?"

"Nothing's wrong. I got something for you." I reached for her hand to help her to her feet.

"What?" she asked, curious. "I wasn't finished with you."

"Yeah, but I want to taste you." I kissed her lips. "Get on my bed and lie on your stomach."

"My stomach?" She began removing her panties.

"With your legs spread and your ass tilted. I wanna suck your pussy from the back." I slapped her on the ass cheek as I escorted her to my bed. I reached for her panties that she still had in her hand and tossed them to the floor. She dove on my bed and lifted her nightie. She tossed her long hair to one side and positioned her face sideways, looking back at me through her peripheral vision, with that voluptuous ass of hers in the air.

I dropped to my knees, gripped her soft ass cheeks with my hands, and parted her pussy lips from the back with my thumbs. Unlike Shamika, who didn't shave her pussy because she liked things natural, Keisha's was clean shaven. I gave it a kiss like it was the lips on her pretty face. Up, down, and around her clit, I began licking with the tip of my tongue, not too fast, but not too slow. I sucked on it with her looking back at me with squinted eyes and with her mouth open like she wanted to scream.

While licking her hot button of love, my door opened. "Kor . . ." I heard Hammer attempt to say my name before he quickly shut my door. Keisha and I both began laughing at him catching me with my face buried between her ass cheeks, eating her pussy. I let up with a solid, hard dick. With Keisha face down and ass up, doggie style, I got on top of her and eased my dick inside her warm, wet womanhood. I began hitting her off slowly. She moaned my name and reached her hand back and pushed at my abs to prevent me from going too deep. But I wanted to fuck her the way I wanted to fuck her. The thug way. Hammer told me that this dick was what she needed in her life. So I reached for her hands and gripped them at her waist like I was arresting her, doggie style.

"Korey, what are you doing?" she moaned.

"Handling my business." I slowly stroked her pussy while holding her hands so that she couldn't prevent how much of this dick I put in her. Around and around, my dick explored her womanhood. In and out, I deeply penetrated, working her middle. Her soft ass cheeks bounced forward and back off my midsection with every hard stroke.

She was moaning and calling my name loud enough for Kolanda and Hammer to hear if they were anywhere nearby. As I sped up my pace, working her middle and hitting her bottom, she cried that she was cummin' and for me not to stop! I let her hands go free and held her at her waist, pulling her to me with every forward stroke of my dick for deeper access. She screamed my name and clawed the bedspreads and mattress. I was fucking the hell out of her from the back, unapologetically.

She was cumming hard, and so was I at this point. I quickly pulled out to avoid nutting inside her. I wiped myself with my towel. She turned onto her side and curled up. I got on top of her and kissed her. "You all right?"

She looked at me and nodded, struggling to recover from her orgasm.

"You sure?"

"Korey," she said softly, touching my cheek with her feathery hand. "That was awesome."

"I thought so too." I kissed her again.

She turned her body so that she could be on her back. I was over her and between her legs. "Did you enjoy yourself?" she asked me, looking me in the eyes.

"I enjoyed every minute of you. I want some more." I leaned in for a passionate kiss. Before I knew it, my dick was hard again. I eased it back inside her with her legs wrapped around my waist. We were at it again.

# Chapter 17

## *Merry Christmas*

"Damn, my nigga," Hammer said. "You and Keisha was up there fucking like a mu'fucka! Was the pussy good, K? It had to be. You had your face all in it!" he exclaimed while we rode to handle some business in his car.

"Like KFC!" I shot back, shaking my head and gripping my crotch, letting him know it was finger-licking good! "She got a snapper, Ham. That's on my solid and my mother's grave!"

"I told you her shit ain't been tatted all up by nigga's dicks. That's that grade A like her sister, Kolanda."

"I can tell."

"She's only had that one dude. The white boy I told you about."

"Man, I love Keisha. And, peep this, her head game, yo, it's off the meter! I love a girl who can blow my horn, no bullshit!"

"Sucked your dick into oblivion, didn't she?" Hammer said, cheesing hard. He was barely able to keep his eyes on the road. He was asking me all these questions about Keisha and me in the bedroom because he wanted to be able to tell me now for certain, "I told you so." Ever since I'd known his ass, he hated for someone to doubt what he believed and knew to be true. I didn't doubt him from the start. Everything he dropped in my ear about Keisha I kept close to my heart. I just needed a little time to feel shit out and see things for myself, Korey's way. Especially since I had been away so long in the joint.

"So, what's up? You going to lock it in with her on a serious relationship-type thing? What?"

I inhaled and exhaled hard and thought about what Hammer just asked. I was falling for Keisha hard, no doubt. But my true, loving heart was still with Shamika.

"To be honest, Ham, I want her and Shamika."

"But I thought you and Shamika has issues."

"Told you we resolved our issue. See, Ham, I thought Shamika had totally fuckin' abandoned me. But, man, nothing was further from the truth. She been raising our daughter right, man. Olivia is very smart and respectful. Other than that, she ain't with no man. All she do, besides spend quality time with O, is work and sleep."

"Yeah, but twelve years is a long time to be gone. How can you be certain she didn't cut out on you for real, for real, K?" he asked, pulling into a car dealership of a guy he needed to hit off with seven ounces of heroin.

"I know because she looked me in my eyes and told me. I know her, Ham. If she was fucking around, she would have told me. Especially after I brought fine-ass Keisha over to her house. Yeah, she would have told. Not to mention, a woman's pussy don't lie to a man, either."

"You fucked her?" He parked the car.

"We got it in good, dawg. It was like I was hitting a virgin."

"So what you're saying is, you're gonna love and keep her and Keisha?"

"Yo, I think your people comin'." I looked and saw a guy walking toward Hammer's side of the car. We were in his Lexus IS. The guy was carrying a briefcase.

"Korey, hop in the back seat."

I hopped into the back seat with my hand gripping my 9.

"Hammer," the guy said, giving my ace a handshake. "Good to see you. Everything's here." He pointed at the briefcase.

Hammer nodded. He was smart when making transactions. He did little talking. In fact, if someone talked too much, he and I both got leery and took it as a sign that they could be wired, working for the authorities. If that had been the case, we'd all die. Going back to the joint was not an option.

Hammer motioned with his hands for the guy to open the briefcase. He got the message and did so. Again, Hammer nodded, seeing that all the cash was present. He pointed with his thumb for him to hand the briefcase to me, which he did. Then Hammer opened the console and handed him a brown paper bag full of heroin. The guy took a look inside, nodded, and shook Hammer's hand. He then exited the car, and Hammer pulled off.

We made two more drops before calling it a night. We went back to the house, ate Domino's Pizza, and played Spades. It was me and him against Kolanda and Keisha. They kicked our ass!

Christmas came fast. I spent the whole day over at Shamika's with her and Olivia. Olivia had so many brand new clothes and shoes, she could have opened up her own clothing store! She loved the tennis bracelet that Keisha picked out for me to give her. I'd gone back to the mall and bought Shamika one too. Hers was hot pink. She too loved her gift. Shamika bought me tank tops, briefs, and socks in different colors, and Egyptian Musk cologne. She loved smelling that fragrance on me. It was one of my favorites as well. Olivia bought me the latest Jordans. She said she didn't know what to get me, so she asked her mother what I liked, and Shamika told her I was a freak for Jordans. In the old days, I had every pair that came out.

After the sun had gone down, Shamika asked me if I would like to join her and Olivia at her mother's house for dinner. I declined. Her mother was never a big fan of me and what I was doing in the streets. She used to tell Shamika all the time that she could have done better than have a baby by a thug. "A nigga in the streets!" she called me. I respected her opinion of me. She wanted the best for her daughter. In her eyes, the best wasn't me.

Before they got ready to go to her mother's, I asked Olivia to excuse us for a moment while we discussed something in Shamika's bedroom.

"Okay, Daddy." She went and put all her gifts that were all over the living room inside her bedroom.

I shut Shamika's bedroom door. She was looking so good with her black drawstring sweat suit with knee-high black leather boots.

"What do you want to talk about, Korey, that's so important that you asked Olivia to leave us alone?" she said, picking through her hair as she looked in the mirror.

I eased up behind her, placing my hands around her waist, and I kissed the back of her neck. "I just wanted you to know that I truly enjoyed the two of you today."

"We enjoyed you too, Korey." She turned around and faced me. "When are you going to come and go to church with us?"

"That's not for me right now. You know I don't play with God, baby girl." I kissed her lips.

"It's not about playing with God. It's about taking time to give Him praise and fellowship with His people."

"I'll get to it, Mika."

"When, Korey?" She gave me a look of concern.

"No man knows the time and day that the Good Lord will call upon him for his services. But I'm sure that day will come. Every person has their own appointed time, boo-boo. Now, let me taste them sweet lips."

She yielded them to me and kissed me with passion. Before I knew it, my dick was hard. "Let me get a little bit before you go to your mother's for dinner."

"Right now, Korey? Olivia's out there waiting."

"Olivia is in her bedroom. Now, let me get a li'l bit."

She looked at me and shook her head. While she was looking, I was dropping my pants and briefs to my ankles. She saw my dick, hard and pointing forward. She came out of her boots, sweatpants, and panties. I got on top of her and kissed her while massaging her pussy with my finger until it was soaking wet. I eased my dick inside her and began grinding in circular motions, nice and slow.

"You must want Olivia to have a sibling, Korey, the way you been making love to me," she moaned. I'd been hitting Shamika off every other day since we resolved our issue.

"You want me to stop?" I teased, knowing better, for she'd been upbeat and showing off her pearly whites since this dick had been back in her life.

"Noooo." She softly stretched the word. "What I want is for us to get married."

"You're already my wife, Mika. We don't need a wedding for you to know that. Do we? I don't, baby."

"We just . . . just need to consider doing things God's way," she stuttered between me slowly grinding like she liked it.

"Love is God's way, Mika. I love you."

"I love you too. But—"

"But what?" I cut in, stroking deeper and speeding up my pace. "But what, Mika?" I teased, working her middle in and out.

"Nothin'," she softly replied, taking air in between her teeth and tightening her arms around my neck. In and out of her womanhood I went in circular motions. She started crying as she always did when this dick was sending her to cloud nine. It was feeling good to her. It was feeling good to me as well. I didn't want to let up, but the more I sped up my pace, the quicker nature took its course with us both. We went to heaven on a "quickie jet" fueled by love and hot lust. Love and lust that I couldn't see myself burying for this beautiful woman, ever!

I went and took a quick wash up, then she did the same while I went to Olivia's bedroom and kissed her good-bye. "I love you, Daddy," she said soft and sweet.

"I love you too, sweetheart."

"Thank you for my gifts."

"Thank you for mine." I kissed her forehead and departed with tears in my eyes. When I was in the joint, I thought about reuniting with my baby girl. I didn't know how I would be able to take care of her, though. Getting back in the drug game was the last thing on my mind to do to assist me in being in a position to spoil my baby girl. Now I was home. And, due to Hammer's situation with the old man, and me backing his play, I had crazy loot stashed. Loot that I planned to use to keep my baby girl and her mother smiling.

I went and spent the rest of my evening with Keisha at her condo uptown. She cooked peppered steak with fried veggies over white rice and banana pudding for dessert. We drank cherry Moscato and exchanged Christmas gifts under the illuminating candlelight that was resting in the middle of her dining table. It gave off a sweet strawberry aroma. She bought me a gold Rolex Presidential watch, which she placed on my arm while sitting on my lap. I had bought Hammer a rack of freaky triple-X DVDs. He and his wife bought me a brand new black and gold Ninja motorcycle, the latest on the market.

"Merry Christmas," she said, smiling. This was one of those moments where I wanted to cry. From day one, Keisha has made me feel like a king.

"Thank you, cutie," I looked her in her eyes and said. "I really appreciate this gift. It's very, very nice." I bought her and Kolanda onyx stone tennis bracelets since she had told me that black was her and Kolanda's favorite color. She was speechless. She received it with tears of joy coming down her eyes and down her cheeks as I placed it on her wrist. I wiped her tears with my palm and thumb.

"You make me feel very special and wanted, Korey." After I placed her gift on her arm, we kissed some more.

"Because you are special," I told her with a feathery rub of my hand up and down her back. She was sitting on my lap with only a designer leopard bra and thong on. I was wearing only leopard briefs that she had also bought for me and suggested I wear for this romantic occasion. She was looking so sexy in her bra and thong. Her bra held her voluptuous breasts incarcerated. Wanting to kiss, lick, and suck them, I lifted her bra up, freeing her tits like the judge freed me of my unreasonable prison sentence. I kissed and sucked one while gently squeezing the other with my hand. I pinched her nipples with my fingertips. She moaned when I did that.

After making love to her warm, soft tits with my mouth, tongue, hand, and fingertips, I lifted her up into my strong, muscular arms. I carried her to her bedroom and lay her on her bed. I removed my briefs, then crawled to her and got back to sucking her nipples, both of them, which caused her back to arch and her to take in air between her teeth. I kissed and licked my way down to her flat stomach and circled my tongue on her navel.

Wanting to taste her sweetness, I pulled her thong off, got on my knees, and held her legs up at her inner lower soft thighs. I buried my face and tongue in her delicious peach pie of pleasure, causing her to squirm and grip my head in ecstasy.

"Merry Christmas," I said, eating her to bliss.

"Thank you, Santa," she softly shot back, enjoying the ride.

# Chapter 18

## *Happy Birthday!*

Six months after Christmas, on a beautiful summer day in June damn near ninety degrees, I picked Shamika up from her job in my Vette. It was her birthday, June tenth. I'd already had a dozen red roses sent to her job with a gift basket of bath stuff, including a gift certificate for a massage, facial, and manicure. She hopped inside my car, kissed me, and told me that all her girlfriends at her job as a cashier at Walmart off South Boulevard were harmlessly jealous of the fact that her daughter's father was home and treating her like a queen on a throne. I smiled hard when she told me that. For all I ever wanted was to make her happy and as comfortable as possible in life.

"You said you had somewhere you wanted to take me, Korey. Where?" she asked as I drove out to Mint Hill, which was on the outskirts of Charlotte. I pulled up to a nice-ass double-wide trailer with nice green lawn and a big driveway.

"Who lives here?"

I turned the engine to my car off, reached into my pocket, and retrieved a set of keys. "You do," I said, handing her the keys.

"I do? Korey, are you serious?" she said, wide-eyed, with her hand covering her mouth.

"It's yours, sweetheart. A two-bedroom double wide and fully furnished. C'mon, let's take a look inside."

Once inside, Shamika could hardly move. She stood still and looked around at her new place of residence. She covered her eyes with her hands and broke down crying.

"No, baby girl, don't cry," I said, wrapping my arms around her.

"I'm just happy, Korey. That's all."

"That's what I'm here for, to make you happy, sweetheart. I love you and our daughter."

She wrapped her arms around me and hugged me tight. "Thank you, Korey."

"Keisha owns a lot of property and houses, Mika. She sold this to me for seventy grand. The paperwork is straight. Everything."

"Seventy grand, Korey? That's a lot of money. Are you serious?" she said as we toured her new place.

"That's nothing. I've been doing a helluva lot of hustling and saving. Trust me. We just got to keep up the property tax. It's nothing, though. Keisha will handle everything for me on that end."

"You sure?"

"Most definitely. She's a business woman and a good girl. A real good friend, she is."

"Okay, but let me ask you this, Korey, because I notice you talk a lot about her—"

"Only because she has helped me a great deal since I've been home. She's really a good friend and business consultant, Mika," I cut in.

"I can understand that. But are the two of you intimately involved? That's what I would like to know," she asked, looking me directly in the eyes for the truth. We had stopped right where our daughter's room was going to be. I looked back into her eyes, knowing how she was and how she felt about me having a side piece.

That was a no-no in her eyes. If I told her the truth, that I was in love with Keisha, but on a level different from the one she and I shared, it would be a truth that Shamika would vehemently contest for lack of understanding my blossoming friendship and soul tie with Keisha.

"Look, Mika," I said, attempting to answer her without saying something I shouldn't that would cause her to slap the hell out of me. I knew her. She was not into sharing her man and throne with no other woman. Oh, no. Not if she could help it. "I just gave you the keys to your own house. The days of you paying rent are over. I got another surprise for you as well. All I want is for you and our daughter to be as comfortable as possible and out of the fucking projects. Now, you know me. I'm never going to outright, on purpose, disrespect you. Neither will I allow anyone else to. All I ask, Mika, is that you afford me the same courtesy and not trip off shit that doesn't really matter at the end of the day."

"Okay, okay, okay. Wait," she said, putting her hand up and staring at me with a look that told me that she was about to get all in her feelings over this. "I understand all that. And it goes without saying as far as whether I love you. You know I do. And I respect you."

"Then, baby girl, you gotta let me be me. I'm not a peewee. I'm a man."

"I challenge you to act like it. Because, listen, Korey," she said, now pointing her finger in my face, "I won't be your fool."

I blew air out of my mouth, causing my jaws to inflate, and I slightly turned my head and closed my eyes. The last thing I needed was for her to start bitchin'! "C'mon, Mika. Let's not do this on your birthday."

"Do what?" she shot back with attitude.

"Start arguing over nothing!"

"I'm not arguing with you, Korey. But you will not be pissing on my face and calling it rain!"

"So that's what you think I'm doing? Pissing on your face and calling it rain, Mika?"

All of a sudden, she got quiet on me. Just stood in front of me, lips poked and arms crossed. When she got all quiet and shit, that was when I had to really watch her. It was in those moments she'd be thinking that what she was saying to me was going in one ear and out the other. When she started feeling like that, like I was not listening to her point of view, that was when she started wanting to talk with her hands. So what did I do next? I gently placed my hands on her shoulders and softly looked her in her eyes.

"I picked you up at your job, baby girl, to give you your birthday present, to show you just what you mean to me. How many niggas you know hustling and taking their baby mama and their child out of the projects to better living? Niggas out here making money and spending it in strip clubs and on fucking rims for a car, while their baby mama and kids are struggling!"

"And I appreciate my birthday gift," she said calmly. "But you're still not answering my question, Korey."

"Because I don't need you asking me shit like that regarding Keisha."

"Why not? What is there to hide?"

"It's irrelevant, Mika. That's why. And, trust me, I ain't got nothing to hide."

"Then give me a direct answer, Korey. Are the two of you intimately involved?"

"No!" I lied. "Now, you happy?" I had too much love for her to tell her the absolute truth. Telling her the absolute truth would only cause her to toss and turn at night wondering if I loved Keisha more than I loved her. Plus, telling her the absolute truth would have gotten me slapped on the spot. Now I knew why they say, "Don't let your left hand know what your right one is doing." Some things you just gotta keep to yourself.

"I know you lying, Korey." She pointed her finger in my face. "I swear you better not bring me no disease. God knows you better not do that. And you better not have Olivia around her like that's her second mother. The devil is a liar! I didn't have our daughter around no man while you were gone because I didn't have one. So you do me that favor and not have her around your woman you're lying about, 'cause y'all got far more than a bizzzness relationship. I should punch you!" She pushed my shoulder.

I started laughing and shaking my head. But this was Olivia's mother. My heart. I loved her to death. "I'm grown. We're grown, Mika. Let's focus only on what really matters. If I had a hundred women, not one of them would be Shamika. There's only one of you. My baby."

"Whateva." She smiled, sucking her teeth. I reached and pulled her to me by her waist.

"You and our daughter got a roof over your head that you can call your own. That's all that really matters to me. You hear me?"

"I hear you."

"Good. Give me a kiss."

She kissed me with her eyes closed, intimately.

"I love you, girl," I said, wrapping my arms around her tightly. "Okay, now, let me show you what else Keisha helped me purchase for you. You do like this crib, though, right?"

"I love it."

"All right then, good."

Shamika and I hopped back into my Vette and drove a couple blocks from the crib I bought her. We pulled up on this busy strip where there were businesses of all sorts,

black and white owned. I escorted her to a spot right next
to a white-owned barbershop. It was a small beauty salon
that had been up for sale. An older Korean lady owned
it who Keisha knew as a client. She had filed bankruptcy
and gone out of business due to tax issues relating to
some of her other business endeavors. I had to have it for
my baby.

"You told me that while I was in the joint, you went to
cosmetology school to be a beautician and that you had
even gotten your license, right, Mika?"

"I did," she confirmed. "Been wanting my own shop
ever since. I swear, Korey."

"Well, now you have your own three-chair shop." I gave
her the key, and we went inside. It was small, but still
very clean and nice. Shamika looked around and nodded
her head.

"I like it. Now I ain't gotta worry about doing hair at my
apartment. Thank you, baby!" She kissed and hugged me.
"How much did it cost you?"

"Almost twenty for this. But, again, Keisha made it
happen."

"Twenty thousand?" she said, surprised. "Korey, not to
be all in your business, but you making money like that?"

I wanted to tell her that Hammer and I were rolling
selling heroin, that sometimes we'd make $50,000
with one drop. We were selling an ounce of good heroin
anywhere from $12,000 to $15,000 a pop. I didn't go all
into that with my sweetheart, though. The less she knew
of my criminal involvements, the better.

"I'm doing pretty good, baby girl," I answered her.
"Mainly, I just been saving." I had learned while in the
joint, in a business awareness class, that making money
was one thing. Managing it was another. There was no
way I was gonna be back hustling, making crazy cash and
not have enough sense to put that cash where I felt it was

needed, securing not only my future, but the future and comfort of Shamika and our beautiful daughter, Olivia.

"Happy birthday," I told her with tears in my eyes from seeing her so happy. "Happy birthday." I wondered if her mother would think I was good enough for her daughter now. Probably wouldn't. But fuck it. I was here to make her daughter happy, not her.

# Chapter 19

## *Fuck Beating Josh's Ass*

**Keisha**

"Fuck beating Josh's ass," I told my brother-in-law while sucking my teeth and dismissing the thought of wanting to see him scared and bruised all up. Hammer had come to my condo with Korey to get confirmation from me regarding the matter. When they arrived at my condo, it was late, like a quarter to midnight on a Friday. They both were dressed in all black and riding their twin Ninja bikes, which I discerned from seeing their bike helmets in their hands. I saw that they were both also packing guns. They had placed them on my kitchen table where we were sitting and sipping on green tea with lemon. Hammer had fired up a blunt and passed it to me for a hit. I hit it and passed it to Korey. He said he was cool, so I passed it back to Hammer.

"Are you sure you don't want this muthafucka fucked up, Ke?" Hammer asked, between holding in the smoke from his mellow grass. He was looking for further confirmation. After all, we had made a deal. I came through on my end. Now he was ready to deliver on his end. I knew he would be, sooner or later. One thing about my brother-in-law, he didn't play with his word. If he said he was gonna do something, he did it.

"Korey and I drove by that cat's crib, and we saw him from a distance, playing with a little boy on his porch. I was ready to serve his ass."

"Yeah, that little boy was more than likely his new bitch's son. Apparently, the bitch had him from a previous marriage. Like I said, fuck him. I'm moving on." When I said that, I noticed Korey nodding as if to say that was the right thing to do. Hammer passed me the blunt again, and I took another drag, then passed it back.

"I was about to serve the dude, but Korey stopped me and said that we should check with you for a final word."

"Well, now you have it, Ham. Let him be. Besides," I said, pouring them some more of my homemade green tea, "the two of you got your hands full doing what you're doing, businesswise. Correct?"

"Business is good. Real good," Hammer replied.

"Not to mention catching up to that rat, Fat Raheem! We all want to see him get his."

"Oh, for sho', Ke. Korey and I will see him soon. Real soon, hopefully." I saw Korey nod when Hammer said that. They both changed their facial expressions as he said that. They put on their thug faces for that one.

Fat Raheem was the chief stoolpigeon in my father's case. I never forgot his fat ass and what he decided to do against my father for the Feds. This rat sat at our father's table and was even referred to as "Uncle Rah" by Kolanda and me. He was extremely close to our father. He was family! But he crossed my father to save his own ass from experiencing prison. It's always the ones close to you that hurt you the most.

While we were talking, Hammer's phone went off. He went to the bathroom to answer it. It was Kolanda. She had gone out of town on business, which was why I had been over at my condo. Korey and Hammer were at the house doing what they did.

"How is Shamika and Olivia?" I asked Korey.

"They good. Love their new place. Olivia is going to finish school out where she is, which will be out in a month or so. Later, Shamika will enroll her in a school near their new place. They love it, though, Ke."

"That's good. How about things at Shamika's new salon?"

"Well, it's only been open a month and a half, but business is starting to pick up for her. She got the other two chairs filled. Some young twenty-five-year-old gay black dude rented one and a black woman, who is, I think, in her mid-forties, got the other. They both seem like good people. All of them had clients the other day when I was over there. So things are coming along."

"I'm happy for her. I know she means a lot to you. I think it was smart of you to get her her own shop. You a good man, Korey."

"You think so?"

"Know so." He leaned toward me and kissed me on the cheek.

"Couldn't have made none of that possible for Shamika and our daughter without you. I appreciate you, Ke."

"I know you do."

"What about you, Ke? I noticed you been working crazy hard lately."

"Just finally got a settlement. $1.6 million."

"What?" His eyes widened.

"My client suffered some serious, debilitating injuries. He should have gotten more. He was beaten pretty badly, walks with a cane, and has problems remembering things. Remember, cops only have the authority to arrest you, not assault you. So Kolanda and I are glad we were able to get a nice settlement for him."

Hammer walked back into the kitchen, phone in hand. "Well, y'all, that was my wife. She's on her way home and wants yours truly to have her bathwater ready."

"She's on her way home right now, Ham?"

"Yeah, like an hour away. Told her we were all over here at your place, talking. She said for me to tell you that things look good with that office y'all hoping to open in Rockingham."

"Oh, great." I clapped my hands, excited. Kolanda had gone to Rockingham, North Carolina, to see about opening an office. She stayed there two days with a girlfriend of ours who was also a successful practicing attorney. She wanted us to partner with her in a firm. Pamela was her name, and she did federal and state cases. Unlike my sister and me, she was a criminal trial attorney. She had clients who had wrongful convictions that she wanted my sister and me to represent in lawsuits. The only reason I didn't go with my sister to help solidify our partnership with Pamela was because I had been busy getting that $1.6 million settlement for my client the Mecklenburg County cops assaulted.

Hammer left so that he could be home when my sister got there. Korey and I kicked back, ordered some Domino's, and watched my favorite movie of all time, *Coming to America*. I crashed in his arms.

When I awoke late the next day around 11:00 a.m., Korey was nowhere in sight. He just left a note: "I'll call you," I read.

# Chapter 20

## *Taking a Trip to Monroe*

**Korey**

"Korey, what it do, dawg?" Hammer greeted me on the other end of the phone. He phoned at nine in the morning on the dot while I was still at Keisha's.

"Man, I'm lying here on Keisha's sofa with her in my arms," I said groggily and as quietly as possible to avoid awakening her.

"Y'all must have gotten it in real damn good after I left."

"Nah, we ordered pizza and watched *Coming to America*. Baby girl was tired. Not to mention high as hell. She went out like forty minutes into the movie, leaving me up to watch it by myself."

"Yeah, well, her and my wife have been real busy lately. I put my baby to sleep after about a good hour of rocking the boat," Hammer said, laughing. "She still out right now!"

"I bet."

"Look, though, my nig. Come on over, get yourself together. We riding out to Monroe. I dreamed last night that we caught up to that Fat Rat Rah and I served him his medicine."

"Word, yo?"

"I woke up sweatin', K! But that's what I called you to tell you. We taking a trip to Monroe."

"A'ight. I'll be there in about thirty."

"See ya, my nigga."

I gently laid Keisha down on the sofa and placed a light blanket over her, being that her A/C was on. I went into her bathroom, took me a long piss, washed my hands and face, then eased up out of her crib without waking her. I jumped on my bike, threw my helmet on, and burned rubber.

Hammer was already at the table, coffee steaming, and smoking a blunt. I drank a cup of freshly brewed Maxwell House with him, then hit the shower and got dressed.

"We driving your car or mine, Ham?" I asked him.

"My Lex, cool?" he replied, ready to bounce. He stuck his 9 inside his pants and covered it with his shirt. I did the same.

We rode to Monroe, which was only like a forty-five-minute drive from Charlotte. We parked not too far from the address where this Fat Rah lived, praying he'd show his head so that we could take it off! From the looks of his crib, this cat was doing the damn thing, as we say in the streets. He was living in a big-ass Southern-style plantation-type crib with the well-manicured green lawn and bushes. Parked in his driveway was a white Rolls-Royce, an old-school Boss Hog–type red convertible Eldorado with the bull horns in front, and a black Mercedes-Benz.

We sat patiently waiting literally for hours for Fat Rah to show his head. We rode back and forth up and down this isolated area where there was a lot of land and roads. We did so, trying to go unnoticed. Then we caught a break. A long-haired blond white woman, a little on the heavy side but cute from a distance, emerged from the house. She was wearing a pink tank top, dark shades, some Daisy Duke tight shorts, and sandals. She got in the Mercedes. As far as I could tell, she was in her early fifties.

"Let's follow that bitch," I told Hammer.

"That's exactly what I was thinking too, K." He pulled off behind her, incognito fashion. We followed her to a nearby convenience store gas station. She went inside.

"Park behind her, Ham. I'ma hop inside the bitch's car after hollering at her. You tail us closely. You got me?"

"I got'chu, my nigga. You know that."

I got out and checked my watch simultaneously. It read ten minutes to six. The bitch exited the gas station with what looked like two packs of cigarettes and a fuckin' lottery ticket. She went to pumping her some gas in her tank.

"Come on, now. A pretty woman like you with those long, well-manicured red nails ain't got no business pumpin' her own gas. Here, let me do that for you," I said, reaching for the pump, which she yielded to me, no problem.

"Why, thank you, young man." She blushed. Her accent was deep Southern. "This here a very small town, Monroe is. Everyone nearly knows each other. I'm surprised I've never seen a handsome fella such as yourself around here before," she said, firing up a cigarette and looking me up and down behind her shades. "What's your name?"

"Rico. Everybody who knows me calls me R," I lied to her ass. "I'm a city boy just passing through this town."

I put on a smile and faked like I appreciated her before hearing her say, "What city you're from?"

"The Queen City," I replied, stealing a glance over at her passenger side. The latch was up, indicating it was unlocked. I knew I didn't have much more time to be rapping with this chick, so I began calculating what to do next.

"I got relatives in Charlotte. Over there off of Albemarle Road."

"Oh, okay. Then maybe if you're ever in the Queen City, you could give me a call and maybe we can have a few drinks. Do you have a pen to write down my phone number?" I said, hanging up the gas pump. She opened her car door to retrieve a pen. I quickly checked my surroundings. No one was near us.

"While you're bent over inside your car looking for something to write with, how about you hop over to the other side and don't make a sound," I told her, drawing my gun.

"Huh?" She looked back and saw my burner aimed at her, and the charming, nice guy look that covered my face was now gone.

I hopped inside behind her and took control of the wheel. "Just do what I tell you and everything will be fine."

"Sir, you're not gonna rape and kill me, are you?" she asked nervously. "I can give you money if that's what you need. Just, please don't hurt me."

I checked the rearview as I began driving off. But while doing so, the bitch tried to open the door and bail. I reached and grabbed her ass by the collar, stopping the car. "Shut that door now, or I'ma blow your brains out and leave you laid out on the concrete pavement!" I aimed my gun at her face.

"Okay, okay, okay. I'll do as you say." She shut the door.

"Try that shit again, you dead!" I pulled off.

I drove to a nearby abandoned school building and parked in the lot. I got out, quickly walked over to the passenger side, and opened the door. "Get out the car and come with me," I told her, grabbing her by the arm. I escorted her over to Hammer's Lex.

"Sir, I'm sorry, but I gotta pee."

"What?" I said, opening the passenger side of Hammer's car.

"I got to pee."

"Get'cha shorts and panties down and make it quick!" She pulled her shorts and panties down with one single motion, squatted and pissed. I got the impression she was hoping someone would come along and see us with her, so she could perhaps scream out for help.

"A'ight, bitch, you been squatting long enough. Get inside the car." She pulled her shorts and panties up and got inside with a push from me. I got in behind her.

"Well, well, well, Blondie. Looks like today is your lucky day. You get to hang out with my partner and me. Do you know this guy here?" Hammer said, showing her the eight-by-ten picture of Fat Rah he showed me in Bojangles.

"Yes, that's Donald."

"Who?" Hammer looked at her like she was crazy. "Who the hell is Donald?" he asked her.

"The man on the picture there."

"This man is Fat Raheem."

"That was his name before the government changed it. The government changed his name to Donald Lee Lawrence."

"How do you know him?"

"He's my husband."

"Where is he?"

"He's at the House."

"That big house we saw you leave from before you stopped at that store to get gas?"

"No. The House is one of his gambling spots." As she made that clear, her phone went off.

"Who is that?" I asked her, giving her permission to check it.

"Him. It's Donald."

"Get your composure and see what he wants." I wanted her to answer her phone because I figured that her husband might be one of those cats who, if he called his wife and she didn't answer, he'd figure something's wrong. She put the phone to her ear and spoke with him nice and calmly. A minute later she disconnected.

"What's up? What he want?"

"He needs for me to give a guy something who is on his way to our house."

"Something like what?"

"Four kilos of coke and two pounds of marijuana."

"When?" Hammer asked.

"In about an hour."

"Why can't he deliver it?" I nodded at Hammer asking her that. He was thinking exactly what I was thinking. What man would have only his woman delivering big weight like that? She had to have bodyguards at that house, I figured. But, then again, if she had bodyguards, I wouldn't have been able to get close to her.

"He doesn't deliver it because, at certain times of day, he be running his gambling house. So at those times, he'll have me taking care of drug deals. He only deals with a select group of people. So it's no big thing."

"We're going to your house. You're going to make that transaction. But the money going to us after you do. And whatever other money is in that house of y'all's, we'll be needing that, too."

"Look, I swear to God, y'all can have the money, the drugs, and whatever else. Just please don't kill me."

"Is anybody else at that house of y'all's?"

"No. We live alone. My husband doesn't trust others like that. Not to stay with us."

"Well, Blondie, like I said, we're going back to your house, but first let me tell you why we're here."

"I think I already know why from seeing that picture you showed. That picture is of Donald some years ago. It had to come from someone who knew him in the past.

This has something to do with him snitching for the government. Am I right?"

"Simply put, he crossed the wrong muthafucka!"

After Hammer told her that, he pointed to the door. "To her house, my nigga."

I hopped back into her Mercedes with her on the passenger side at gunpoint. Hammer tailed us closely.

"How long you and your husband been married?" I asked Blondie.

"Twenty years," she answered with her face buried in her palms, crying. She'd been crying nonstop the whole way.

"You went into witness protection with him too?"

"Yes. They changed both our identities. Donald hated being in the program. I did too. They had us way out in Los Lunas, New Mexico, which is on the other side of Albuquerque. Donald wanted to leave mainly because he still had lots of money and drugs stashed that the Feds didn't know about."

"Did you know Mr. Melvin Harris, who your husband snitched on?"

"Of course. Everyone knew Melvin. Melvin was a sweet man. Took my husband from nothing to having everything. I told my husband not to cooperate with the government. But the Feds convinced him otherwise. They said he was looking at thirty to life. My husband said that there was no way he was going to prison, so he decided to cooperate."

"Wow," I said, shaking my head. "Shame on him."

"Yes, and shame on me for marrying his ass!" She began crying harder.

I pulled up at their house and parked her Benz. I got out, rushed over to her side, let her out, and at gunpoint had her escort Hammer and me inside.

# Chapter 21

## *Girl, You Cold!*

**Keisha**

"Keisha," my sister yelled my name from downstairs, interrupting me doing some legal research. "C'mere. You ain't gonna believe who just pulled up in our driveway!"

"Who is it?" I yelled, removing my glasses and turning my ear toward the direction her voice was coming from. She had gone downstairs to do some dusting and cleaning earlier. My sister was a freak for cleanliness. My father always said that Kolanda was more like our mother, the real clean, homebody, domestic, wifely type to stick by her man. We never knew our mother. She died giving birth to us. But he said I was more like him. The type with a big heart, but the type who got upset easy and rarely forgave a fault. Both my sister and I were very loving, though, a trait our father said we inherited from both him and our mother. One thing was for sure, I definitely hated domestic work. Household chores and all that. No, I'd have rather hired someone to handle that for me. My condo stayed a mess. Every time Kolanda came over she cleaned it for me out of being a clean freak!

"Come and see. You ain't gonna believe it!"

I put my glasses on my desk next to my computer and headed downstairs to see what my sister was talking about. I checked my watch on the way down. It was

8:10 p.m. I wondered why Hammer and Korey weren't back yet from Monroe, where my sister told me they had gone. Neither one of them was answering the phone, either. But they rarely did when handling business. *Oh, well.*

"Who is it, Kolanda?" I asked her again, standing before her in my sleeveless, short sundress and house slippers.

"Girl, it's Josh!"

"What? Who? You're lying." I walked over to the window and peeked under the shade. Sure enough, his ass was walking up the drive to our front door. "I don't wanna see him." I turned to walk back upstairs.

Kolanda grabbed my hand. "Girl, see what he wants. That boy didn't come all the way over here for nothing."

The doorbell rang. Kolanda politely answered, with me behind her.

"Hey, Josh," she greeted him with a smile. She could be so phony when she wanted to because she hated the fact that that bastard cheated on me.

"Hey, ladies," he greeted us back, slightly smiling. He looked past Kolanda at me. "Keisha, you . . . you mind if I come in and speak with you a moment? I know it's been awhile, but—"

"But what? Your newfound love leaving you?" I cut in, loaded with attitude.

"I'ma leave you two alone so y'all can talk," Kolanda said, about to walk away.

"You ain't gotta go nowhere, Kolanda. What he has to say to me, he can say in front of you. Now, you got thirty seconds, Josh. What do you want?" I said, looking at my watch and setting it to alarm me after thirty seconds was up.

He looked at me all defeated and took in a deep breath, then exhaled. "What I want is for you to know that I still love you. And that I made a mistake."

"Oh, really?" I said, hands on my hips. "You hear that, Kolanda? He's admitting he made a mistake. What attorney you know would do that?"

"Seriously, Keisha. I swear to Jesus I haven't been happy since you left me," he continued.

"Well, I doubt if anything will change, because I don't plan on returning to make you happy. You had your chance."

"Please, Keisha, just give me one more chance to show you that I love you and that I will leave Amy right now if you take me back."

Deet, deet, deet, deet, deet, deet. My alarm on my watch went off. "What'ya know? Your time is up, playboy. Sorry." I waved him good-bye.

"Please, Keisha. I love you."

"Love doesn't fuck around," I spat, pointing my finger in his face. That love shit coming from his mouth angered the hell out of me. "I gave you my heart, and I was damn good to you, Josh. And what do you do? You cheat on me, on a woman who was loyal!"

"You were loyal, Keisha. And—"

"I know damn well I was, punk! You messed that up by wanting another bitch over me. It's over! O-v-e-r!" I spelled it out loud and clear. "And I would appreciate it if you never came back over to this house again looking for me. Now, bye!" I turned and walked away. "Kolanda, you can shut the door now. I'm finished," I told her.

"Sorry, Josh," she said to him and shut the door. "Girl, you colder than ice cream! A true Virgo!" Kolanda said and went back to dusting the living room.

I stopped at the base of the stairway and broke down crying. This guy was my first love, the man I gave my virginity and heart to. And like broken glass, he shattered my heart into pieces, hurting me. *That's not love; that's a lousy, no-good loser!* The presence of Korey and his caring heart toward me and my feelings had helped me to pick up the broken pieces of my heart and begin to love again. All seeing Josh's face did was make me fucking angry with hate for what he did to bring our relationship to an end. Right now, I needed Korey. I needed him to hug and hold me. I needed him to kiss me and tell me that if no one else truly and sincerely loved me, he did, and that, unlike Josh, he wouldn't ever break my heart.

# Chapter 22

## *Take Me to the Safe*

**Korey**

Hammer and I sat inside this plush mansion of a crib. It was nice and cool inside, courtesy of central A/C. The furniture inside this joint was all new and covered with plastic to preserve it. The floors were shiny white marble, and the huge staircase was shiny wood grain. The staircase led to an inside balcony where one could stand on it and see everything and everybody below. This joint for real reminded me of that crib Al Pacino had in *Scarface,* where he was shooting mu'fuckas from his inside balcony, the scene outside his in-house office, the one where he said, "Say hello to my little friend!"

Fat Rah's wife led Hammer and me to a room upstairs that was filled with nothing but kilos of coke and pounds upon pounds of weed. She put four kilos in a garbage bag along with two pounds of weed to serve the cat who was coming over, who her husband had phoned her about.

About twenty minutes later, we heard the doorbell. Hammer and I stayed close by, but out of sight, while she handled her business. The customer was a white hillbilly-looking, dirty mu'fucka. I guessed that's how they looked in this neck of the woods. Mu'fuckas selling big coke, though! There was little chitchat between them. She served him and he left, leaving her with a big Ziploc bag full of cash. She didn't count it, so I assumed he was a trusted regular customer of Fat Rah. But she said it was 102 Gs. That meant Fat Rah was selling kilos for twenty-five Gs a pop and a pound of weed for a G.

I handed the cash to Hammer. He wasn't all that concerned about getting more cash. Not as concerned as he was about confronting Fat Rah.

"Take me to the safe," I told her. I figured if it was going down, and it was, we may as well take every fucking dime we could. Besides, like my ace and brother told me when I first got out, you can never have too much money!

She led me upstairs while Hammer watched things down below. While upstairs, she stopped in her bedroom. "I need to call Donald first."

"For what?"

"Whenever I make a transaction, he likes for me to phone him that everything went smooth."

"Then hurry and call him."

She called and let him know things with that hillbilly cat went smooth. Then she led me into a walk-in closet where, behind a rack of very expensive-looking casual dress suits, was a little four-foot door. She opened it, and there was a safe. She opened the safe after a few spins of the combination lock.

"There it all is," she said, stepping back so I could view it for myself. Stacks upon stacks upon stacks of cash was all I saw.

"Dump those two suitcases over there and put every dime in 'em."

"Nothing's in those suitcases," she said, retrieving them. "They're brand new."

"Load 'em up right got'dayum now."

She got busy.

"How much you think all that is in that safe?" I asked her while she was sweating, dumping it in.

"I don't know. Three or four million, I reckon. He has more, but it's in off-shore accounts. My husband is filthy rich. I swear to God he is."

"Your husband is a filthy snitch is what he is."

"There's jewelry in here, too."

"Fuck the jewelry. Cash only." I looked and saw some-thing chrome and shiny. It was a .357 Magnum. "Don't touch that gun. Let me get that." I grabbed it. The mutha-fucka was fully loaded. *Dayum,* I said silently. *If I had turned my head, the bitch would have had the ups on me!* I unloaded it, wiped my prints from it, and tossed it to the floor.

"The money, it's all there," she said. Both suitcases were full to capacity and heavy as hell. I made her carry one while I carried the other with the hand I wasn't holding my burner on her ass with. We took the suitcases to the car and got back inside the house. "He's got lots of guns, too," she squealed once back inside. This bitch was just like her husband. She'd tell everything just to save her life.

"Where?" I asked.

"In that room over there." She pointed, walking me to it. She opened the closet door and hanging all over the wall of this walk-in closet was big weaponry. AKs, M16s, Uzis, you name it. This muthafucka was ready for war.

"Ham," I called, "peep this."

He came inside. "Got'dayum!" he exclaimed. He was as shocked as I was to see such high-powered weaponry.

"This nigga ready. We ain't fuckin' with none of this, K. Fuck it. That's too much heat to ride with. Besides, we got our own burners," he said, walking back inside the living room. We followed.

"Can I please smoke me a cigarette, guys? I need one badly."

"Then smoke one, bitch," Hammer told her. He fired up a blunt he rolled from a pound of reefer he grabbed for himself while upstairs. "This some good-ass shit here!" he exclaimed, holding in the smoke, then seconds later releasing it from his lungs. "You smoke this here shit, Blondie." Hammer handed it to her.

Without saying yea or nay, she took it and hit it hard, with her hand shaking like she had Parkinson's disease.

"I knew this day would come, when someone would come looking for my husband for what he did," she said, hitting the blunt again before nervously passing it back to Hammer. "He just told on too many people," she added.

"My father-in-law received a life sentence on account of your husband being the government's star witness. From my understanding, your husband spent three days on the stand with diarrhea of that mouth of his. Rat muthafucka told it all."

"He told me the Feds told him that if he held anything back, they would forfeit the agreement."

"The Feds. Humph!" Hammer muttered with a crooked smile and put the blunt out with his fingertips. He hated the Feds. We both did. "The Feds think they're God. Got all these soft, weak, so-called gangsta-ass niggas bowing at their stinking feet! Not my father-in-law, though. Oh, no. That man . . ." Hammer said, shaking his head and crossing his body like he was in a Catholic church. "God bless the dead. That man was one of the last of a dying breed, a real solid OG." When Hammer said that, her phone went off.

"Y'all want me to answer this? It's him."

"Answer the muthafucka," Hammer told her.

She answered, spoke with him briefly, responded with some yes's and no's, then disconnected.

"What's up? What he want?" I ask, beating Hammer to it.

"He's on his way."

"Good," Hammer said, retrieving his burner from inside his pants. "That's real fucking good!"

# Chapter 23

## *Tipsy*

### Keisha

"Are you okay, sis?" Kolanda asked me, seeing that, shortly after Josh left, I went to her bedroom bar and poured myself some gin and grapefruit juice. She sat beside me and poured her one too.

"I'm fine."

"No, you're not. You're lying," she shot back, knowing me better than anyone. She placed her arm around me. "You been drinking away since Josh came over. Wanna talk about it?"

"I hate that bastard! And he got the nerve to come over to our house, talking about he still love me!"

"Maybe he does, Keisha."

"What is there to love, Kolanda, when you have shattered your woman's heart? C'mon now, riddle me that."

"The broken pieces, the memories, I guess. People do come to their senses after a while. Sometimes it just takes them being with someone worse before they realize they had someone better. Men are notorious for that shit."

"That bastard definitely had the best when he had me, Kolanda." I took a sip.

"Of course he did. I think he finally realizes that now, too."

"So, tell me," I said, taking another drink and looking into my sister's sweet face and eyes. She'd always been there for me. And although I was born three minutes and seven seconds before her, she always took up the role of big sis. "Tell me, do you think I made a mistake by not giving that bastard opportunity enough to express himself to me tonight? Or should I have slammed the fuckin' door in his face at first glance?"

"Regardless of what he wanted to say to you, he blew his chance to have you and love you unconditionally. That's all that matters. He blew that by cheating. It's okay to forgive him, Ke. Nothing wrong with that. But you don't have to take him back. As far as I'm concerned, if a man will cheat once, he'll cheat twice, and a third."

"And a fourth, and fifth," I added while continuing to sip away.

"Precisely. Best thing is to move on and don't look back, no matter how bad it hurts. You hear me, sis?" Kolanda kissed me on my forehead and squeezed me tight for comfort.

"You know I'll toast to fuckin' that!" We touched glasses and turned up our drinks. By now, I was pretty damn tipsy. "Okay, now, forget about Josh," I said. "Tell me this, Kolanda. What do you think about Killa Korey? You think he's right for me, like Ham's right for you?"

"Korey's a sweet guy. I like him. I think he really, really likes and respects you—"

"But do you think he loves me?" I cut in.

"I think that's a question only he can answer, Ke. I do feel that he believes in you and deeply enjoys your company and friendship. He tells my husband all the time that you're like an angel to him, real special. He thinks a lot of you, Ke. I like Korey."

"He thinks Keisha is special," I repeated to my sister, slurring my speech, thinking of the nightie Korey bought me. The gin was taking its course. "But he has a baby mother who he thinks is special also."

"So what? She was before you, Keisha. You can't change that. Most importantly, she's not Keisha! You're Korey's angel. His baby's mother is his baby's mother."

"Do you think I would make a good mother?" I asked, rubbing my stomach.

"Not drinking as you do whenever you're feeling emotional about something, no."

"No, really, Kolanda. Do you?"

"You'll make a good whatever you set your mind to become. But not drinking so much!" she said, helping me off the barstool and taking my drink from me. "You need to lay it down. I think you've had one too many drinks." She helped me to my bedroom where I laid my tipsy ass down.

"I love you, Kolanda," was the last thing I remembered saying before I was snoozing.

# Chapter 24

## *You Crossed My Father-in-law*

**Korey**

"Bae, I'm home," Fat Rah yelled as he stepped inside his house alone, carrying a small leather bag. "Whose car is that out in the driveway? Do you have company?"

"Donald, is that you, honey?" she yelled from the bathroom downstairs after flushing the toilet like her ass was really using the muthafucka. She was there with me as Hammer and I planned.

He walked toward the base of the staircase to go up. Unbeknownst to him, that's where Hammer was in a blind spot.

"What up, bitch!" Hammer stepped out of hiding, burner out, and aimed at Fat Rah's face, startling him.

"Hey, what's going on here?" He lifted his hands and backed up a little.

"I got a message for you, muthafucka!" Hammer barked with venom.

He looked past Hammer momentarily and saw me with my burner at the back of his wife's head. She was crying. "Do whatever they tell you, please, D."

"What's going on here, fellas? Is this a robbery?" He looked at me, then back at Hammer, who couldn't wait to address him the thug way.

"Nah, nigga," Hammer said, screwing his face up and holding his burner sideways at Rah's forehead. "This a reality check!"

"Reality check?" he repeated Hammer, confused.

From his pocket, Hammer retrieved the picture of his father-in-law. He held it up in Rah's face. "You know this man, muthafucka? You don't have to answer that. I know you do. You crossed him!"

"Look here, guys. Shit happens. I didn't have a choice in the matter."

"The main code in the game and in the streets is that if you get jammed up, you don't under any circumstances cooperate with the authorities to the extent you cross your friends and associates!" Hammer exclaimed with a hard stomp of his foot to the floor to stamp his seriousness.

I'd known my ace for many, many years. We grew up together, hustled together, went to prison together, and were still together, and I'd never seen him this serious, backed by the deadly emotion of uncompromising anger.

"Thing is, bitch, you took the easy way out," he carried on. "You crossed my father-in-law, who sent me to give you a message from his grave."

"Wait, wait, please wait. Maybe we can work this out. Maybe I can make this right. Would y'all like to have a lot of money? I got plenty. I swear I do. I'll take you to it right now. I got drugs galore, coke by the kilo, marijuana by the pound. Guys, y'all can have it all. Just let my wife and me be," his fat ass pleaded just like he did with the government, looking for the easy way out.

"My father-in-law had mad love for you," Hammer said, nose flared, shaking his head. A tear fell from his eye. "But you crossed him like Judas did the Lord Jesus. This ain't business. This one personal!"

Hammer quickly squeezed three shots off like his trigger finger was in a squeezeathon! One bullet penetrated his forehead, knocking his big body back. The other two went into his face, causing him to drop to the floor, dead as a doorknob. I knew exactly why Hammer shot him only three times. The three bullets represented the three days Rah sat on the witness stand telling the courtroom of the underworld activity he and Hammer's father-in-law were involved in.

Rah's wife wept hard with her hands at her face at seeing his body slumped over on the floor, blood pouring from his face and the back of his head, leaving a red puddle on their white shiny marble floor. Hammer rushed over to her, grabbed her by her collar, and pushed her so hard in the direction of where her husband was lying dead that she stumbled over him on the floor.

"Please, don't kill me. I cooperated with you guys to the fullest."

"That dead rat there," Hammer said, pointing at Rah with his gun, "that's your husband. A wife must ride and die with her man, bitch." He squeezed one off into her forehead, killing her instantly.

Before leaving, I ran upstairs, cut open a kilo of coke, and brought it back downstairs, leaving a trail of powder coke on the way down. I sprinkled it all over both Rah and his wife's bodies to make the scene look like a drug-related homicide. Then we set everything that looked flammable on fire and got the hell up out of Monroe.

When Hammer and I got back to the Queen City, it was a little after midnight. We grabbed the suitcases full of money and headed inside, him carrying one and me carrying the other. We went straight into the den, placed the suitcases on the sofa, and unzipped them. Hammer couldn't believe the money we now had in our possession. "How much bacon you think this is here, K?"

"I asked Fat Rah's bitch the same thing while she stuffed it all in these suitcases. She said anywhere from three to four mil. Yo, this it. We ain't got to hustle drugs no more, Ham. We set for real!"

Hammer went and grabbed his money counting machine, which was on a table to the left of us. He set it up to count our riches, then gave me some pound and a hug. "You dead right. We straight for real now, my nigga."

"Tell me 'bout it." I smiled, nodding.

Hammer grabbed a few stacks of cash out of the suitcases and put them in the money machine. Each stack was fifty grand.

"Yo, did you see the fear in that fat muthafucka's eyes when I put my burner in his face, K?"

"Looked like he saw a ghost, yo!"

"I dropped that snitch for that man right there," Ham said, pointing over at a big, blown-up, framed picture of his father-in-law on the wall. "That dear man is the reason we all are able to eat good right now. You, me, my wife, and Keisha. All of us are indebted to that dear man. Tonight, though, K, I paid my debt with the undying loyalty and help of the only brother I have ever known and have mad love for: you."

We shook hands this time, Partnerz in Crime style, locking our trigger fingers together. I was about a year and a half out of the joint, and I had said I wasn't going to get tangled back up in the game of criminal activity. But, here I was, with blood on my hands from backing my brother's play. I guess undying loyalty should not be underestimated.

"Baby, I didn't know you and Korey was back. Why didn't you come upstairs to give me a holler?" Kolanda said, walking in on us embracing and running money through the machine.

"My bad, sweetheart," Hammer said, giving her a kiss. "I thought you were asleep. I didn't want to wake you."

"Well, I was upstairs resting. Then I heard this machine and figured you and Korey were back. I see business is good," she said, looking at all the money we had out all over the sofa.

"Baby," Hammer said, stopping what he was doing, which was putting more money into the machine. He looked his wife in the eyes. "You see all this bacon? Korey and I took it all from the muthafucka who ratted on Pops."

"Fat Rah?"

"Yeah."

"You caught up with him?"

"Sweetheart, he and his wife got murdered tonight. I stretched his ass out like a Cadillac coupe!"

"Yeah." Kolanda made a fist and smashed it into her palm. "The fat snake got what he deserved!" she said, excited.

"He damn sho'nuff got it. Hammer didn't play no games delivering the nigga and his wife the murda mail, special delivery," I chimed in.

"Good. That's damn good. Like I said, the snake got what he deserved!"

"One thing, though, babe," Hammer said, putting his hand up with a serious look suddenly blanketing his face.

"What's that, Ham?" she shot back, catching on to the sudden change of face.

"And Keisha should know this too: never, ever, under any circumstance, mention to anyone what I just told you."

"I know, babe. You know I don't have loose lips. Neither does Ke."

"You take it to the grave with you. I got back at that nigga, Rah, because he crossed the man who loved me enough to introduce me to you, the woman I love more than any woman in this world. You hear me, baby girl?"

"Of course I hear you. I know the game. Keisha and I both do. Never talk!"

"There you go, baby," Hammer said, giving her a kiss. "That's all I'm saying."

I nodded, knowing from being in the game long enough that loose lips sink ships.

"Partnerz in Crime, baby girl," Hammer said, locking trigger fingers with Kolanda like he and I had been doing for many years as an embrace of inseparable union and loyalty.

"I will back my man's play, come what may." She uttered those nine words Hammer taught her that she must never go back on ever as long as they were alive and together.

"Oh, and by the way, Korey, Keisha's in her bedroom. Josh came over, trying to talk her into taking him back."

"Word?"

"Hell, yeah. She dismissed him. But, Korey, him coming over only opened up wounds that Keisha hasn't completely healed from."

"I feel you."

"She went and took in one too many drinks. But she's up there in her bedroom sleeping. You might wanna talk to her in the morning. She could use your presence."

"I'ma go up right now and check on her."

"Yeah," Hammer said, waving me forward. "Go 'head, K. We'll get back to counting all this money tomorrow."

"A'ight. Bet that."

I walked upstairs to check on Keisha. Sure enough, she was in her bed in her bra and panties. I covered her with her bedspread that was partially covering her buttocks. I came out of my clothes, leaving my briefs on. I lay beside her on my side, with my arm wrapped around her. She moved and opened her eyes enough for her to see it was me.

"Korey," she said softly, with a drunke
came over here, talkin' about he love me.
leave and never come back."

"You did, baby." I gently rubbed her back up
through her bedspread.

"I don't love him anymore. I love you."

"I love you too, Keisha."

"I wanna have your baby."

"You do? A little boy or little girl?"

"A little Korey Jr." She snuggled closer to me a
kissed me on the lips, smiling. She was really tipsy. H
whole bedroom reeked of alcohol, plus I could taste it o
her lips.

"We're gonna have to work on that then, aren't we?"

"Can we start now?"

"Not now, cutie," I replied softly. "Maybe in the morning. For now, get some rest so you can sober up. Okay?" I
kissed her on her sexy, narrow nose.

"Mm-hmm."

# Chapter 25

## *I Want to Have Your Baby*

The following day after Hammer and I handled that dire situation with Fat Rah's rat ass, I awoke to Keisha giving me a killa blowjob in her bed, where I slept with her overnight.

"Damn, thank you, baby," I said to her softly as her head went up and down on my erect pole of pleasure, making me feel like I had awakened in heaven itself. "Thank you so much!" I couldn't thank her enough for the wonderful feeling that her moist mouth was delivering over my jimmy.

"My pleasure," she said, smiling. Then she slapped her face with it, got over me, and lifted her bra, which freed her tits. She put them where she felt they belonged: directly in my face where my mouth was. "Suck my titties. I love it when you do that."

I licked and gently sucked on her nipples while squeezing her tits like I was begging for milk. While I was doing so, Keisha reached and pulled her panties to the side, gripped my throbbing hard dick, and eased down on it. She gently and slowly rode up and down what little she could before she was completely wet enough to take it all up inside her.

She rode me in upright fashion, with her hands resting on my chest. Her tits bounced as I gripped her ever-so-soft ass cheeks to assist her up and down on my pole.

Every time this dick hit her bottom, she let out a deep, soft, "Uhhh," and pressed her nails in the flesh of my chest.

"Cum inside me, Korey. I wanna have your baby. Cum in me," she freaked, looking me in the eyes the whole ride to let me know that she wasn't kidding me. To ensure that I watered her garden of pleasure and sheer delight, she began twirling her pussy down on this dick, and she turned up the volume on her moans. "Sss, uhhh."

Kolanda fucked around and peeped inside the room, being that Keisha's door was cracked and the sound of us having sex was loud. Kolanda saw my tree of life planted deeply in her sister's soil of love. She shook her head, smiling at us getting it in early. She shut the door quietly, leaving Keisha and me in the boxing ring of love and lust to duke it out sexually until we had enough.

I knew that Shamika and Olivia would be at church being that it was Sunday morning, so I drove out to Mint Hill to love on them for a while. I also had to put away some cash at a safe I had at Shamika's place. I had damn near $2 million as my cut from what Hammer and I took last night from that rat Fat Rah. Hammer and his wife stayed up counting it. $3.9 million it was in all. I took the $1.9 million that Hammer put to the side for me in one of the suitcases. But here in my Vette, I was travelling with only 150 stacks. I gave Keisha fifty stacks just for taking $300,000 to her condo and hiding it in a safe that I had over there full of loot already. I left the rest over at the crib, in my bedroom closet, stacked away neatly in five of my Air Jordan sneaker boxes. I was finally a rich-ass young nigga, just like I always dreamt of being.

When I got to Shamika's, I didn't see her electric-blue BMW minivan that I gave her money to buy. She'd always wanted one, so I told her to trade her used Honda

Civic in on it and I gave her the rest of the down payment. I could have had her pay the whole nearly $30,000 that the dealership wanted, but doing that would have only raised eyebrows. I didn't need muthafuckas checking all into my baby mother's financial status and whatnot. I'd have rather she made payments. After all, she owns a salon that's bound to be successful. This would allow her to account for being able to afford what she was riding in, not to mention that just because I was getting mad loot with my ace, Hammer, that didn't give me a license to spend recklessly. I learned in the business course I took that a fool and his money would soon part. I wasn't going to be that fool!

I put my $150,000 up in the safe in the closet of Shamika's bedroom. It was after 1:00 p.m., so I put one of Shamika's Smokie Norful CDs in and pressed play. "I Need You Now" began playing, not too loudly, through the speakers of her entertainment system of her bedroom. While I was in the joint, I used to listen to this song a lot on the Christian radio station. I couldn't count the times I heard it and prayed to God for Him to bless me out of prison early because I needed to be with Shamika, raising our daughter. Looking back on those moments of praying to God in the joint, while listening to Smokie Norful's heavenly voice, brought tears to my eyes as I considered the fact that God had indeed answered my prayers.

I was not a person who was deeply religious, but I did believe in God. My mother always went to church just like Shamika went now. In fact, my mother used to write me in the joint and tell me to get me a nice churchgoing woman and settle down with her when I did get out. I missed my mother tremendously. With her, it was all about God and not about the gangsta life I elected to be a part of to earn my daily bread.

I silently thanked God for answering my prayers. I thought He was the reason I got an early release from the joint. Me and Hammer both, as well as so many others who benefitted from the change in the crack law. Since I was silently thanking God for my freedom, I humbly asked Him to forgive Hammer and me for our sins and to bear with us because old habits and ways were hard as hell to break.

As I was pacing Shamika's bedroom floor, silently praying, which really felt good and peaceful being that no one was around, I heard keys jingling and Olivia's voice. "My daddy must be here because his car is in our driveway," she said loud enough for me to hear her.

I walked out of Shamika's bedroom into her living room and saw them coming in. "Told you, Mama, my daddy was over here," Olivia said, smiling and quickly walking over to me, arms open wide.

"Hey, baby girl." I wrapped my arms around her and gave her a kiss.

"How long have you been over here, Korey?" Shamika asked, placing her purse and keys on her coffee table. Her mother was behind her, but she took a seat saying that her feet were killing her.

"About an hour," I replied, giving her a hug and a kiss on the cheek. "How you doing, Mrs. Washington?" I greeted Shamika's mother.

"Tired, honey, and my feet hurt. This here is a nice place, ah, Mika got here. She say you bought it for her. You must be doing real good now that you're out of prison."

"I can't complain."

"Daddy, I'll be back. I gotta use the bathroom," Olivia interrupted, walking toward the bathroom.

"So what'chu doing for a living now, ah, Korey?" Shamika's mother asked.

"I invest in real estate. I'm doing pretty good with that right now."

"Really?" she hissed, looking at me like, "Who do you think you're fooling?" For as long as she'd known me, I'd been a drug dealer and street cat, but I didn't give a damn what she thought of me. I wasn't obligated to tell her the truth of what I did to earn my daily bread and a better living for myself, Shamika, and our baby Olivia.

Before I could say anything further, Shamika cut in and said, "Mama, you gon' help me fix this chicken I got thawing in the kitchen?"

"Don't I every Sunday?"

"Well, we might need to be getting to it, don't you think?"

"Go on and get the flour and seasonings out and whatnot. I'll be in there. Told you my feet hurting. Been ushering in these o' tight heels," she said, picking one of the heels up and looking at it. Shamika's mom was like 280! Everybody who knew her called her big mama!

I knew by Shamika cutting in what she was trying to do. She was interrupting her mother's attempt to ask me questions that Shamika knew I didn't have the patience and temper to answer and put up with. Her mother was a nosey and somewhat miserable woman. She wanted Shamika to so badly meet a doctor or a lawyer or a pastor of a big church and be the wife of one of those types. I mean, like someone with one of those titles in front of their name made them better than a man with real love for Shamika, a man like me.

Now, her father, who ended up losing his life on the battlefields of Iraq, he was cool. Before I went off to the joint, he used to tell me that as long as I didn't mistreat Shamika by beating on her and stuff like that, and as long as I had true love for her, it was all good with him. Pops was a real cool dude. May God rest his soul in peace. I never put my hands on his daughter other than to love her with them or to stop her from slapping the hell out of me for doing or saying something she felt I shouldn't have.

"So, ah, Korey," Shamika's mother said, focusing back on me. I knew she would. She just couldn't help herself. My phone started going off while she was talking. "Are you going to keep yourself out them streets?"

"I haven't been in the streets since I been home. I'm definitely through with the streets," I answered her while checking my phone. It was Hammer. "Excuse me a moment," I said to Shamika's mom, putting my hand up. I spoke to Hammer briefly. He was just checking up on me.

When Shamika's mother saw me put my phone away, she said, "You and Shamika plan on marrying each other?"

I looked over at Shamika, who was standing not too far behind her mother. She shook her head, saying no quietly, indicating that was how she wanted me to answer her mother.

"We haven't talked about it in detail, but I do love your daughter very much."

"The pastor at our church thinks that Mika would make a good wife."

When she said that, Shamika closed her eyes and shook her head and walked off into the kitchen like she didn't want that coming from her mother's mouth.

"Does the pastor have a wife?" I asked, picking up on the fact that he must have had a thing for my girl.

"No. He's a young thirty-five-year-old God-fearing man. Comes from a good family and he has no kids. He always be saying that Mika would make a good wife. I reckon he likes her."

"Mama, are you coming?" Shamika yelled.

"Let me get in there, 'fore this girl worry me to death about getting that chicken fried." She got up and went off into the kitchen. "You keep yourself out of trouble," she said on the way.

I walked into Olivia's bedroom, wondering why Shamika hadn't told me about this preacher fella who liked her. Olivia had changed out of her Sunday clothes into one of her short outfits and sandals. "I was just on my way back out there, Daddy."

"You wanna go get some ice cream?"

"Sure. I love ice cream."

"I know." I placed my arm around her neck. We walked to my car.

Shamika met us on the way out. "Are you having dinner over here, Korey?"

"If I'm still wanted."

"What's with the attitude all of a sudden?"

"Wait for me in the car, O."

Olivia walked to my Vette and got inside, leaving her mother and me alone a moment.

"Were you ever going to tell me about this pastor cat who thinks you would make a good wife, Shamika? What's up with that? Are y'all two kicking it on the fuckin' low?"

"My mother talks too much."

"Maybe so, but was she right?"

"He's nothing to worry about, Korey. Trust me. I am not interested in him at all. You trippin'."

"Trippin'? Let me tell you something, Mika," I shot back, looking her squarely in her eyes with my serious face and pointing my finger in her face. "You better not be kicking it with this cat on the low, leading him on and, shit, flirting! If y'all got anything going on, you better be cutting it off now! And I'm dead serious!"

"Korey, you trippin'."

"Yeah, well, let me find out!"

"Whateva, Korey." She sucked her teeth, rolled her eyes, and went inside.

I hopped inside my car with my baby girl and burned rubber. One thing I didn't play was sharing Shamika. That wasn't going to happen! There was only going to be one bull in her pasture. Me!

# Chapter 26

## *Partnerz in Crime*

Olivia and I went to Dairy Queen and copped us some ice cream. She ordered a banana split. I had a chocolate sundae with a big red cherry on top. After leaving Dairy Queen, I took O shopping at Foot Locker. Like me, she had a fetish for sneaks. I bought her two pairs of Jordans and matching Chicago Bulls jersey skirts. I really didn't want to buy her the jersey skirts because, at fourteen years old now, my baby girl's jewels were noticeably visible. I mean, her breasts were like li'l well-ripened oranges, her waist was small, her little booty was plump, and her thighs and legs were semi-thick and muscular from her running track for her school. I would have hated for a guy to see her in one of these jersey skirts and say the wrong thing to her. But being that she wanted them, I paid for them. I just could not look her in her pretty light-skinned face, with those pretty hazel-green eyes looking back at me, and tell her no to anything she wanted.

When we were done, I took her over to Hammer's. Him, Kolanda, and Keisha were all there and showed my baby girl mad love.

"Ms. Keisha, is she your twin sister?" O asked her, pointing at Kolanda as we all chilled in Hammer and his wife's bedroom at the bar.

"Mm-hmm," Keisha replied, smiling. "But, tell me the truth, Olivia, who looks the best? Her or me?" Keisha stood up from sitting on the barstool and placed her hand on her hip with a pose, trying to look sexier than she already was naturally.

Olivia looked over at Kolanda, who was sitting at the bar, looking as beautiful and as sexy as Keisha, but poking her lips and shaking her head at Keisha daring to ask O that question.

"I can't tell the difference. Both of you are very pretty," she said, then looked at me. "What do you think, Daddy?" she asked me as if looking for me to bail her out of this one. Keisha had truly put her on the spot.

"Well," I said, "you supposed to pick Ms. Keisha. Don't you see that fifty dollar bill in her hand?"

"No, no, no, no, no," Hammer interjected while gently pulling his wife close to him by her waist and pointing at her as he stood next to her. "You're supposed to pick this one. Besides, what's a fifty dollar bill compared to this, Olivia?" Hammer reached inside his pocket and pulled out a wad of hundred dollar bills. He held it up for Olivia to see clearly.

"Okay, she wins," O said, pointing at Kolanda. "She's the prettiest." We all began laughing, seeing that the offering of more money motivated and persuaded her final decision.

"Baby girl, never let any amount of money offered to you stop you from speaking the truth! You got me?" I lifted my hand for a high five.

"I got you, Daddy."

"Your dad's right, O," Hammer walked up to her and slid her a one hundred dollar bill like he would slide someone a drug package on the low. "However," he said low, "you made a good final decision to pick my wife."

"Oh, whateva!" Keisha said. She handed my daughter the fifty dollar bill that she had in her hand anyway. "Here's for telling the truth from the start. Sometimes it's always good to go with your first mind."

"Thank you, both," O said, smiling and looking at me like, "You need to bring me over here often. Your friends are nice!"

"You know, Olivia," Hammer said while taking a seat next to his wife at the bar, "you are a very pretty girl yourself." He reached for O's hand and gently pulled her to himself.

"Thank you."

"You must get your looks from your mother because your old man right there, well, he's not so good-looking."

"My dad's good-looking. In fact, everybody says that we look so much alike that he couldn't deny me even if his life depended on it!" She began laughing.

"That much is true," I heard Keisha chime in.

"There you go, baby girl. Defend the man who loves you beyond measure," I said, walking over and giving her a kiss on the cheek. Hammer still had her hand in his. He waved me off with the other one.

"I was just kidding, baby girl, about your dad. That's a good man right there. When we were inside the joint, all he did was talk about how much he missed his daughter. You mean the world to that guy right there. Which means you mean the world to me, to that woman, and that one," Hammer said, pointing at Keisha and Kolanda. "You know who all of us in this room here are together, O?" he carried on with a question for baby girl. He answered it before she could. "We're all Partnerz in Crime."

"Partnerz in Crime?" she repeated, with an inquisitive look suddenly blanketing her pretty face. She turned from looking at him and looked over at me. She was looking for an explanation.

Hammer wasn't going to leave her hanging, so he continued what he started. "Yeah, O. Partnerz in Crime. That mean we're family. We stick together. We don't let anyone or nothing come between the unity, love, and loyalty we all have for each other."

"Oh, I see. So y'all are like a gang?"

"Mmm," Hammer said with a pause, thinking on how to respond to that. "We prefer the term 'family,' O. Your dad is my family, as is Keisha and her sister here, Kolanda, who is my wife. Now, we're not blood related. Keisha and Kolanda obviously are, but we're all bond related. Our common bond is our love and loyalty toward one another. When your dad hurts, we all hurt, and vice versa. If Keisha here needs a helping hand with something, she has all of us, and all of us have her."

"Oh, okay," O said. "I understand."

"That's how those of us in this room here roll. And, look, O, this here is how we shake hands to show that we are of one family, which is the family of love and loyalty for each other. Stick out your index finger."

Olivia stuck her index finger out like she was pointing, giving directions. Me, Keisha, and Kolanda all looked on as Hammer schooled my daughter on who we were to each other and how we did things. At fourteen years old and very intelligent, Olivia was catching on to everything he was sharing. He pointed his finger out along with hers.

"Okay, now, O, lock your finger into mine and I'ma do the same with yours." They locked index fingers, which Hammer and I referred to as trigger fingers. Hammer didn't use the words trigger finger with Olivia because he was wise enough to choose his words carefully. What he was schooling her wasn't about anything criminal in essence, but about the science of our bond. As their index fingers locked together, Hammer asked Olivia, "What does our fingers locked together look like to you, O?"

She thought a second. "Mmm. To me, it looks like a chain link."

"Precisely, baby girl," Hammer said, nodding. "As Partnerz in Crime, all of us in here are linked by love and loyalty. Those two elements, components, are what keep your father, Keisha, Kolanda, and me in unbreakable companionship. If there is no love and loyalty among us, the link is broken. Thus the chain of unity becomes of no effect. You feel me, baby girl?" He unlocked his finger from hers and rubbed his hand over her pretty long hair that she wore hanging.

"Yes, sir."

"Okay, then. Give the family a summary."

"Well, it's like what I learned in Sunday School earlier today. Be true to those of your own household of faith, and do unto others, especially family, as you would have them do unto you. And don't be a traitor or someone who turns his or her back on his or her loved ones."

"There you go, baby girl," I said to her. We all gave her high fives before I had to get her back over to her mother's. Not to mention, dinner over there had to be ready by now. We'd been gone almost three hours. I could hear Shamika's ass now: "Where the hell y'all been? It doesn't take three hours to go get no damn ice cream!"

"Keisha, I got something special for you later. Will you be here or at your condo?" I said to her before getting into my car. Olivia was already waiting for me inside.

"I'll be here. What do you have planned?"

"You'll see."

# Chapter 27

## *Get Out Them Panties*

"Daddy, I gotta ask you something," Olivia said to me as we mobilized back to Shamika's house.

"Then ask, baby girl. You know you can ask me anything."

"Who do you like best? My mother or Ms. Keisha? Tell me the truth, Daddy. Which one?"

"I like 'em both, O. Why you ask that?"

"Okay, nothing wrong with liking them both. That's cool. You're a man. But, if you could only pick one, who would it be? Mom or Ms. Keisha?"

"Your mother, of course."

"Why?" She looked over at me, fully attentive to know why I chose Shamika.

"Your mother and I been together since we were like in our late teens, O. I love her. She's a real good woman. She's a partner in crime to me. Keisha's a good woman too, don't get me wrong. But your mother, she gave me you. And you are the joy of my life!"

"Am I your favorite girl in the whole wide world? Like over my mother and Ms. Keisha?" she asked with excitement in her voice.

"You got my DNA in you, O. No girl in this world means more to me than you. And you know what? I'll do anything to make you happy. So listen. Whenever you do find your Prince Charming in the future, if he can't match your daddy's love for you, then what does that tell you, O? It should tell you that he wouldn't make a very good partner in crime for you."

She held her index finger out with a smile when I said that. Then she said, "Linked by love and loyalty, Daddy?"

I locked trigger fingers with her and smiled and replied, "Damn right. That much you should never get twisted. You hear me?"

"I hear you, Daddy."

"I love you, baby girl."

"I love you too. And I'm glad you are home. I hope you never, ever leave Mom and me again."

"I won't. Don't worry about that. Now, did your mom tell you that she's enrolling you in private school up here in Mint Hill?"

"Yes, sir. She told me."

"I want you to have the best education possible. You're gonna have to if you plan on being an attorney one day."

"I know. I just want to make you and Mom and my grandmother proud of me. Nothing else matters."

"I'm sure you will," I said, pulling up in Shamika's driveway. "But, listen." I faced her. "Whatever you do in this life, do it because it's the right thing to do. Nothing wrong with making your parents proud. A child should want to do that. It's a good thing, for parents are special. They're a gift to be cherished. But, ultimately, do whatever you do out of it being the right thing to do, O. That's the only way to roll."

"How do you know when you're doing the right thing, though, Daddy?"

"You'll know, O. You'll know because God inside you will tell you. Now, peep this and be honest with your dad," I said. "The pastor at the church your mom attends, does he like your mom? Tell me the truth."

"I think he does."

"And what makes you think that, O?"

"Because every Sunday, after church service is over, he always pulls my mother to the side to talk to her. And he's always like extra nice to her. I think my grandmother wants to see them date, but I doubt if Mom likes him. She talks about you too much to give him any play. She loves you, Daddy. You got the playa card to her heart. That I know for sure."

"Are y'all coming inside, Korey? Or are y'all gonna sit in the car like I'm supposed to bring plates out there to you!" Shamika shouted, interrupting my convo with Olivia.

"Let's go inside now, O, before we both be in trouble with your mother."

Shamika had the table set with fried chicken, mac and cheese, greens, black-eyed peas, and sweet potato pie for dessert. To wash it all down, she made sweet lemon tea. I tore off into that food and, like everyone at the table, walked away with a full belly. Olivia went and helped her grandmother with the dishes.

I couldn't get it out of my head that Shamika's pastor was trying to holla at her, backed by her mother wanting to see them together. Her mother hated the fact that I was me and not some Joe Blow she could control or manipulate into being what she wanted me to be: a lame-ass nigga with her approval to fully have her daughter. This was one of the main reasons I secretly refused to put that ring on Shamika's finger and wed her. I didn't want her mother at our wedding, pretending she approved of us marrying when nothing could be further from the truth. Korey didn't cater to nobody, male or female, who couldn't care less about him.

My dear mother told me a long time ago, "Korey, always be yourself. If others can't respect you being yourself, that's their problem. Not yours!"

Seeing that only Shamika and I were now at the table, I looked at her with my serious face and said, "So, you wasn't going to tell me about your li'l pastor who likes you, huh?"

She looked behind her for the presence of her nosey-ass mother. She was still in the kitchen doing the dishes with O and putting food away. "Can we go to my bedroom and discuss this?"

"Let's go, shit. 'Cause you got some explaining to do."

I followed her to her bedroom. I looked at the short skirt she was wearing and got mad inside. It was one of those skirts that was so short that when she sat down, you could damn near see her panties! I bet her pastor was seriously loving the sight of that in his church.

"And why the hell you all at church with a short-ass skirt like the one you got on for?" I said the moment we stepped inside her bedroom. She shut the door behind us.

"You know I wear these types of skirts all the time, Korey. So don't go there." She sucked her teeth and gave me a dismissive wave of her hand.

"If you're going to church, you need to wear skirts that come down to your knees!"

"Are you serious? We are not living in the 1950s."

"You heard what I said." I looked her in her eyes to show I wasn't gaming her.

"Why are you so upset and hostile all of a sudden? I told you that I'm not interested in my pastor."

"You still could have told me that he likes you."

"For what? So you can be all upset like you are now?"

"No. So that I can be informed of what's going on with you and around you. That's why!" I raised my voice while pointing my finger in her face.

"Well, I'm sorry, Korey," she said, with her eyes beginning to water. "Damn, I apologize for not letting you know."

I just stood in front of her and looked her in her eyes without saying another word, leaving her to wonder what was going through my head. I had to catch myself so that I didn't allow myself to be overtaken by anger at her keeping from me the crush her pastor had on her.

"Like I said, I don't like him like that. Honestly, I don't. Now stop looking at me like I'm lying to you because I'm not, Korey."

"I swear, I better not find out otherwise, Shamika."

"Boy, please. You won't. I wouldn't lie to you. Now, give me some suga." She placed her arms around my neck and kissed me on the lips. I played stubborn.

"So that's how it's gonna be? All stingy with your love? You not gonna kiss me, Korey?" She looked at me like, "I can't believe you."

"Korey, I love you. Not my pastor or any other man. So, damn, get it out of your head that I'm holding something back from you. I know how you think. 'Ain't nobody gonna have my girl but me!'" she said in a baritone voice, trying to imitate me.

"Play with me if you want, Shamika, but I'm telling you I better not find out you flirtin' with that nigga, leading him on and shit."

"Boy, please. I ought to karate chop you in the throat for even thinking I would do that. But since we trippin', Korey, I better not find out you effin' that lawyer chick, Keisha, since you wanna insist on going there!"

"Get out them panties," I told her. "Get out of 'em right now." I began dropping my jean shorts and briefs and then stroking my dick.

"Oh, so now you wanna get between these legs? Just a moment ago I couldn't even get your lips to poke for a kiss!"

Before we both knew it, she was out of her panties and on her back with her legs open, and I was between them, reminding her that this good pussy between her legs belonged to Korey Taylor.

"I hate your ugly ass!" Shamika pushed me in my chest before putting her panties back on. We got a good five minutes of fuckin' in.

"Earlier, you were telling me you love me. Which is it?"

"I lied."

"Yeah, right."

"You coming back over here later?" she asked while straightening her hair in the mirror.

"Not if your mother's over here."

"She won't be. I'm about to take her home in about thirty minutes."

"Good."

# Chapter 28

## *I'm Grown*

I opened Shamika's bedroom door to go wash my dick. Guess who was at her door, fucking eavesdropping? Her nosey-ass mother!

"Oh, excuse me," she said, seeing my face, then Shamika's behind me. "What were y'all doing up in there, ah, Mika? You know you shouldn't be having sex and y'all not married. God don't like ugly!"

"Mama, will you please mind your business? I don't snoop around your bedroom door when I'm at your house. Why are you doing that while at mine?"

"Don't you dare, ah, sass me, Mika."

"I'm not, Mama. But right is right, and wrong is wrong. You in my house! You can't tell me what I can do in my own house. I'm grown!"

"You know what? I'ma grab my things so you can get me back to my place. You were doing real good before this heathen here got out of prison."

"Heathen?" I cut in, seeing that she was referring to me.

"Yes, heathen! You always been a bad influence on Shamika! What, you think I'm blind and don't know that you out of prison and back selling dem, ah, drugs again?"

"Mama, you wrong," Shamika cut in to defend me.

"No, Mika. You wrong. And he's wrong. Talking 'bout he into real estate. You ain't a bit more vested in real estate than I am in the devil's work! And if my daughter knew what's good for her, she would stop seeing you!"

"Grandma, why you putting my daddy down like that? My daddy bought us a new house and helped my mother get a salon. He spends time with us and has never said bad things about you to me. Don't put him down like that, Grandma. That's not right. I don't like you doing that!" Olivia said with emotion, then quickly walked to her room.

"Honey, if you only knew. Mika, I'm getting my stuff so you can take me on home." She walked away. Shamika was so upset she walked in her bedroom and began crying, face inside her palms.

"Baby girl," I said to Shamika with my arm around her. "Don't let how your mother views me and your love for me ruin your day. That's your mother. She has a right to her opinion."

"But she is always so judgmental and critical of you. And I hate that about her. You are not the devil."

"You know that. I know that. Our daughter does too. That's all that matters. Besides, only God can judge me. Only God can judge your mother. It's all good, baby girl. I ain't trippin'."

"I love you, Korey. Don't let what she said ruin your day either."

"I won't. Now, get cleaned up. I'm going to O's room to talk to her."

"Okay." She wiped her face with her palms and got up from sitting on the bed and went to the bathroom.

On my way to my daughter's bedroom, Shamika's mother walked right past me. Inside, I wanted to hate her for always seeing me as the devil and feeling that I was not good enough for her daughter. But then I remembered what the old man in the joint taught me. *Hate destroys the hater.*

"Olivia, sweetheart, are you okay?" I asked, stepping into her room and sitting beside her on her bed. She too was crying.

"If don't nobody else love you, Daddy, I love you."

"I know you do. I ain't trippin' on what your grand-mother said. People are who they are, O. I've learned to take the bitter with the sweet."

"Are you staying over here tonight? I want you to. My grandmother isn't going to be here."

"I gotta make a run for a minute, but I'll be back later. I love you, though, sweetheart."

"Daddy, I want you to know that I don't care if you sell drugs. That's your business if you do. You're still my daddy. That's all that counts with me. But I don't want you to go back to jail."

"Baby girl, look at me. I don't sell drugs anymore. I'm through with that. That's my promise to you. You hear me?"

"Yes, sir. I hear you, and I believe you."

"Give me a kiss." O gave me a kiss, then I went into the bathroom to wash my dick! When I came out to finally leave, Shamika, O, and Mrs. Washington were gone. Knowing Shamika, she couldn't wait to take her mother home.

Being that seeing Josh again caused Keisha to be down a little, on account of their love affair crumbling for reasons of infidelity, I thought I'd do something thug special for her, which I had secretly prearranged. I picked her up in a white limousine with dark, mirrored tint on the windows. It was driven by a paid driver courtesy of the limousine company. It was complete with champagne and snacks. Keisha was speechless, and so was Kolanda and Hammer when we pulled up in the driveway to pick her up.

"Romantic-ass nigga," Hammer said, smiling. "I see ya!"

Keisha was looking sexy as ever with her li'l Charlotte Hornets jersey skirt and matching Air Nikes. Keisha had all kinds of jersey skirts. Every team in the NBA was in her closet. She knew I loved seeing her in her jersey skirts because they fit her curves to a T and gave me the chance to adore and drool over her Tina Turner million-dollar legs! She had her hair parted in the middle and hanging.

"I just wanna take you riding," I told her while kissing her ever-so-soft lips that were covered with strawberry lip gloss.

We cruised the highway with Stevie Wonder's "For Your Love" playing softly through the speakers. We were going nowhere in particular. Just riding and drinking Dom Perignon. I turned down the music and read her a poem I wrote while on the way over to pick her up. She began shedding tears and telling me thanks and that she really appreciated the moment. I told her that she was more than welcome. For she was a queen chick like my other queen, Shamika, one who I highly adored and never would part with.

I told her to relax back on the soft cushion seat. As she did, sipping on champagne, I got on my knees in front of her. I lifted her short jersey skirt and removed her panties. She gapped her legs, knowing what time it was. Shamika loved this dick penetrating inside her. Keisha liked that too, but more than anything she loved getting her pussy sucked and licked.

I kissed, licked, and sucked Keisha's pussy and watched as her eyes slightly closed and her mouth opened to take in air. "Eat it, Korey. Sss. Dayum, it feeeels so good!"

I ate Keisha's sweet, juicy pussy until I felt that she felt her breakup with Josh was a blessing in disguise. Then I dropped my shorts and briefs. I placed one of her legs over my shoulder and held the other leg out. I gripped my dick, hard as a rock, and slid it inside her with ease until it was all the way up in her. I deeply penetrated her pussy, stroking it slowly around and around, in and out. All I could seem to think about while hitting her off like a man was supposed to hit his off queen, were all the days and nights I spent in the joint, restricted from doing this. The thought caused me to speed my pace and hit her off harder. Before we both knew it, we'd been making love, drinking champagne, and cruising the highway for two hours.

I had the limo driver, who was an older white male, take me to get my Vette. I had left it parked at the limo service place. I drove Keisha back to the crib. She was tipsy and ready to bathe and hit the bed. She had a busy week ahead of her, she told me.

I showered, got dressed, and headed back over to Shamika's. By now, it was late. Very late. I used my key to Shamika's house. I walked into O's bedroom. She was sound asleep. I gave her a kiss on her forehead. She opened her eyes and saw it was me.

"No, no, no, baby girl. Go back to sleep," I said softly. "Just wanted you to know that I was here, okay? I love you."

"Love you too," she responded, half asleep.

"Get your rest," I told her. "I'll see you in the morning."

"Okay."

I let her get back to her beauty rest. I headed to Shamika's bedroom. She too was in bed asleep. I removed my clothes, all of them, and hopped in bed with her. I got under the bedspreads and placed my arm around her. Her eyelids slowly lifted.

"Korey," she said softly. "What time is it?"

"Time for you to give me a li'l bit." I rubbed my hand gently up and down her soft booty and squeezed it.

"No, seriously. What time is it?" She removed my hand.

"It's a little after one."

She sat up, facing me, with her hand at the side of her head and her elbow propping her up. "It's what?"

"It's a little after one, babe. I was coming back sooner, but I got caught up."

"We're not going to start this, Korey, coming over here all late in the night. No, no, no. Where's the respect? O's in bed. I'm in bed. Are you serious?"

"You're right, babe. I'm wrong. My apology."

"Don't let it happen again, Korey. Now I'm dead serious about that because it's not right."

"Baby, I said I was wrong. What more can I say?" I said, ready to smooch. She looked at me and just shook her head because she knew that, at the end of the day, Korey, the nigga she loved so much, was just gonna be Korey.

I placed my arm back around her and pulled her close to me, but she acted like she didn't want to move and be intimate with me. I kissed her soft lips that she didn't poke out to meet mine. I gently rubbed up and down her soft booty and squeezed it.

Seeing that she was still unresponsive, and just looking at me all mad like, I said, "Don't be like that, Mika, damn. Let'cha boy get some." As I was saying that, I took and lifted her bra, freeing her tits. I pulled her over me, easing under her in the process, all uncontested.

"You think you can just come over here and do what you wanna do, don't you?" she said, unlatching her bra and removing it so that I could suck on her nipples, which I did while gently massaging her pussy lips through her panties.

"If you don't wanna give me any, then why is your pussy all wet? Huh? Why you all wet, Mika?"

"Shut up," she said and came out of her wet panties. We began kissing and having a tongue party. I fingered her while our tongues collided.

Not the one to be teased between her legs, she reached and gripped her pussy's best friend, my hard dick. She directed it to the entrance of her most prized possession and eased down on it a little at a time until it was filling her to maximum capacity. She began riding it slow.

"There you go, baby girl. This your dick. Ride it until your anger over me coming over late subsides," I said, assisting her by gripping, squeezing, and lifting her soft ass cheeks up and down on my hardness.

"Oooo, sheiiit!" she softly moaned, taking it all up inside her!

"It feel good, doesn't it?" I teased.

"Oh, gosh, yes. It . . . it always does." She began picking up her pace the wetter her pussy became. "Ssss." Her breathing increased. Since I'd been home, she had seriously been taking advantage of this dick. Up and down and around, she rode my pony like there was no tomorrow coming. Her pussy was so good, wet, and warm that it made me want to holler! But I held it in because I didn't want to wake our daughter.

After a good-ass four minutes of this dick deeply penetrating and filling her pussy up, Shamika's body began to jerk. She was in heaven at this point. Hell, so was I. She slowed her pace, grinding in a circular motion, getting the fullness out of her orgasm.

She began kissing on my chest as my dick softened and slipped out of her loveliness. "Korey," she said, suddenly bringing her kisses on my chest to an abrupt halt, "what is this?"

"What is what?"

"Scratches all over your chest! Who did this?"

I ran my hand across my chest. It was all marked up. "You did this."

She got up and turned on the light for a better view. "What the hell?" she said, touching my chest with inflated

eyes. "I don't remember doing this. You been effin'
someone else!"

"You don't remember a lot of things when this dick up
in you, Mika! But you're the one who marked my chest all
up like this."

She looked at me suspiciously and waved her finger
at me like, "I know your ass lying to me." But knowing
that sometimes, when on this dick, she got caught up
in the moment, she couldn't remember if she did it. She
turned the light back out and got back in bed. She turned
sideways, facing me, but was still silent.

Smack! I suddenly saw stars. She slapped the hell out
of the side of my face! "That's just in case I didn't put
those marks there!" she viciously barked, then turned her
back to me and curled up.

"See, Mika," I said, placing my arm around her, "there
you go trippin'."

"No, move, Korey." She twisted her body and removed
my arm from touching her body. She reached for her
pillow and buried her head underneath it, crying.

*Damn,* I said silently, lying on my back, eyes toward
the ceiling with my arm across my forehead. *I'm really in
trouble, now.*

The next morning, I awoke a little after 11:00 a.m.
Shamika and O were gone. I got my naked ass up out
of bed, showered, and put on some clothes that I had in
Shamika's closet. At about twelve-thirty, I was hopping
in my Vette and dialing Shamika's number.

"What'chu want, Korey?" she answered with an attitude.

"Where are you and my baby?"

"We're at the shop. Where else?"

"Why didn't you awaken me this morning with some
breakfast like you usually do when I stay the night?"

"Because I didn't feel like it. Besides, you know how
to cook!"

"So that's how you're feeling today? Like giving me the cold shoulder and shit?"

"Here's your daughter."

"Hey, Daddy. Where you at?"

"Hey, baby girl. I'm on the highway, mobilizing."

"On your way over here to Mama's shop?"

"Probably later. You all right?"

"Yeah, I'm lovely. Helping mom with a few of her clients. She's letting me wash, condition, and blow dry some of her clients' hair before she gives them their professional 'dos. It's a li'l crowded in here, too."

"A'ight. I'ma let y'all get back to work. See ya later on, okay? I love you."

"Love you too."

"Tell your mom I love her."

I heard her tell her mom that I said I loved her.

"She said, 'Mm-hmm,' Daddy."

"A'ight. See y'all later."

I disconnected, feeling extremely bad about Shamika busting my ass with scratch marks from Keisha's nails all over my red chest. Although I knew that Shamika didn't know for sure if she had put them there, I knew that she was a woman of keen discernment. She was hard to fool. From now on, I was gonna have to just fuck Keisha from the back.

I phoned Hammer, but he wasn't answering his phone. Figured he and Kolanda were probably together, handling some business. He and I only had like nine ounces of heroin left to get rid of, which he told me he and his wife would take care of.

I phoned Keisha.

"Hello?" she answered after two rings.

"Hey, cutie. What's up?"

"At the office, Kolanda and me. How is everything?"

"All is well. On my way to the house right now."

"You talk to Ham?"

"Tried to call him. He's not answering his phone."

"He's over at my dad's gravesite."

"Where is that?"

Keisha gave me directions. It was in Matthews.

"He just left about ten minutes ago because he called Kolanda. I think you should talk to him because, since that business was handled, he's been fairly quiet."

"I'm on my way to your father's gravesite too, then."

"Okay. And, Korey, baby?"

"What's up?"

"Thank you so much for last night. I truly enjoyed it."

"It's all good, baby girl. I enjoyed it too. I always enjoy you. Just want you to be happy and not think about that clown who hurt you."

"Thank you, baby."

"Give me a kiss and we'll talk later."

"Mmm, mah," she kissed me through the phone. Thing I loved most about Keisha, next to her just being a sweetheart of a woman to me, was the fact that she wasn't tripping on my seeing baby moms. Keisha just wanted me to be there for her in little special ways. Between me and her career keeping her busy, happy, and smiling, baby girl was just fine.

And me? I was loving the hell out of the both worlds, having two queen boss chicks who loved me, Korey Taylor, a G who would do anything to see my queens smiling.

# Chapter 29

## *Burying My Flag*

I pulled up at the location of Kolanda and Keisha's father's cemetery. Sure enough, Hammer's Vette was there. I looked around for him and, after walking through this massive cemetery, I spotted him at a gravestone. He was kneeling down with his eyes closed and his lips moving. When he finally opened his eyes, he looked and saw me standing not too many feet from him. I walked over to him and reached for his hand to help him to his feet.

"Killa. What's up, baby? How did you know where I was?"

"Keisha told me."

"You probably been trying to call me, huh?" Hammer said, dusting his knees off.

"Yeah, I was."

"Thought I'd come out here to Pop's gravesite and let him know that he can rest in peace now, since Fat Rah's ass out of the picture."

"Nothing wrong with that."

"I dreamed about Pops last night, K, man."

"Word."

"Unlike when I met him in the joint, he wasn't in a wheelchair. He looked younger, and he was dressed in all white. He just stood in the doorway of my bedroom, smiling. Then he said, 'Get out the game and live your life.'"

"Wow, yo. That's deep, Ham."

"That's why I had to come out to his grave. I think he's watching over me, K. You, me, Kolanda, and Keisha. Man, we gon' be all right."

"I believe that, Ham. Think we should take the loot we got in our stashes and just invest and, like the old man said in your vision, live. 'Cause mu'fuckas make lots of money out here and some are so caught up in this and that, they never take the time out to enjoy it and live."

"So true, man," Hammer agreed. "You know I was thinking about converting this small house Pops got off Independence that my wife and Keisha aren't doing anything with. I was thinking about converting it into a nice li'l studio, gather some talent up, niggas who can rap and sing and shit, record 'em under our own Partnerz in Crime label. What'chu think about that?"

"I'm with whatever you want to do. You know that. Long as it's legit, now."

"Oh, yeah, speaking of legit," Hammer said, reaching in his back pocket. He retrieved from it his black flag. He and I both had them. They represented that thug life we were so dedicated to from day one of us street hustling and whatnot. He held it up with tears in his eyes. "Korey, would you be mad at me if I told you that today I'm burying my flag?"

"Nah, my nigga. I wouldn't be mad. In fact, hold tight." I rushed to my car and retrieved mine from my console. "If you're burying yours, I'm fuckin' burying mine."

Next to Hammer's father-in-law's grave, he dug a nice, deep hole. He placed his black thug flag and all the negativity it represented into the hole, which represented a grave. I placed mine in it as well. We both covered those two flags until they could no longer be seen. Hammer hugged me with a tear falling from his eye. There was one falling from mine as well.

"It's over, my nigga," he said. "It's over. Doesn't mean we're not gonna want to bust a nigga's bubble out here in this world if he violates, K. Just means we can decide to seriously think twice because today is a new day."

"I love you, bruh," I told Hammer, feeling something magical that I didn't think either one of us could explain.

"Love you too, yo. Forever and always. P.I.C."

"Yeah, P.I.C., my nig." We locked fingers.

With that all said and done, and us drying our damn tears, we bounced in our cars. I told Hammer via phone how Shamika slapped the hell out of me for the marks on my chest and how she was still mad at my ass because she suspected me of fuckin' around. Told him how I told her she put the marks there.

"Nigga, you gotta be out of your mind if you actually think Shamika gonna really believe that. A woman knows her own lovemaking, K. What planet you on, yo?" Hammer said, laughing. "You better do something nice for her is all I can tell you."

Hammer followed me to a florist shop where I copped Shamika a dozen fresh red roses. We headed to the salon where Hammer followed me inside. "What up, everybody?" I greeted everyone the moment I stepped inside.

"Hey, Korey," all the workers greeted me back, except my daughter.

She said, "Hey, Daddy." She was washing some older woman's hair. Shamika saw me and went back to doing some chick's micro braids.

Hammer greeted everybody. Shamika even told him, "Hi."

He walked over and kissed Olivia then sat down. Then Hammer said, "Do y'all cut hair up in here?" while running his hand over his hair, which did, in fact, need a cut.

"Sure," the gay guy, who calls himself Rayshawn, responded. "What'chu want? A low-cut Caesar? And your goatee shaped?"

"Yeah. You can handle that for me?" He got up.

"C'mon. You right on time. I'm just finishing her up." He referred to the client who was now paying him. Hammer didn't discriminate. He was like me, treated everyone like he wanted to be treated: fairly, gay or not.

While Hammer sat in the chair to get his haircut, I walked over to my sweetheart. My hands were behind my back the whole time. "These are for you, sweetheart." I revealed the dozen roses I bought for her. "I love you."

"Oooo," Rayshawn said, "That's so sweet! Wish I had a man so thoughtful."

"Honey, I know that's right," the other worker chimed in and said. She was older and was also doing someone's hair. Her name was Myra.

Olivia looked over and smiled. "I see you, Daddy."

"Thank you, Korey," Shamika said. She even cracked a smile, but what woman wouldn't while receiving a gift with her friends looking on? She continued braiding away.

I leaned in and kissed the right side of her lips then whispered in her ear, "You mean the world to me. Let's never go to bed mad at each other again. Please."

She nodded, then whispered in my ear while still braiding away, "Let's not see you again with scratch marks from sex all over your chest ever again. I'm not stupid."

I didn't say anything further to insult her intelligence. Just gave her a kiss on her neck and took in a handful of her soft booty and gave it a thug squeeze.

I saw Olivia looking at me and smiling while my hand squeezed Shamika's booty. O shook her head. "Daddy, you a playa. I gotta give that one to you. A real, true, charming playa!"

"There you go, sir," Rayshawn told Hammer, handing him a mirror. He'd finished cutting his hair. It looked good, too.

"Now, that's what I'm talking about. You just got you a new customer," Hammer told him, running his hand over his fresh cut.

"Hell, you may as well trim me up too, Shawn," I cut in. "Give me a one and a half with the grain and shape my goatee up just like you did Hammer's."

"Well, c'mon, 'cause we through." He waved me forward.

"Thanks," Hammer said to Rayshawn. "By the way, I'm Hammer, Korey's brother by another mother." He reached his hand out for a friendly shake.

"Rayshawn. You can call me Shawn." He shook with Hammer.

"Nice meeting you, Shawn. What I owe you?" Hammer went into his pocket.

"Just fifteen."

"Take fifty. You did a good job." Hammer peeled Rayshawn off a fresh fifty from his wad.

"Thanks, sir, and God bless'chuuu!" he said, smiling. He was happy to receive such a big tip.

"You know that fifty paid for both our haircuts, right?" I said to Rayshawn.

"Oh, did it?" He flipped his hand like a woman while leaning back a little.

"Just joking. But you about to make another five-oh. Just hook a brother up. Make me look young enough to hang out with my beautiful daughter over there, who thinks her old man is a playa."

"I'll do my best."

After Rayshawn hooked me up, I kissed Olivia and then Shamika, and Hammer and I rolled out. Before hopping in our cars, Hammer stopped me. "Korey," he called, like something important suddenly hit him to tell me.

"What's up, dawg?" I gave him my undivided attention.

"Inhale and exhale a minute, my nigga. I mean, just take a moment to notice that we're free. Like actually free. No more locking in a cell with another man. No more punk-ass correctional officers shaking a nigga down, telling us when to go here and when to go there. And no more fucking not being able to touch your woman on a visit like you would like to. That's over with. We free. And, guess what else we are? We two rich-ass niggas from the hood, who paid our fucking dues the thug way. That life is over now, yo. A lot of niggas don't get a chance to say that, K. Plus, we got good-ass women in our corner. Man, K, that's all we ever wanted."

"Damn, you so right," I cut in just to agree. It made me briefly think about many cats we knew still in the joint with thirty years and life sentences and shit. Cats who may never see the light of freedom if something didn't change for them. Not to mention the many street cats who had lost their lives chasing that almighty dollar while in the drug game and a part of that thug life. This was a beautiful moment for Hammer and me. I felt exactly where he was coming from. He wanted us to savor it.

"Again, inhale and exhale the air of freedom, my nigga. Nothing can stop us from doing so now, but us."

# Part 2

*Eight Years Later*

# Chapter 30

"Whatever you do, O, I would advise you to not tell your father about this," Shamika warned, standing before her crying and distraught daughter.

"I have to tell Dad. It's the only way this is going to be rectified," Olivia tearfully replied.

Shamika placed her hands on each side of Olivia's shoulders and leaned in slightly, locking eyes with her. "O, listen to me. I'm your mother. I know your father. He—"

"I know him too, Mom."

"Yes, you do. Which means you know, O, that if you inform him about what happened to you, your father is going to kill those two guys. Now, do you want your father going back to prison, possibly for the rest of his life, for doing something crazy?"

"Mom, are you serious right now?" O shot back with a stomp of her foot to the floor for emphasis. "I was forced to do something that I'm going to have to live with for the rest of my life! Two men raping me! Dad has got to know about it. He's the only one, he and my uncle, who can get me justice."

"Why didn't you just call the cops, O?"

"Mom, I was drunk! I didn't even realize what had been done until one of the guys, who was supposed to be my boyfriend, showed it to me the next day."

"He recorded it?"

"On his phone, yes! All calling the cops would have done was publicize my shame. I would become a walking public spectacle, viewed as sluttish all over my college campus. I can't afford to be vilified."

There was silence for a moment. Shamika was trying to figure out what could be done other than calling Korey, but nothing registered other than Olivia should have called the cops.

"Besides, Mom," Olivia said, interrupting her mother's thoughts on the matter, "Dad told me that if I ever have a problem, wherever I am, to call you, him, or uncle Hammer about it. So I called you. You want me to call the cops but, Mom, I don't trust the cops to handle this. I trust my father. That's who I'm calling."

"Your father is not law enforcement, O."

"In my life, he is! Especially when it comes to something like this. You and I both know, Mom, that if law enforcement gets involved with this, they're gonna see me on that video doing something I would have never done in my right mind. They're gonna drag this thing out. Defense attorneys, in a long, drawn-out trial, will paint the picture of me being some type of promiscuous girl who, while in a drunken stupor, had sex with two guys willingly. Even if I were to get them convicted, I would have been so embarrassed that it would be unbearable for me to live with. I'm just gonna have to trust my father's judgment on this one because I am calling him."

Shamika inhaled and exhaled hard. Her head was beginning to throb with pain over this. She walked over to her drawer and retrieved an Extra Strength Tylenol. She took it with a swig of ginger ale.

"You know, O," she said, turning back around to face her daughter, "your father and your uncle Hammer don't need any unnecessary drama in their lives right now.

Look at them. They're running a very successful record label now. They're no longer a part of that life and trouble that sent them to prison. They're completely legit. People like their recording artists and others are depending on them to be there for them for the sake of their careers flourishing. Why ruin that by telling him what happened to you? He's only going to approach the situation with no understanding. That's the way of your father and your uncle Hammer. They will kill over you."

"No one deserves to be mistreated, Mom. Some men think that they can treat a woman any kind of way and get away with it. I think that's where a dad like mine comes in."

Olivia dialed her father's number with Shamika looking on. Shamika inhaled and exhaled through her nostrils, knowing the drama dialing Korey's number would bring. She wanted to snatch the phone from O's hand and stomp it with her foot on the floor, but she knew that her daughter was extremely hurt and disgusted over what happened to her. Shamika didn't like it herself but, in her mind, her place as Olivia's mother was to comfort her, not seek revenge like she was a vigilante.

She listened as O began to talk on the phone, crying and sniffling.

"Daddy," she said after Korey answered his phone. "I need to see you."

"Is everything okay, baby girl? What's up? Talk to me."

"Nooo, everything's not okay. Can you come over to Mom's? I been here since early this morning. I need to talk to you."

"Where's your mother?"

"She's right here."

"Put her on the phone."

Olivia handed Shamika the phone. "Hello?"

"Mika, what's up, baby?"

"Over here with O. She drove in from Chapel Hill early this morning."

"She told me, but what's wrong with her? Why is she sounding sad and crying? Talk to me."

"She'll tell you when you get here, Korey. I'ma leave it at that."

"I'll be over there in less than an hour. Bye!"

Korey hopped in his Benz with KJ riding shotgun. He'd been in a recording session that he decided to wrap up earlier due to Olivia calling and asking him to come over to her mother's place. He knew that She'Cute, an up-and-coming R&B young female artist he and Hammer were working closely with, had a CD due out very soon. She had two more tracks to lay, which were supposed to be completed by tomorrow, and no later than the day after. But Olivia was like a goddess in his life.

At twenty-two years old, she still had him bowing at her every beck and call. Part of Korey being there for her so voraciously had a lot to do with the fact that she was his one and only daughter. He believed that a father should spoil his daughter, no exception. Moreover, Korey was at O's every beck and call because he was still feeling the guilt of being out of her life those twelve years he served in the joint. She'Cute's CD would have to wait if it came down to him being there for O.

"Daddy, where are we rushing off to in such a hurry?" KJ asked.

"We're going to see your sister."

"Oh. We going to her college like we did last month when we surprised her for her birthday?" he said with excitement in his voice. He loved his sister very much.

"No. She's at her mother's. We're going over there."

"In Mint Hill?"

"Yeah. Look, call your mother on your phone and see what she's doing."

"Okay." He retrieved his phone from his pocket and dialed her number. While he was doing so, Korey's phone vibrated.

"What's up, yo?" he answered, seeing that it was Hammer.

"Ay. You a'ight? She'Cute said you had to make a run, wrapping her session up earlier. What's up?"

"Yeah, I did. O phoned me crying, said she needs to talk to me. She's at Shamika's. Something's wrong."

"You think so?"

"Know so. She didn't drive all the way from UNC just to talk. I know my baby girl better than that."

"I feel you. Well, let me know what's up when you find out."

"I got you, you know that. By the way, you still over at the studio with Mad Loot, right?"

"Yeah, Mad recording now. That cat nasty, K."

"Of course he is. That's why we signed him."

"The boy gone' blow up something nice, K."

"Might be the next Lil Wayne."

"Or better, yo."

"Just like She'Cute might be the next Mary J.B.," Korey added. "The girl like that!"

"Man, they both got the juice, K."

"Oh, yeah, what I was getting to, though, was since you're still over at the studio with Mad . . . Well, first, is She'Cute still there? She told me that she was gonna hang around. Did she leave?"

"She's here."

"Cool. Look, Ham, have her and Mad go ahead and lay that track they wrote together."

"Talkin' 'bout that joint 'Shining'?"

"Yeah. She'Cute told me that she perfected the hook on that joint. From my understanding, that's all Mad was waiting on to complete it."

"Yeah, it was. I'll have them get on it as soon as Mad finishes the track he's spitting on now."

"A'ight, bet that. I'll hit you up about what's what with O after I talk with her."

"A'ight. Oh, and before you go, K, your babe just walked in. She's on the phone, though."

"She did? More than likely, she's on the horn with KJ. I just told him to call her. Tell her I'll see her later."

"A'ight, holla, yo."

"Daddy, Mama asked what time are you going to have me back home?"

"Tell her I said I got this and that I will have you back home before nightfall. I know it's a school night."

KJ relayed his father's message to his mother. Seconds later, they were pulling up into Shamika's driveway where, parked directly behind her BMW minivan, they saw Olivia's white Porsche. He and Hammer had bought it six years ago for her sixteenth birthday.

*Maybe my baby girl just pregnant and, being that this is her fourth year toward obtaining her bachelor's degree, she's debating whether or not to have the baby. If that be the case, I'm not fucking signing off on her having no damn abortion. Career or no career. I love kids too much to not wanna see their beautiful faces on this earth,* Korey said to himself before turning the car off and stepping out with KJ alongside him. "Lord, let this be good," he silently prayed. "Please let this be good."

# Chapter 31

Shamika was sitting next to Olivia on her midnight black soft leather sofa set with Olivia's hand in hers when Korey and KJ walked in. Both of them looked to have been crying to Korey. They had been.

"Hey, Mama Mika," KJ greeted Shamika with open arms. He loved himself some Shamika, who has embraced him with love ever since he was born.

"Hey, KJaaaay," she greeted him back, stretching his J initial and smiling, happy to see him. She gave him a big hug. Korey hadn't brought him over for like two weeks. This was because Korey and Hammer had been away with several of their artists on tour in New York City, New Jersey, Philly, Baltimore, DC, and Virginia.

"Hey, sis," he greeted Olivia, wrapping his arms around her neck.

"What's up, boy?" She hugged and kissed him. "What you been up to?"

"Rappin' in the studio. Dad and uncle Hammer both said that when I step my skills up, they're going to let me record a CD."

"So you wanna be a rapper, huh?"

"Not wanna be. I'm gonna be, sis. What? You don't know?" KJ looked her up and down and said. Then he looked at his dad who was giving Shamika a hug and a kiss. "Dad, you better tell my sister about me. Can I rap or not, Daddy?"

"You working with a li'l some-somethin'," Korey vouched for him, nodding.

"Whateva." Olivia playfully pushed him softly at his forehead.

"I can rap. You'll see one day."

"If I know Dad correctly, you'll be 'rapping' your life around getting some knowledge on how to run a successful company. Spell 'rapper.'"

"R-a-double-p-e-r."

"Ohhh," Korey said out loud with his fist to his mouth, happy that his almost seven-year-old son could spell very well.

"Okay, okay." Olivia smiled hard. So did Shamika. "I might have to take you out to eat on me for that one! That was good. I'm proud of you!" She hugged him again.

"My mama makes sure I do all my homework. Dad be on me about taking my education serious as well. Mama Mika does too."

"That's right, KJ," Shamika said. "Because, at the end of the day, ignorance is a cure for nothing. Now, do me a favor, KJ, and come out here with me and help me water my flower garden," she said, looking at Korey and winking her eye.

"Okay."

KJ followed Shamika outside to her flower garden. Korey knew that Shamika asked KJ to help her water her flowers only so that he and Olivia could be alone. At the moment, Korey understood that whatever Olivia needed to talk to him about, it had to be serious.

He kissed her on her forehead and sat as close to her as he could. "So, what's on your mind?" Korey asked her.

She looked at him, took a deep breath, then dropped her head in the palms of her hands and began crying.

Korey placed his arm around her shoulder. "Baby girl, lift your head and tell your daddy why you're shedding tears. You can talk to me. That's what I'm here for. What's wrong?"

Olivia lifted her head and face from her palms. She wiped her tearstained cheeks and looked her father in the eyes as best she could. "My boyfriend, Daddy, he took advantage of me while I was drunk at a party he had and—"

"What do you mean, he took advantage of you? Are you telling me he raped you?" Korey cut in with hot anger beginning to surface with jet-like speed at the thought of someone violating her.

She dropped her head again and buried her face in her palms, crying.

"Did he rape you, Olivia?" The volume of Korey's voice raised as he asked her for a second time, fearing the worst answer.

She nodded, with her face still inside her palms. "Yes, sir," she tearfully confirmed. "Yes."

"Look at me right now, O." He reached and gently placed her hands in his as she looked into her father's eyes as best she could through her tears. Her father's eyes were stone cold at this point. She'd never seen them look that way. "Tell me exactly what happened. I wanna know everything. And, O, don't you leave nothing out. Now, what happened?"

Olivia wiped her cheeks with her palm and said, "My boyfriend threw a party at an apartment he has in Chapel Hill. A lot of people were there, and we all were drinking heavily. It was his twenty-first birthday. Some of his boys were there. One of them was like his very best friend who is home on leave from the military."

"Okay, O, just get to what happened. Get to him violating you," Korey rushed her. Even though he had told her to tell him everything, the anger that was surfacing within him had him growing increasingly impatient. For he found it extremely difficult to look into his baby girl's pretty eyes and face and know that someone did the unthinkable to her. He wanted her to get straight to the heart of the situation now, without delay.

"Okay, so when the party was over and everyone left, he asked me would I stay. I told him I didn't mind. Mainly because I was pissy drunk and unfit to get behind the wheel. Anyway, like I said, everyone had left. Only him, his best friend from the military, and I were there. He asked me if I would do him a favor for his birthday. I told him yes, I would do anything for him on his special day. He said, 'Then make my best friend and me happy. Give us both blowjobs.' I told him that I cannot do that because I'm not having sex of any kind until I'm married. That's when he pulled a gun out, put it to my head, and forced me to blow him and his best friend or he would kill me! He even recorded me blowing the both of them, but the recording doesn't show him with a gun. But he had one. The following day, he showed me the recording. He told me that he was just playing with the gun and that he wasn't really gonna kill me."

"Did they have intercourse with you, too? Be honest."

"Dad, I wouldn't lie to you about any of this. They just wanted blowjobs. And I did it because I was drunk and scared."

"Had your boyfriend done something like this before to you?"

"Never. I believe his military buddy put him up to it. Mama told me that I should have called the police, but I remember what you told me years ago. You said if I ever have a problem of any sort to tell Mama, you, or Uncle Hammer."

"That's correct. To hell with the cops. They don't love you like I love you."

"So I told Mama. Then I told her I was calling to tell you."

"You did right. Listen, what happened to you was not your fault, you hear me?"

Olivia nodded with tears running down her face.

"Some guys are just straight up ignorant, with no real respect for a lady. Now, tell me, O, do you love this boyfriend of yours?"

"I thought I did because, like I said, he has never asked me to do what he asked me to do. He has always been like real nice to me. I know his military buddy put him up to do what he forced me to do."

"Well, that's bullshit. No one can make you do something like he forced you to do if he didn't want to do it. I don't give a damn how nice he's been to you previously. Guys are notorious for being nice one minute, then dirtball nasty the next. A real man, with real love for you, would never do no shit like that to his woman. What's his name?"

"David. David Blakely."

"What about his friend?"

"I heard him call him Tim."

"Is Tim older than him?"

"Yes, sir. Like two years older, I think."

"Where does he stay? This Tim guy. You know?"

"I think on a military base in Fayetteville. I can find out. See, my boyfriend—well, my ex now—he doesn't know that I'm really upset about what he made me do because I downplayed it when he showed me the recording on his phone. I just pretended it didn't affect me because I was drunk. But, deep inside, I knew I was gonna contact you about it."

"I want you to keep your composure about this. You only have, what? Two more months before you graduate college?"

"One more month."

"Good. I want you to get that recording, even if it means you steal his phone."

"I'll get it."

"And I want you to get me the full name and address of this Tim fellow. Okay?"

"Yes, sir."

"And, O, listen to me. You're twenty-two years old. A grown woman. You can do whatever you wanna do. But, please, never take more than one drink of alcohol outside of the presence of the family, people who love you and have your best interests at heart. You hear me?"

"I hear you, Daddy," Olivia said, nodding and looking him in the eyes almost in a trance-like state. But she was in deep thought over what Korey was really saying. He was transmitting to her that this world was cold and that no one in it but her family could be trusted to clothe her with the warmth of a real, true, trustworthy love. No boyfriend, no associate, no nothing, but family. And her family consisted of her father, mother, little brother, Uncle Hammer, Aunt Kolanda, Keisha, and her grandmother.

"When do you have to be back at your school?" Korey carried on.

"I'm leaving in a couple hours. Got class in the morning. I'll be free for the weekend. I just needed you and Mom to know what had happened."

After making that statement, her phone rang. She checked it. It was David. "This him right here, Dad."

"Answer it, but don't act mad or anything. Pretend all is well."

She answered and began talking to him. Korey walked outside, but he was so upset over the thought that someone had dared to take advantage of his daughter that all he could seem to think of was doing something very, very devious and brutal to the parties involved.

Seeing a look of serious anger written all over Korey's face, which he was trying his best to conceal, Shamika left KJ to continue watering the flowers while she walked over to Korey who was just standing on her porch, chewing on his bottom lip, nose flared and hitting his fist in his palm.

"So what you think about what happened to O?" Shamika asked softly, standing in front of Korey and placing her hand gently on his shoulder.

"I think somebody is in grave trouble. That's what I think. And I don't think you should have told her that she should have called the police."

"Why not? It's their job to handle criminal matters, Korey."

"It's our job to take care of our daughter. Don't nobody love her like we love her. Not the cops. Nobody!"

"Taking care of her is one thing. Doing something stupid is another. The cops don't have to love her to do what they have been hired to do, Korey. Protect and serve those who have been harmed and those in harm's way. Are you serious right now?"

"Protect and serve? Yeah, right. Give me a break, Mika. Our daughter was violated, simply put, by two cats who, in their pursuit to get their rocks off, used her as sport. What father you know would allow guys to do that to his daughter and get away with it? Huh?"

"Getting the cops involved is not letting them get away with what they did, Korey. The cops will do something about it."

"You keep talking about the cops, Mika. Okay, they're gonna come ask a few questions, take a damn report, then they're gonna maybe arrest the guys, and that's a big damn maybe. Because where is the evidence of rape?"

"Olivia said there's a video."

"That will be the first thing those guys get rid of. Then what? Our daughter gon' be made to look real stupid. I know the system, Mika. That's why I told O a long time ago that if something ever happened to her to call you, me, or her uncle Hammer, no exceptions. Now, law enforcement has its place, but that's my daughter in there who was violated. And she's your daughter. She cried while telling me what happened to her. She's hurt, and she wants justice. Besides, Mika, O's mouth ain't never been on a nigga's dick. She's still a virgin, for crying out loud! Them niggas in trouble! I swear on my mother's grave, they're in trouble!"

Shamika inhaled and exhaled hard with her hands locked together on top of her head. She knew this would be Korey's mindset. "Fine," Shamika said, "go. Go get yourself in trouble. Act like you don't have a company to run and people depending on you and Hammer to help make their dreams come true."

"So what should I do? Act like this shit never happened, Mika? You know me. You know I can't do that. Not when it comes to my baby girl! Hell, I've checked cats for far less, put them in their place for merely looking at you wrong—"

"Then do what you feel," she cut in, not really wanting to discuss it further. "But don't call my house from jail; because, deep down inside, you know better, Korey, than to take matters like this into your hands at this stage in your life. You can think. You just too angry right now to think, but you can. You can come up with a better solution than to go and destroy some mother's child. Yes, your daughter has been hurt, violated as you may call it; but, Korey, who in this life hasn't been hurt? Things happen. Mistakes are made every day among young people. You know that.

"All I'm saying is that I know that's your baby girl. I know you will do anything for her, but if you keep playing judge, jury, and executioner in her life and being at her every beck and call, you're gonna be the one who hurts her the most because you're gonna become a crutch she can't do without. That would make her a cripple. Now is that what you want for your baby girl? For her to be handicapped?"

Without allowing him to respond, Shamika then looked over at KJ, who was still watering her flowers, and said, "KJ, that's enough. Let's wrap that hose up now." She walked over to him to help him do just that, leaving Korey alone to think about her take on what happened to their daughter and what she felt should have been done as well as what she felt he shouldn't go do. But she knew Korey. She knew he was hardheaded and stubborn when it came to being there for Olivia and any other family member he loved dearly. At this point, she just hoped that what she had to say didn't go in one ear and out the other. She determined in her mind and heart that she would pray about it later.

Korey walked inside the house. "O," he called. She was in the bathroom, freshening up. When she came out, he said, "You talked to that clown?"

"Yes, sir."

"Well, you make sure you get all the information that I asked you to get. You hear me?"

"I will."

"And you coming home for the weekend, right?"

"Yep."

"Good, because me, you, Uncle Hammer, Kolanda, and Keisha having a meeting Saturday about this incident. We'll decide then what action will be taken. Until then, hold on to this. Follow me."

She followed Korey into Shamika's bedroom. Korey stepped inside her walk-in closet and retrieved a shoebox he had stashed in a safe location. Inside was small weaponry, from .25 automatics to .380s. He handed Olivia a chrome .25 automatic with a shiny pearl handle, a weapon small enough to have on her without anyone knowing. It was fully loaded.

"That's for your protection. Here's how you put one in the chamber." He cocked it back, showing her how to ready it to fire. "Now, put this away," he said low, looking back and forth for any sign of Shamika coming. Shamika would chew him out severely if she knew he was putting a gun in Olivia's hand. "Keep it secured inside your purse. You got me?"

"I got you, Dad." She took it and placed it inside her pocket until she could place it in her purse, which she left inside her car. Korey put his shoebox of guns back in the secured spot he got it from. Right when he did so, Shamika walked in.

"So, O," Korey said, "don't cry over what happened to you. Your mother and I talked about it, and we concluded that people make mistakes." He winked his eye at her without Shamika seeing him do so, to throw her off from what he and Olivia were really doing in her bedroom. He wanted to make it seem like they were just talking about what happened to her. "But I do want you to cut ties with your boyfriend and just strictly focus on finishing up your bachelor's so you can go straight on to law school. Nothing else matters. You hear me?"

"I got you, Dad."

"Give me a hug and I'll see you tomorrow when you come home for the weekend."

She embraced her father with a tender hug, but as her arms were wrapped around him, Shamika caught a glimpse of the butt of the pearl-handle .25 automatic she placed in her front pocket. "Olivia, do me a favor," Shamika said, interrupting her and her father's loving embrace. "Excuse yourself to the living room where KJ is for a moment. I need to speak to your father in private."

Olivia left them alone, shutting Shamika's bedroom door behind her.

"Are you kidding me, Korey?" she looked at him and said, hands on her hips.

"What's up, Mika? What's on your mind?"

"You gave our daughter a gun? Are you losing your mind?"

"A gun?" Korey played senile, but his theatrics were fruitless, not enough to fool Shamika. She saw the burner with her own eyes.

"Yes, a gun! The one in her pocket," she shot back, pointing her index finger in Korey's face. "Do you want our daughter going to jail? She's not a street-thug-oriented person, Korey."

"Does she have to be to be able to protect herself, Mika? Yeah, I gave her a piece to protect herself. She shoulda long ago had one for protection!"

"She need a license to carry a weapon, Korey! You know that."

"She's going back to Chapel Hill alone. I just don't want her feeling unprotected. It's just until she gets a permit to carry one legally, that's all. Why you having a fit party over it?"

"No, Korey. Uh-uh. No." Shamika shook her head. "If she gets caught with that thing and it's not registered to her, she's going to jail. Not to mention, what if she goes and does something stupid with it, like shoot the two guys who took advantage of her? So call her in here right now before you leave and get that gun from her."

"Get it from her?" Korey looked at her like she done lost her mind.

She didn't say anything, just gave him a look like, "Play with me if you want to. I'll call the police."

Korey knew not to chance her doing something crazy like that, so he reluctantly called Olivia. "Let me get that gun back, O," he said to her the moment she stepped into her mother's room.

"Huh?" She looked at him, then at her mother, then back at him.

"Give it to him, O. You don't need that in your life," Shamika said before Olivia could say anything. "I know Korey wants you to be protected, but carrying that gun without a license is illegal. Give it back to him right now."

Korey rolled his eyes behind Shamika's back, a gesture to indicate she was tripping. He held his hand out. "It's okay, O. Hand it over," he said.

She reached in her pocket, retrieved it, and handed it to him.

"But let me say this," Korey held up his hand and said. "You will register for a firearm as soon as possible. That way, you'll be legit. And if someone fucks with you—"

"Watch your mouth!" Shamika cut in, hitting him over his shoulder with her palm.

"If somebody disrespects you, you'll be in the right to protect yourself." When Korey said that, Shamika sucked her teeth and shook her head.

"Girl, take your problems to God," she said. "Guns will only get a person but so far. And, Korey, you should know that by now. Oh, I forgot. The hardheaded never learn."

"Yeah, whatever."

# Chapter 32

"KJ, call your mother," Korey told his son as they pulled up in her driveway at her condo. He parked next to her car. Seeing her car let him know that she was inside. "Tell her we're outside in the parking lot and are on our way inside."

KJ did as his father instructed him, then disconnected. "She said okay, Dad," he said, putting his phone away. Seconds later they were inside Keisha's condo. The smell of fried pork chops immediately arrested Korey's and KJ's nostrils. "Mmm, Mommy. That smells good," KJ said, rubbing his belly then giving her a kiss.

"You hungry?"

"Yes, ma'am."

"Well, by the time you take your bath, dinner will be ready."

"Okay." KJ began walking to his bedroom to get ready to bathe.

"Afterward we'll go over your homework. You hear me?"

"Yes, ma'am," he replied from a short distance, then disappeared into his bedroom. Keisha continued frying her pork chops.

"What's up, babe?" Korey eased up behind her, wrapped his arms around her waist, and kissed the back of her neck. She tensed up a little.

"Had that business meeting, sold two properties, then Kolanda and me had to make a couple of court appearances. Went by the studio, Kolanda and I. Hammer told me that something came up with O," she said, having turned to face him.

"It did. Not something I wanted to hear, either."

"She okay?"

"Something happened. Baby girl ran into a little problem."

"Little problem?" she repeated him. "Korey, I don't think Olivia would have driven home from UNC to talk to you if her problem were little. She would have called." Keisha then turned from facing him to transfer her pork chops, which were now well done, onto a big plate where the rest of her well done pork chops were. "So what was the problem?" she asked, facing him once again while wiping her hands of pork chop grease residue with a towel.

"Baby girl'll tell you."

"Why you can't tell me? What is it? She pregnant?"

"When she comes back home for the weekend, me, you, her, Hammer, and Kolanda gon' meet up at the house and discuss what her problem is. Then we'll come up with what should be done about it."

"Okay, then, if you say so. You hungry?"

"I am, but I gotta get back over to the studio. She'Cute and Mad Loot supposed to be laying a track down that I need to oversee and approve. You feel me? So I got to get back over there. We got a deadline to meet."

"I believe they were about to record something before I left. I know I saw Mad Loot recording. He's pretty good."

"Yeah, he is. She'Cute gon' kill 'em too."

"How old is she again, Korey?"

"Just turned twenty."

"She's real pretty and very talented! I think if she can keep the boys away and stay focused on her craft, she can go far."

"Well, I been working closely with her as Hammer has been with Mad Loot. They know that their ability to become successful artists, for the most part, is in their hands. Hammer and I and the crew over at the studio are gonna push them as far as we can, but they're the ones, at the end of the day, who are gonna have to put in the work. Feel me?"

"Yeah, they gotta come up with the hits," Keisha cut in.

"Precisely. Other than that, babe, I'll be back later, okay?" Korey said, having eased up to her and placed his hands at her waist.

"I'll probably be asleep," she said, seeing Korey's lips coming in for a kiss.

"So I'll wake you up." They began tonguing. He caressed one of her tits through her blouse while their lips and tongues made brief love.

Keisha couldn't believe that almost ten years after picking Korey up from the bus station his first day home from the joint, he would become the one she would come to love and have the mad hots for. She couldn't believe she'd become the mother of his six-year-old son, Korey Jr. She loved the fact that Korey had always been her best friend. He allowed her to be herself and do her thing as a woman of substance, who was career-oriented and a loving and caring woman. One who understood her position next to a G who had nothing but real love for her.

"Why you gotta wake me from my beauty rest, babe, when you can take me in my bedroom right now and introduce me to that bulging cobra in your pants? I know it's awake and looking for a desirable target to strike," Keisha said softly in between them tonguing.

"You right." Korey lifted her in his arms and carried her into her bedroom. He kicked the door shut behind them and laid her down with their tongues still greeting each other hungrily. Keisha was wearing a short skirt. When

Korey laid her down on the bed, she just opened her legs, and there was the target for his now fully awakened cobra to strike hidden behind the crotch of her candy apple red G-string panties. Seeing it, Korey dropped his shorts and underwear in one single motion, freeing his cobra.

"Come up out of them panties right now, Ke. I'm 'bout to beat this pussy up."

"You take them off of me," Keisha said, legs open wide and unbuttoning her blouse to fully free and expose her lovely set of double-D twins. Korey reached and eased her panties down while simultaneously taking one of her nipples into his warm, moist mouth. He sucked on her tits and fingered her with two of his fingers until Keisha was so wet and hot all over that she begged him to let his erect cobra strike her most sacred love target.

"Put it inside me, babe. Do it now."

"Say please," Korey teased, gently pinching her nipple and rubbing the head of his cobra around and around the lips of her loveliness.

"Please," she softly begged.

Seconds later, she felt Korey's big, juicy, long, warm cobra entering and growing inside her. "Ahhh." She slightly opened her mouth and closed her eyes, legs up in missionary position. She wrapped her arms around his neck and held on tight as Korey manipulated his hips in a circular motion and forward and back, hitting her off at a medium pace, deep and hard. He wasn't En Vogue, but he was giving her something she could feel.

# Chapter 33

Having hit Keisha off real nice between her legs, making her feel extremely good after a long, busy day, Korey got in his Benz to make his way over to the studio. A helluva lot was going through his head as he mobilized to his old-school *Smokey Robinson's Greatest Hits* CD. He was at the moment listening to "The Tracks Of My Tears." He was thinking about how his day started early this morning. Keisha had phoned him around five o'clock, informing him of a very important business meeting she had to attend and, as a result, she needed him to pick KJ up and take him to school and pick him up when school was over.

After scooping KJ up and taking him to school, he got with Hammer over at their studio around nine o'clock to begin recording and putting finishing touches on Mad Loot's and She'Cute's upcoming CDs. She'Cute, who Korey had been working very closely with being that he discovered her, was a petite cutie with short blond hair who wore a small diamond nose ring to look sexier. People said that she put them in mind of Miley Cyrus. She sang with the vocals of Mary J. Blige, but her swag was like that of a Lil' Kim.

Korey took a liking to her and so did Hammer after overhearing her in the parking lot of a club late one night. She was singing as she was walking with some other girl to the other girl's car. Korey looked at Hammer in amazement at her heavenly voice. So, having called her over, he introduced himself, along with Hammer, and gave her his recording studio card.

Three days after that introduction, She'Cute called him. Korey set up a meeting with her over at the studio in the presence of Hammer and some of the studio engineers. Korey told her to get on the mic and sing the late, great Whitney Houston's version of "I Will Always Love You." She'Cute killed that song. That's when Korey and Hammer knew that they had to sign her. Now, after a whole year of working with her closely, it was nearing the time for her CD to drop. Korey just had to have her perfect her vocals on a few tracks previously recorded.

Korey had been working with her since this morning; then, after breaking around 3:00 p.m. to pick KJ up from school, he had returned only to receive that call from Olivia.

The news Olivia dropped on him hit him like a slug to his chest from a twelve-gauge shotgun. Someone had dared to mistreat his baby girl without knowing who her father was. Moreover, who her uncle was.

Korey's head was hurting now, thinking about getting to his daughter's assailants. But at the same time, while mobilizing on his way to the studio, he was thinking about what Shamika dropped in his ear on the matter as well. He knew that Shamika loved the hell out of their daughter. Olivia was her only child. They were also like best friends. If anyone wanted justice for what happened to Olivia, it was Shamika. She would move heaven, earth, and hell for Olivia's well-being and safety. But she wasn't a stupid mother who would dare risk her freedom just to get revenge. Korey knew this about her. He had to respect her point of view. She was just being Shamika. But he was a street-oriented cat. He loved Shamika tremendously because she, if no one else, had his very best interests at heart. He just couldn't see himself being the "call the cops, let them handle their daughter's gripe" type. That mentality was foreign to him and the Partnerz in Crime circle, where there the motto was, "Eye for an eye. Tooth for a tooth. Fuck over anyone in this family and we're comin' to see you!"

"Yo, Ham. What's up, babe?" Korey had phoned him about fifteen minutes away from the studio. He turned the volume down on his music.

"Over here recording a hit, my nig. What it do?" Hammer said, raising his voice over the loud music in his background from the Mad Loot recording.

"On my way over."

"Good. How's O, yo? Baby girl a'ight?"

"Nah, we got a problem. But I'll put it in ya ear in a moment."

"Okay, bet that. Look here, She'Cute right here. She wants to holla at'cha."

"Put her on."

"K, this you?"

"Yeah, what's up, Cute?"

"Are you coming back over?"

"I am. In fact, I'm on my way now."

"Mad and I laced and laid that track. It's hot, I swear. You gotta hear it. Hammer said it's a hit!" she said with mad excitement ringing through her voice.

Korey smiled on the other end of the phone and said, "Word, yo?" In the music business, a hit song and record meant mad cha-ching, as in lots of dough. For her to tell him that Hammer called what she and Mad Loot had worked on a "hit" meant a lot. Because, like him, Hammer had a seriously keen ear for good music. He had predicted that two other artists on their roster had hits when he heard their singles. He turned out to be absolutely right. Both of their singles made Billboard's Top 10 and went gold.

"Yeah, it's that fye. I promise you."

"Well, I'll definitely hear it for myself in a li'l bit. Besides that, Cute, everything's a'ight with you?"

"Things couldn't be better for me right now, K. I'm working with you and Hammer. Y'all are like the Berry Gordy and Smokey Robinson here in the Queen City. Everybody and their mother with talent trying to get signed by y'all. P.I.C. Records is the Motown here. Like I said, things couldn't be better, K."

"If you and Mad laced that track like you said, it's going to get better."

"Oh, we laced it. You'll see," she cut in, still with that exuberant excitement echoing through her voice. She was mad confident over having combined her vocal skills with the highly potent lyrical rap skills of Mad Loot, who she considered an up-and-coming heavyweight in the rap game.

"The team at P.I.C. Records is going to push you and Mad as far as we can. I just want you to continue working your ass off."

"I am, K."

"Hard work and dedication is the key. Our other two artists, Gurl Squad and Juice, are back on tour and selling mad CDs. So just keep working hard. Y'all next."

"Like I said, K, I am, and I know Mad gon' continue working his ass off. He wants to be just as successful as I do."

"Tell Hammer I'm pulling into the lot now and to come out and meet me."

"Okay. I got you, K. See you when you come in."

"Bet."

Hammer checked his watch as he was walking out of the studio to meet Korey in the parking lot. His watch read 8:28 p.m. He saw Korey with his elbows on the hood of the driver's side of his Benz and his chin resting on his hands, which were locked together by his fingers. He was looking out into the darkness that was blanketing the atmosphere, being that the sun had long rested.

"What's up, K? Why you wanted to talk out here?" Hammer asked, placing his arm around Korey's shoulders. He knew his ace well enough to know that the look of him being in deep thought meant that Korey's spirit was disturbed.

"Two bitch-ass niggas violated baby girl, yo," Korey looked Hammer in the eyes and face and said as calm and cool as he could.

"Say what?" Hammer shot back, hoping he didn't hear what he thought he just heard. "In what way?"

"One was her so-called boyfriend. The other, his best buddy. According to O, they were celebrating the nigga's twenty-first birthday. They all were partying hard and drinking. When the party was over—"

"K," Hammer cut him off and put his hand up. "You better not be about to tell me that my niece got raped. Is that what O drove from college to tell you, my nigga?" Hammer looked at Korey with thug eyes, nose flared and lips tightened.

A tear suddenly fell from Korey's eye while he nodded slowly. "The muthafuckas forced O to suck 'em off."

"I don't wanna hear no more." Hammer whipped his phone from his pocket. "I'm calling O right got'damn now."

"Call her. But, Ham, don't say nothing crazy over the phone. You and I both know that those two niggas are on borrowed time right now. They will not get away with what they did."

"You know what?" Hammer said, putting his phone back in his pocket and pacing back and forth in front of Korey, thug mad. "Where them niggas stay?"

"O gon' have everything we need to know by the week-end. I already told her what to do. Plus, she graduates next month. So—"

"Yeah, but we're not waiting until she graduates to holla at them niggas who violated and disgraced her, K. Are you buggin'? Them niggas didn't wait to get their dicks sucked by my got'damn niece. Fuck that! I wanna know where they can be located, bottom line, K! And we gon' make 'em come up missing."

"We'll know when O come home for the weekend."

"Man!" Hammer exclaimed, hitting his fist in his palm. "O, my got'damn baby. Ain't no nigga touching her inappropriately without having to answer for it. Fuck that!" Hammer was hyped and ready to see Olivia's perpetrators dealt with, if possible, right now, even in the face of putting their new artists on hold. He didn't give a damn. Violating someone in their family was the worst thing someone could ever do in his eyes.

Korey was the same way, but he was a little more nonchalant and composed about it. Not that he wasn't mad as hell over the matter; but he had learned, while taking anger management classes in prison, to control his anger and not let it control him. It was a reality that even Shamika put him in remembrance of. This was why after Olivia had shared the news with him he walked outside to calm himself down, as well as to give her time to gather information. He wanted to see how he would be feeling in a couple days. He knew that "day one anger" over a matter was the deadliest. Moreover, he knew that no matter how much he cooled himself down, it was just a matter of time before O's violators meet her father.

# Chapter 34

As Korey and Hammer continued working with their artists in the Queen City and contemplating murder, in the small town of Monroe possible trouble for both of them was brewing. A story that was aired all over the news eight years ago of a vicious execution-style murder that was speculated to have been drug related was suddenly back headlining nearly every local news station there and in surrounding areas.

"Authorities say that it was one of the most gruesome murder scenes ever witnessed in an upscale, quiet suburban neighborhood in Monroe. It looked to have been a murder of two, but one miraculously survived: a female, Sheila Malinda Lawrence, who suffered a gunshot to her forehead. Authorities believe that she knew that she was about to be shot because her Life Alert was pressed, alerting 911 that there was an emergency at the residence. When authorities arrived, they found her home on fire. Police personnel were able to drag both bodies from the house. A male body, that of Donald Lee Lawrence, was said to be deceased on arrival. The female was unconscious, but she had a pulse. They both suffered severe burns from the fire. She was immediately rushed to the emergency room, where she underwent surgery after surgery before slipping into a deep coma.

"Authorities say that after eight years of being in a comatose state, her eighty-nine-year-old mother, who refused to pull the plug on the life support system her daughter was supported by, was elated when her daughter slightly opened her eyes. Authorities are hoping that she will soon be able to open her mouth and provide them with information regarding who shot and killed her husband and attempted to kill her, leaving them both for dead."

Kolanda was watching Channel 9 Eyewitness News at 11:00 p.m. when this story began to air. When she saw Fat Rah's face as the one who was shot to death and his wife's face, who survived, she quickly got Hammer on the phone.

"Kolanda, what's up, sweetie?" he answered, seeing that it was his wife.

"Hammer, babe, I need to see you. Where's Korey?"

"Korey's in his car behind me. We're just leaving the studio. Been over here working hard. What's up, though? Something wrong?"

"Listen, dear heart, whatever you and Korey do, y'all need to get here right now."

"What's wrong?" Hammer turned his music down, sensing the urgency in his wife's voice.

"Can't discuss it over the phone, but you and Korey are not going to believe what the fuck I just saw on television."

"This ain't got nothing to do with Korey's daughter, O, does it?"

"No, it doesn't. But it's dead serious. Don't y'all stop nowhere. Come straight here."

"A'ight, babe. See you in a minute."

Hammer immediately phoned Korey, who was tailing him closely. He told Korey that Kolanda had just called and needed to see them right away.

"What for, yo?" Korey said, with Olivia's situation still weighing heavily on his mind.

"Don't know," replied Hammer. "She didn't say. But something's not right. I know my baby. It was in her voice, K. Something's wrong."

They pulled up at the house, parked, got out damn near in unison, and went inside, with Hammer leading the way. In the living room, standing in front of a big, widescreen television mounted on the wall, Kolanda pointed to it. The newswoman anchor was about to mention again what Kolanda had heard earlier that made her pick up the phone to call her husband.

"Look at this shit, y'all."

"What is it, babe?" Hammer looked at her, puzzled. So did Korey; then he looked at the television. A second later, Fat Rah's and his wife's pictures were being shown. The headline read, WOMAN IN COMA EIGHT YEARS AFTER BEING SHOT IN THE HEAD AND LEFT FOR DEAD NOW SHOWING SIGNS OF LIFE.

"What the fuck?" Hammer exclaimed in disbelief. He'd put a bullet in her head, at point blank range. He and Korey both knew that when they exited Fat Rah's crib eight years ago both he and his wife were unresponsive.

"How in the hell could that bitch have survived?" Korey said, shaking his head.

"Earlier, I was listening to this shit," Kolanda said, "and they were saying she'd been in a coma the whole time, and that her mother refused to pull the plug on her. However, they say they don't know if she can talk."

Hammer placed his hands on top of his head and locked them together. He began pacing the floor. Her survival befuddled him and had him in a serious state of disbelief. His mind quickly and repeatedly replayed the moment he pulled the trigger. The bullet greeted her forehead, and she fell to the floor.

"Kolanda," he said, putting a halt on his pacing back and forth. He stood in front of her. "I need you to get your people on this."

"I'm going to see someone tomorrow," she replied. "Right after my court appearances."

"Find out this woman's condition in its totality. Can she see? Can she talk? Can she remember anything? Can she walk? We need to know every damn thing."

"We'll know. I'm certain of it," she assured him.

"This too much info for one day," Korey cut in. "Look, I'm on my way back to Keisha's. I'll get with y'all tomorrow."

"Oh, Korey," Kolanda said. "How is O?"

"She'll be all right. Hammer's gonna let you know what's what. Like I said, I'ma see y'all tomorrow. Too much on a nigga's head right now," he said, giving her a kiss on the cheek.

"A'ight, my nigga. See you tomorrow. Get you some rest, if you can," Hammer said, embracing him and locking trigger fingers with him, P.I.C. fashion, before letting him be on his way.

# Chapter 35

Fridays at Got'cha Lookin' Good beauty salon, owned by Shamika, were always busy days for her. Shamika had more clients than she actually wanted to do today. When she awoke, she noticed that she was feeling like she hadn't slept at all last night. Actually, she hadn't gotten but about two hours of rest, if that's what you wanted to call it. Truthfully, all she'd done was shut her eyes, doze off here and there, and toss and turn. For the most part, she and Olivia spent most of the night talking on the phone. She spoke with Olivia her whole drive back to Chapel Hill. She wanted her to feel safe and to not worry or fret over those two guys taking advantage of her in the name of them having fun. She knew that immature individuals did immature and stupid things, especially under the influence of alcohol.

"This too shall pass," she told Olivia. What she wanted Olivia to know above all was that God doesn't like ugly. He would repay her perpetrators when He deemed it necessary.

In Olivia's mind and heart, God was gonna use her dad and her uncle to see that justice was truly served regarding that situation. But she didn't make mention of that to Shamika. She knew all too well that, over the years, her mother had become churchgoing and seriously religious. The only thing holding her back from becoming like a nun was her daddy's dick.

Oh, Olivia wasn't stupid. She'd overheard, many times, her dad and mom in the bedroom, getting their freak on. Her dad would be putting it on Shamika, too! Afterward, her mother would have a different glow and happy demeanor about herself. Olivia knew that her mother loved herself some Korey. Bad boy or not, she couldn't get enough of her father's love. Like Samson was for Delilah, it was no secret to Olivia that her mother was weak for her father.

As she got up out of her bed feeling extremely sluggish from lack of sleep, Shamika slipped into her house robe and slippers. She checked her clock over on her nightstand. 5:55 a.m., it read. She had to have the shop open by 7:45. Her first client was scheduled at 8:00.

She stepped out of her bedroom to go into her kitchen to put on a pot of coffee, but having walked to her living room first, she was surprised to see Korey lying on her sofa, sound asleep. She shook her head, having no idea whatsoever that he was even in the house. *Now, I wonder, what time did he get here? And how come I didn't hear him when he came in?* she said to herself.

His phone began vibrating on the table where he had it next to his car keys. She walked over, picked his phone up while he was still asleep, and saw that it was Keisha on the caller ID. She quickly sent it to voice mail.

Ever since Korey broke the news to her more than seven years ago that Keisha was carrying his child, she hadn't cared too much for her. Shamika long knew that the two of them were having sex. The night that she busted Korey with all those scratches over his chest assured her of that. When he broke down at her house and told her that Keisha was pregnant by him, for the first time ever Shamika punched him in his eye as hard as she could; then she ran off into her bedroom and cried her eyes out for three hours. Korey had a black eye for a week!

Feeling the presence of someone's shadow over him, Korey twisted out of his sleep and slowly opened his eyes. There was Shamika, directly in front of him, putting his phone down.

"What'chu doing, Mika?" he asked groggily.

"Your whore just called. I sent her to voice mail."

"Damn, Mika baby, why you do that? It could be something important she's calling me about. Something could be wrong with KJ. Don't be doing that," he scolded her and reached for his phone.

"Ahh, whateva." She gave his response a dismissive wave of her hand. "There's nothing wrong with KJ, nothing at all. Bottom—"

"You don't know that!" he cut her off. "Don't ever do that again wit'chu crazy ass."

"Bottom line, if your little lawyer whore wants to talk to you, she'll have to do it outside this house."

"Or what, Mika?" He reached for her arm and pulled her to him and squeezed her tight. "Or what, huh?" He pressed his forehead to the side of her face, grinding playfully.

"Yeah, you betta grab me, because you know you 'bout to get slapped."

"You ain't gon' do nothing."

His phone began to vibrate again.

"You need to get up and go brush your teeth, 'cause your breath stinks," she told Korey.

"Whateva." He loosened his grip on her so that he could answer his phone. While he held his phone to his ear, Shamika mugged his forehead, then ran off into her kitchen for coffee, cheesing.

"Yeah, you betta haul ass."

Keisha was on the other end of the phone. She called Korey to inform him that he needed to pick KJ up from school later today because she was gonna be in court until about four.

While Shamika's coffee was getting ready, she went to take a shower. Needing to refresh himself as well, Korey went into Shamika's bedroom closet when he got off the phone to pick out some clothes; then he went into the bathroom where Shamika was bathing, stripped naked, and joined her in the shower.

"I didn't tell you that I wanted company up in here, so what you think you're doing?" Shamika said, looking him up and down as he entered the shower uninvited.

"Shut up," he replied, smacking her on her soapy, wet buttocks.

"And don't be hitting me on my booty like that."

"Or what?" He got behind her and pressed his instant hard-on against her soft butt cheek and kissed the back of her neck.

"Or I'ma squeeze these balls." She took a handful of his testicles.

"Okay, okay, Mika. Damn, I'm sorry, baby," he began pleading. The last thing he wanted was for her to have his balls in a vise grip.

She loosened up. "That's what I thought," she said, showing who really had the power. She got back to soaping her body.

"I just wanna li'l bit before you head off to work." He reached and cupped both her soft tits and kissed on the back of her neck.

"You always talking 'bout you wanna li'l bit," she said softly, feeling his hard-on pressing against her booty.

"You know I can't see all these goodies of yours, Mika, and not wanna taste."

He caressed one of her tits while, with his other hand, he began exploring her womanhood and massaging it with two fingers. Shamika was wet and feeling hot all over all of a sudden.

"This all you wanna do, Korey, is have sex." She poked her booty more toward his hard-on and twirled it. "Here," she said, looking back at him over her shoulder and placing her hands up on the wall.

"There you go," Korey said, easing his strongly erect pleasure plug into her wet and warm love socket. She tensed as he entered her.

Korey eased in and out of her at a nice, slow pace. She became wetter with each stroke, making it easier for him to gain full access. She threw her body back to meet his forward thrusts.

"You love entering my heavenly gates, don't you, Korey? You just can't get enough of it, can you?"

"It got candy in it, it's so good!" he softly acknowledged, digging deeper and harder, hitting her spot.

"Hit it, baby. Hit it," she begged. It felt so good she began crying as she always did when Korey was working her insides just the way she liked it. Shamika bit her bottom lip and hung her head down to prevent a scream from escaping her lips as a wave of indescribable pleasure rushed over her.

"Damn, girl, this juicy fruit of yours too damn good to be true," Korey said, having gotten off with Shamika. "Now you can get ready for work."

"You make me sick," Shamika said, playfully pushing him away farther in the tub.

"No, I don't," he responded about him making her sick. "I make you well."

"You ain't getting no more, either." She began soaping her body.

"That's what'chu always say."

# Chapter 36

Korey drove to McArthur Street off Statesville Avenue to an apartment that She'Cute was living in. Korey didn't know who she lived with; it wasn't his business, so he never asked. He turned his music down a little and parked with the car running. He tapped his horn a couple times. Korey told She'Cute last night, while listening to the track she and Mad Loot completed, that since he cut her studio session short due to him having to talk with his daughter, they could come this morning and pick up where they left off.

He hit his horn again and checked his watch. It was 8:20 a.m. Some young-looking dude came to the door with his shirt off and holding up his hands up like, "What up? What do you want this early?" Korey stepped partially out of his Vette and looked over the hood. "Tell She'Cute to come to the door."

"What?" The dude put his hand to his ear. Before Korey could repeat himself, he saw She'Cute coming out wearing a house robe and slippers, with her hair in a ponytail. She attempted to walk toward his Vette, but the dude who answered the door pulled her back to the apartment by grabbing her wrist.

"You're not going to see that nigga in that short-ass robe, bitch. Are you crazy?" Korey read his lips. He could feel where he was coming from. The robe she had on was so short, Korey could damn near see her panties from the back as she reluctantly went back inside. Seconds later she returned with some black leggings on. She leaned into Korey's car through the passenger window.

"That's my boyfriend. He trippin' on some o' jealous-ass shit."

"Yeah, well, you a'ight?" Korey asked with concern. Her boyfriend, who was standing in the doorway, didn't look too happy to see Korey.

"I'm good."

"Well, you know, it's studio time. I know it's early but, hey, we gotta make up for lost time yesterday when I had that emergency."

"Yeah, I know. Look, K, I'm glad you came over. If you will give me about twenty minutes, I'll ride to the studio with you. That way I won't have to take a taxi."

"A'ight, bet. Go ahead and handle your business. I'll be out here waiting."

"Okay, thank you so much. I'll hurry up." She quickly walked back into her apartment.

Korey sat out in his car listening to "If I Ruled the World" by Nas and Lauryn Hill. He was thinking about that chick, Sheila, Fat Rah's wife, and how in hell she could have survived a 9 mm bullet to her head. If she fully recovered, it could mean disaster for him and Hammer. They didn't wear masks when they handled their business with her and Fat Rah. And although eight years had passed, Korey knew that Sheila got a good, good look at his and Hammer's faces. As he was thinking on that situation, he looked and saw She'Cute's boyfriend walking toward his car.

"Yo, Nickie said she'll catch a taxi," he said, referring to She'Cute by her real name and rubbing the knuckles on his right hand like he punched something.

"You sure, yo? She told me to wait right here for her. Now she's saying for me to go? She'll take a taxi?" Korey looked at him a little strange. He wasn't feeling what was said.

"Hey," he shot back, lifting his hands, "I'm just telling you what she told me to tell you."

Being ever observant, Korey saw the butt of a gun in his waistline when he lifted his hands. "Why couldn't she come out and tell me what you're telling me now?" Korey wanted to know. Something about this cat just wasn't clicking with him. He seemed to be the controlling type with a chip on his shoulder.

"'Cause she's in the bathtub and wanted me to do it. Is there a problem with that, yo?" he said, now suddenly mean mugging Korey like he wanted trouble.

Korey looked this cat up and down a moment. He had brown skin and was about five foot eleven and sort of muscle bound like he'd just gotten out of the joint. He had his hat turned to the back. From what Korey could discern, from appearance and from this cat's swag and attitude, he was a thug playing the serious tough role. Korey didn't like nothing about this cat. He seemed to be the type who would be a bad match for a good girl trying to make something of herself, like his artist. He had his burner under his seat, but he saw no need to use it when he could use his head, ego and pride to the side.

"Just tell her I'll be at the studio waiting."

"Yeah," the cat replied like, "Whatever." He then walked back into the apartment.

Korey felt an uneasiness in his gut that he only felt when he sensed trouble. He went to the studio and waited for She'Cute to arrive, but she didn't. Nor did she call. This was the first time this had ever happened, but it was also the first time he had been over to She'Cute's apartment while her boyfriend was there.

He went and picked up KJ from school, took him out to eat, then had Keisha come to get him from the studio. By then it was late in the evening, and everyone who was supposed to come to the studio had come. Korey was seriously troubled at this point. He and Hammer had a lot invested in She'Cute. They knew that at the right time, her soon-to-be-released CD was gonna blow up. There was no way Korey was gonna let some wannabe hard thug cat ruin what P.I.C. Records had worked so hard for, which was to see She'Cute become a star under its label.

He called Hammer to the side as Hammer was in the studio booth with Mad Loot and another artist, talking on one of his songs.

"Yeah, what's up, K?" Hammer came over to Korey outside to another room where it was quiet.

"It's She'Cute," Korey said. "She's still not here. I'm worried."

"Yeah, where is she?"

"Don't know, but she was supposed to have arrived by now. Something's not right on her end."

"What makes you feel that way, K?"

"Went to her crib early this morning and some li'l nigga came to the door, supposedly her boyfriend. She was supposed to ride with me over here, but then as I was waiting on her to get herself together out in my car, this li'l boyfriend of hers comes out of her apartment about ten minutes later, talking about she sent him out to tell me that she's gonna take a taxi."

"You serious, K?" Hammer cocked his head and caused his eyes to squint. He wasn't feeling what he was hearing, just like Korey wasn't feeling She'Cute's boyfriend.

"She ain't called or nothing, Ham. I'm about to go over there. Besides, I didn't like that nigga of hers, and I believe he may have kicked her in her ass a li'l bit out of jealousy."

"Oh, one of those types?"

"Yeah, a pussy-ass nigga. I'm going back over to her crib to check his ass."

"Not without me, you're not."

"I know that. How much longer you gonna be with Mad?"

Hammer checked his watch. It was a quarter to 9:00 p.m. "We 'bout to wrap it up right now."

"And I'm telling you now, Ham, if that li'l nigga done put his hands on Cute—"

"Look, K, I already know what time it is. I know you. We're going to see what's up. Don't even trip. Try calling her again, though, while I go tell the boys that's it for tonight."

Korey tried She'Cute's number again. Nothing. Nothing but voice mail.

One hour later, he had Hammer knock on her door. Her boyfriend, having never seen Hammer's face before, answered the door. That was all the leeway Korey needed.

# Chapter 37

"Where's Nickie, you pussy-ass nigga?" Korey stepped forward and spat with his 9 mm aimed straight at her boyfriend's now startled face. He lifted his hands as if being robbed and he began stepping back slowly.

"Where is she, muthafucka? I swear I ain't asking you again! Grab that burner from his waist," Korey told Hammer. Hammer reached and snatched it.

"She's in the back bedroom there, yo. Why y'all coming all up in here like this?"

Korey pushed him in front of them with his burner to the back of his head. "Take us to her."

He led Korey and Hammer to a back room. It was the worst thing he could have ever done. There She'Cute was, lying in bed with a black eye and swollen face.

"Cute," Korey called her. "Get up. Help her out that bed," he looked at Hammer and said. Just to look at her swollen purplish-blue eye and face made Hammer want to punch this boyfriend of hers out as he helped her out of bed.

"Cute, look over here at me," Korey said, his gun aimed directly at her boyfriend's head. "Who did that to you?"

"He did," she answered. No hesitation. "He punched me and knocked me completely out earlier when you was over here," she said, beginning to cry.

"Get on your knees, muthafucka. Get on them right got'damn now!"

"Look, I told her I was sorry. I just lost it, that's all," he said, making his way to his knees.

"C'mere, Cute." She came to Korey. "Go take a look at your face in the mirror and come right back."

"I saw it earlier."

"Did you like what you saw?" Korey rhetorically asked, knowing she didn't. She was an extremely pretty girl, but now her face looked like Tina Turner's did after Ike Turner beat her: awful!

"No, that's why I didn't call you. I didn't want you and any of the guys at the studio to see me like this. I look terrible!" She placed her face in her palms and began crying some more. Korey and Hammer both looked at each other in disgust over her situation and shook their heads.

"Where your brothers at, Cute?" Korey asked.

"I don't have any brothers," she said through her tears, wiping her palms over her cheeks as gently as she could. Touching her face hurt.

"Where are your sisters?"

"Don't have any of them either."

"Where's your mother and father?"

"Somewhere in Atlanta, strung out on dope! I don't have nobody. That's why I be over at the studio working so hard, because I want something out of life."

"You can never have something out of life, fuckin' with a no-good piece of shit of a guy like this! A nigga who would make you look ugly to the public, beating on you and shit! A real tough guy don't hit women. Now, what do you want to happen to this piece of shit?" Korey bitch-slapped him, but he put on like he wasn't even fazed by Korey smacking the hell out of him.

She'Cute looked at him and slowly shook her head. He returned the stare with his lips tight and nose flared like he was a real serious hardcore gangsta.

"I want his ass dealt with," she spat with venom. "Dealt with in the worst way! Because all he does is slap me around and try to control my life. I'm sick and tired of it!"

"Then deal with this nigga." Hammer handed her the cat's own gun that Korey had ordered Hammer to take from his waistline. Without hesitation, she took the burner. Korey then moved himself away from being in the line of fire as She'Cute moved closer to her abusive boyfriend with a perfect aim at his chest area.

"This is for all the times you slapped me around and I couldn't do anything about it, Marco."

"Bitch, if you're gonna shoot me, then shoot me. Fuck you and these niggas. I ain't afraid to die!" he coldly and heartlessly cut in.

"Oh, you don't have to worry about that, you son of a bitch!" she spat before squeezing off three times. Bam! Bam! Bam! She hit him up with hot lead so close and personal in his chest that his body jerked when the bullets touched him. His shirt even began to smoke.

Korey grabbed the gun from her hand, which was shaking tremendously, and he took a good look at the corpse. He was dead as a tooth without nerves after a root canal.

"Get all your personal belongings and wait for us out in the car," Korey told her.

As she was going to do that, Hammer stopped her and said, "Are there butcher knives and garbage bags in here?"

"In the kitchen, yes."

"Grab two butcher knives and some garbage bags. Bring 'em in here now. Then get'cha personal shit and wait for us out in the car."

She did what she was asked to do. Korey grabbed the biggest knife she passed them. The joint looked like a miniature machete. While Hammer used the knife he had to cut fingers and toes, Korey took the one he had and placed it at this cat's throat. He stood in his Tims on one corner of the very sharp blade and pressed his weight on it. The blade sliced through the victim's neck, leaving Korey to only have to cut some neck extremities to have his whole head off. He placed the head in the garbage bag that Hammer tossed his fingers and toes in.

They were both a semi bloody mess, which they wiped off after placing the remainder of the body in garbage bags that they tripled to make stronger holding power. They found an empty suitcase and put the remainder of the victim's body inside it and zipped it up. Doing all this felt like a lifetime, but it was efficiently done all in ten hot minutes. They both carried the suitcase out the back door to a nearby Dumpster and tossed it inside. Then they returned only to set the apartment on fire.

By now, She'Cute was inside the car waiting for them. She was glad that there were no neighbor's apartments close by. All the apartments were spread out. Korey and Hammer made their exit, hoping by all means that the now blazing fire would destroy any forensic evidence that could later link them to what just went down inside that apartment. In Hammer's hand was the bag that they placed She'Cute's ex's head, toes, and fingers in, along with the towels they wiped the blood off with. By taking those body parts off the victim, they knew that if the remainder of his corpse were ever to be discovered, it would be nearly impossible to ID him.

"I'm taking you to the Fairfield Inn off Sugar Creek," Korey said to She'Cute, looking back at her through the rearview mirror as they began to mobilize. "Want you to stay there a few days and nights 'til your face heals and things blow over. A'ight?"

"That's cool."

"I don't want you to call nobody; and, whatever you do from this night forward, 'Cute, don't ever mention, under any circumstances, what happened in that apartment with that nigga. You hear me?"

"Certainly, K. What about me finishing up my CD?"

"It can wait for now. We don't want you doing anything at this point but lying low and healing up. Feel me?"

"I feel you. I hate y'all had to see me like this." She began to cry.

"Shiddd, we don't," Hammer interjected. "Ain't no nigga got no business beating your ass 'til your face all swollen and shit, and your eye all big and black. Fuck that! You with P.I.C. now. We're not letting you go out like that."

"I appreciate it, guys. I really, really do."

Up to this point, She'Cute had only perceived Korey and Hammer to be nothing more than fly, handsome businessmen, who by all means would help her singing career blossom into something beautiful. She had no idea that these two brothers had a past rooted in dealing drugs and them being ruthless bad boys when need be.

"Like my brother K said, 'Cute, just don't ever in this life mention what happened with your boyfriend," Hammer reminded her, knowing that a snitch would not be tolerated as a part of the company they kept.

"I won't. Besides, I'm the one who shot and killed him. Tired of that bastard slapping me around!"

"Yeah, but you killed him with the assistance of my brother and me."

"I'll never, ever say anything about it. I swear to that." She crossed her heart.

"Good. Neither will we. On a criminal level, my brother and I only have a select few that we deal with. Like us, they never discuss outside our circle what we do in the dark. That would be a fatal, fatal mistake, 'Cute. Are you hearing me?" Hammer looked back at her in her good eye to show his dead seriousness.

"I understand. Believe me, I understand."

There was an awkward silence in the car for a few seconds. She broke it. "How did y'all know to come over?"

"My brother was very concerned about you all day today. He felt and knew something was wrong with you. Particularly because you've never missed a studio appointment. Moreover, K wasn't feeling your boyfriend."

"You wasn't, K?"

"Not at all. I knew me and that nigga was gonna violently clash if he had done something to you, which I deeply felt he had as I was patiently awaiting your arrival at the studio. When you didn't show up, I said to myself, 'That nigga did something to her.' And, trust me, after seeing your black eye and swollen face, had you not murked him, I would have," Korey assured her, nodding.

"I appreciate you guys for coming to see about me," she reiterated, wiping her tearstained cheek as Korey pulled in to the Fairfield Inn.

She 'Cute been on her own since she was sixteen. Feeling like her heavily drug-addicted parents cared more for their addiction than her, she fled her hometown of Atlanta with her boyfriend, who was nineteen years old and on the run from state authorities for a past robbery attempt of a convenience store. In Charlotte, her boyfriend peddled drugs, but he was really a nobody.

"It's our job to check up on you. Hell, like Ham said, you with P.I.C. now. We ain't letting nothing happen to you if we can help it. Now, peep this," Korey said and parked. "I'ma go in here and cop you a room for a week. It's just until your face and eye heal. Afterward, shit, we'll try to find you a nice li'l apartment somewhere and finish up your CD. Not to mention, your face gotta be pretty for all those photographers whose magazines you're gonna be all up in as the next big thing in the R&B genre."

When Korey said that, She'Cute managed to smile. Smiling was painful. Her face hurt severely, but the mere thought of her becoming a star made her happy.

# Chapter 38

"Babe," Kolanda said to her husband inside her office where he had come to have lunch with her before having to later meet with a prominent hip hop magazine reporter for an interview with Mad Loot. "Our source tells me that it's a miracle indeed that Rah's wife is still breathing now on her own, no life support machine. Says that ninety-five percent of people who get shot in the head don't survive. They die immediately."

"That's why I capped that nigga, Rah, and his bitch in the dome, Kolanda," he said with the volume low on his voice as he sat across from her at a shiny wooden table inside her office, eating a salad. She was having the same thing. "I had no intention of sparing either of their lives."

"I know," Kolanda responded, wiping her mouth with a napkin. She then continued dropping on him what her source dropped on her. "The ones who do survive a shot to the head are usually seriously impaired for life. Some never come out of a coma."

"Look like this bitch coming out of hers, though."

"Yeah, but she's in such an amnesiac state of mind that our source tells me she doesn't even recognize her own mother. She's severely senile at this point. She has also been slipping in and out of consciousness. Doctors are contemplating hooking her back up to the machine. Honestly, I doubt if she'll ever recover."

"Hate to say it, but hopefully the bitch doesn't recover."

"She'll be so mentally impaired that, even if she does, she wouldn't be able to finger you or Korey. I mean, babe. Who in their right mind would take the word of a retard? Think about it."

"Is there anything else? Mad Loot and I got a meeting with this magazine reporter."

"Unfortunately, there is something else." Kolanda walked over to her desk and retrieved a folder. She walked it over to Hammer, who was now wiping his mouth and hands. He was preparing to leave so that his wife could get back to work. Kolanda fingered through the many papers inside the folder while standing next to Hammer, who was still seated.

"Look at this," she said, placing a composite drawing in his hand. Hammer studied it and knew immediately who it resembled. Small beads of sweat began surfacing over his forehead as he felt himself suddenly getting angry.

"Who the fuck gave this sketch of Korey to the cops, Kolanda?" He tossed it on the table, thinking it was becoming one thing after another. First, there was the Olivia incident, then Rah's wife showing signs of recovery, then the She'Cute situation that ended up with her boyfriend losing his life, and now this damn drawing of his ace.

"Some teller at a gas station in Monroe," Kolanda answered while placing the sketch back inside the folder.

When she mentioned a gas station, Hammer's mind immediately replayed Korey and him being at one. It was where Korey rocked Fat Rah's wife to sleep with his good looks, mannerisms, charm, and wit before Korey kidnapped her at gunpoint.

"When everything went down, investigators went all through Monroe, questioning whomever they could get to cooperate with them on anything suspicious that they may have witnessed around the time of the shootings."

"And a fuckin' gas station teller comes forward, huh?"

"Unfortunately. Sources say the teller remembered seeing a man talking to this Sheila woman, Rah's wife, out in the gas station's lot. He gave the cops that description. Why they never followed up on it, I don't know, but now they're back taking a fresh look at the case."

"You know the name of this teller?"

"Not yet. I'll get it."

"Male or female? You know?"

"If I'm not mistaken, a male."

"Well, babe, find out his name. Find out if he still works at that gas station and even where he lay his head. He can't be allowed to finger my ace. That's like fingering me."

"I'll get on it ASAP."

"Fuck!" Hammer exclaimed, hitting his fist in his palm. The possibility of Korey and him going back to the joint after all these years of being out and living their dreams was something he'd do anything to avoid. Like Korey, Hammer hated the joint. Being in the joint would take him not only from the life he loved, but also from the very people he loved, like his dear wife and Keisha. If he could help it, he wasn't going back to being locked in a cage like an animal where he would be told when to do this and when to do that. For a man like Hammer, prison was hell on earth. Again, a fate he would avoid at all costs.

He ended the meeting with his wife and went and handled business with Mad Loot and the hip hop magazine reporter. But next to his artist getting some publicity, all Hammer could think about was that sketch of Korey and getting to the person who gave it.

"You ain't doing nothing but digging your own grave. You know that, Korey?" Shamika said to him. "That's all you doing when you use your mind to think like a thug."

They were inside her salon alone. It was well after 8:00 p.m. and she was closing up. He had She'Cute with him along with his son KJ, both of whom he had sent to wait for him out in his car while he hollered at Shamika about Olivia's situation. The only reason he had She'Cute with him and his son was because he had gone over to the hotel earlier to check up on her after having taken KJ shopping. He didn't want her feeling alone with the incident that they took care of last night weighing on her mind, so he took her with him and KJ to Mint Hill and had Shamika do her hair.

"Digging my own grave, Shamika?" Korey repeated her. "I wish you wouldn't talk like that. I hate it when you do," he said, trying to get her to see his point of view, which was that a father was in the right to do whatever possible within his power to see to it that his child was protected as well as respected in this world of sin.

"I don't see why I shouldn't talk to you like this. No one else is, Korey. Are you even for real right now? I'm telling you the truth. You're digging your own grave."

"That's not the truth." Korey shook his head. "Truth is, I'm standing in defense of our daughter."

"Really?" Shamika stopped wrapping up her salon appliances, and she looked at him from a short distance, for he was sitting in one of her worker's chairs.

"Yes, really. I'm standing in defense of our daughter by any means necessary. Bull jive ain't nothing."

"No, you're not," she refuted, now shaking her head and her index finger. "Don't even sit there and tell that lie."

"Lie?"

"Yes! You're not defending Olivia. Who you fooling, Korey? Certainly not Shamika! I know you. You're defending your li'l reputation as her no-nonsense father who would rather walk through hell's fire with gasoline poured all over him before it is said that he lets someone get away with disrespecting his daughter."

"Am I wrong? I'm her father."

"But you thinking like a fool!" she exclaimed and clapped her hands for emphasis, cutting him off.

"There you go trippin'. I ain't gotta listen to this shit!" Korey got up to leave, offended by her calling him a fool, but Shamika blocked the door, preventing him from doing so.

"Get out my way, Mika." He gave her a slight push on her arm. She stood her ground.

"I ain't doing nothing! What's up? Now all of a sudden you want to leave? You wanna leave 'cause, for real, Korey, you're a coward!" She pointed her index finger in his face to punctuate her statement. "A stone-cold coward!"

"First I'm digging my own grave. Then I'm a fool. Now I'm a coward, Mika?" he shot back and looked her directly in her eyes.

By now she knew he was heated. The eyes were never untruthful. Plus, she knew him well enough to know he didn't care for being belittled. You would think she would have retreated and let him be on his way for the purpose of cooling down, but Shamika was the one person who wasn't afraid to confront Korey with what she believed to be the truth and right. So she continued standing her ground, knowing that if she stood on her ground of truth unapologetically, all of heaven would back her play. Not to mention she'd been praying on Olivia's situation earnestly.

"I called you what I called you because that's exactly what you been acting like: a coward, someone afraid to use his head."

"That's your opinion. Now, excuse me." He reached for the door handle to leave. Shamika didn't budge.

"You ain't going nowhere 'til I finish saying what I got to say."

"Then say what you gotta say, Mika, 'cause I'm done talking!" he cut in quickly because he was getting really upset.

"Boy," Shamika said through clenched teeth while pointing her finger in his face, "I'm praying for you. That thug pride in you and that ego of yours need to die! Look at you. All ready to go over to Hammer's place, where Olivia is right now waiting on you because y'all supposed to have a meeting on what should be done to the guys who violated her. O told me y'all was having a meeting."

"You her mother. She can tell you whatever she wants." Korey shrugged.

Shamika slowly shook her head and tears were now forming in her eyes. "I rebuke the devil in you, Korey. What are you trying to turn our daughter into by having her around a bunch of folks who think like you? Huh? A thug? Is that what you want for our daughter? Even if you and Hammer were to do something crazy, why O gotta meet with y'all on it? Why she gotta be a coconspirator, Korey? Huh?"

"O grown. She can go where she wants. You trippin'!"

"I ain't trippin' and you know it!" She pushed him in his chest. "I'm telling you what's real. And what's real is you're digging your own grave, both you and Hammer! Y'all think that the only way to solve a problem is by thuggin'. That is not the only way to solve a problem, Korey. Whatever happened to someone just thinking before they react? When you were in prison, you used to write me all the time saying, 'I hope you are out there in that world using your head.' You used to say that in all your letters. Well, now you're home. You're out here in this world. Why aren't you using your head?"

"I been fuckin' thinking—"

"Don't curse around me," Shamika cut him off, hating him using foul language around her, or what her mother and church would call "the devil's language."

"I was thinking when I took you out the projects and bought you your own house and this here salon," Korey countered. He knew he was a thinker. The things he'd done for her and Olivia were the proof. "Our daughter is in college behind me using my head. Now, I'm not Mr. Perfect, but don't stand here and act like I don't use my head, Mika. 'Cause that's where you're wrong. I do use my head!"

"Not disputing your ability to use your head. I know you can use it. To stop using it would be your downfall. That's all I'm saying! Listen to me. Olivia is your heart, Korey. Don't use your heart when seeking revenge for what happened to her. Use your head. We both know that the penitentiary and the graveyards are full of individuals who, for whatever reason, stopped using their heads. I don't want Olivia and KJ's father to be one of them. That's it. That's all I'm saying. You can leave now if you want to."

"Then excuse me."

She moved out of his way. Korey then walked out of her shop, hopped in his Benz, and headed back to the Queen City to drop She'Cute back off to the hotel and prepare himself for the meeting at Hammer's.

Having arrived at the house, Korey stepped inside along with KJ. Upstairs were Hammer, Olivia, Kolanda, and Keisha. They were all in Hammer and Kolanda's huge bedroom at the bar sipping on gin and grapefruit juice and listening to the golden voice of the late, great Luther Vandross, which was playing through Hammer's high-amped speakers.

As Korey walked into the room where they were, he noticed Kolanda, Keisha, and Olivia were chatting about something while Hammer was sitting at the bar, quietly looking at the screen of his phone. However, it wasn't Hammer's phone that he was looking at as Korey supposed. It was the phone of Olivia's ex. Hammer was watching the recording of what her ex and his buddy forced her to do to them.

"What's up, y'all?" Korey had to somewhat shout over the music to make his and KJ's presence known.

"What's up, dawg?" Hammer looked up and shouted, giving Korey a military salute. Hammer then reached for his entertainment system's remote to turn the music down a little.

Korey returned the salute with his hand positioned straight at his temple and shooting it straight forward. KJ quickly walked over to his mother, who kissed and hugged him. Korey walked over to Olivia. "Hey, baby." He kissed her. He then kissed Kolanda on her cheek. "What up, sis?" he greeted her before making his way to Keisha to give her a kiss and hug.

"We been waiting on you," Keisha said. "But I swear, K, I don't think you wanna really see that recording."

"Did you see it?"

"Twice already. So did Kolanda. Hammer is watching it now. Those guys made O look like she was a whore who was getting paid to make them happy. She told us all how it all went down. I think you and my brother-in-law already know what them dudes' punishment should be. That's the conclusion that Kolanda and I came up with: just letting you and Ham do what y'all feel needs to be done," Keisha said in Korey's ear, because KJ was standing between her legs as she sat on a barstool.

By then, Hammer waved Korey over. "Look at how these niggas made sport of our baby girl," Hammer said through clenched teeth, handing the phone to Korey for him to see for himself.

On her knees, inside of what looked to be a bedroom in the background, was his daughter. Her violators were laughing and pouring champagne over Olivia's head and watching it run down her face while her ex's buddy's cock was being reluctantly sucked on by her. She moved from the buddy's cock to her ex's. While sucking her ex off, his buddy could be heard in the background saying that Olivia sucked cock so good that she didn't need to be in college; she needed to be in the call girl business circle! Olivia could be heard vomiting on the recording from her ex ejaculating in her mouth.

Madder than he ever found himself in his life, Korey threw the phone to the floor with all of his might. He then began stomping it with the bottom of his Tims until the phone was destroyed. Like Keisha predicted, the content of the recording angered him. It did more than anger Korey; it made him weeping mad internally knowing that this was a disgraceful incident that his daughter would have to live with for the rest of her life. The mental and emotional trauma that she was experiencing from it was something he knew she was dealing with, but on what level? How would this influence her trust in men later in life? And how would she view him as her father if he didn't take this matter seriously enough to avenge her dignity and womanhood as one under his and her uncle's umbrella of protection? He stomped some more on the now completely destroyed phone.

Everyone in the room was looking at him express his anger. They didn't move. They didn't make a sound. They all, but one, knew what was on his mind: murder! KJ, the one who had no clue, tapped his mother on her leg and said, "Mommy, why my daddy mad?" He looked in her eyes with his innocent and pure light brown ones for an answer.

Keisha pulled KJ closer to herself and wrapped her arms around him. "That phone was showing an ugly picture that your dad didn't like. He's a'ight." But she knew that he wasn't all right. She knew Korey was deeply disturbed by seeing his baby girl in such a seemingly helpless and compromising position.

She called his name, "Korey," and waved him over to her, but Hammer looked at her and shook his head as if to say, "Now is not a good time." He knew his ace well enough to know that, when highly upset, he didn't like to talk. Not to mention there was nothing needing to be discussed at this point because not only had Olivia given her uncle Hammer the phone with the recording of her situation, she gave him her ex's apartment address. Better than that, in Hammer's view, was her informing him that her ex's buddy, Tim, was still in town at her ex's apartment, but would be leaving for military duty the coming Monday.

However, in spite of Hammer not wanting Keisha to bother with Korey at this very moment of being angry, she insisted he come to her. After all, she knew him too and had even come to love him very much, as the very mother of his junior!

He walked over to her with a look on his face that she'd never seen before. It was cold. Scary would be an understatement.

"Are you gonna be okay, babe?" she asked softly.

"I'm good," he said. He then turned to Olivia, who was messing with her little brother. "O, did you get that other info I wanted and needed you to get?"

"I got it, K," Hammer cut in, knowing immediately and exactly what he was referring to before Olivia could say a word in reply. "Matter fact, K, peep this." Hammer waved him back over.

"I'm straight," he said to Keisha before stepping back close to Hammer, seeing the look on her face that she wasn't sure of his mental state.

Hammer walked Korey into Korey's bedroom of the house with his arm around Korey's neck. "My nigga, O gave me all we needed. I say we load up right now, handle business with these niggas, and be out of Chapel Hill by early morning. I'm fuckin' ready. I know you are. What's up?"

"Let's go," Korey shot back in a hurry. He didn't even have to think about what he wanted to do at this point. It was already evident.

# Chapter 39

Shamika cried her eyes red nearly her whole way home after having an argument with Korey. Inside, she felt disrespected and hurt by him waving off what she had to say to him concerning their daughter's situation and how she felt Korey should go about handling it. Walking out on her as he did, all angry, made her sense that what she had to say was of no value to him.

The tears kept coming as she entered her house. She was extremely tired and exhausted already from just having an extremely long and busy day at work. She had seven hairdos, two of which were micro braids that took two and a half hours of finger exercising apiece to complete. Such was a tedious task within itself. Add that along with her other time-consuming hairdos and trying to talk some sense into Korey's head and that equaled a serious migraine headache.

She took two 200-mg ibuprofen to calm her thumping head and prepared to bathe. While making preparations to bathe, she was thinking that if she didn't love Korey so very much, she would joyfully abandon the task of trying to get him to stop reacting to certain situations the thug way. She knew in her heart and mind that him reacting the thug way to the hand he felt life dealt him had somewhat to do with being raised by a single mother and all.

His mother struggled when he was younger to make sure he had food on his table and decent clothes on his back. Korey had told her once that before his mother ultimately gave her life to Christ, he awoke late one night to use the bathroom and overheard her having sex. When he finished using the bathroom, he saw a man he'd never seen before coming out of his mother's bedroom. He later asked his mother if that man was his father, because he never knew his father. She told him no, that the man was someone she met and needed to help pay their rent. Korey knew from that moment that his mother had given up her body in exchange for cash. He hated that she had to do that.

Shamika knew that this was one of the reasons that when Korey had come into a lot of money, he bought her a house of her own. He never wanted her to be in a compromising position to have to pay her bills. Shamika didn't want him to have to thug and do street things to ensure that he and their family didn't go without. All possessing that thug mentality did was cause Korey to have to do twelve long years. Shamika remembered vividly missing him while he was away. She missed his warm, gentle smile and touch, the smell of his cologne, his passionate kisses, the way he would take his time and make love to her most prized possession. The last thing she wanted was for him to end up going back to the joint. But she was a wisher. A dreamer, if you will. Korey was his own man.

Him being his own man meant to Shamika the same thing it meant for her to be her own woman. That being, he would do what his conscience told him. But just thinking about what he would do to an individual who has disrespected their daughter was frightening. She saw the recording of those guys seemingly making sport of Olivia. She didn't like what she saw. She wanted justice. No doubt about it. But not the type of justice she knew Korey would deliver.

She soaked her body in a tub of warm bubble bath and listened to Yolanda Adams's "The Battle Is Not Yours" and silently prayed for her baby daddy and for his ace, Hammer. She knew them all too well. They would seek to avenge Olivia's most shameful and embarrassing moment. Oh, how right her premonition would be.

Hammer and Korey, with a mean vendetta against Olivia's perpetrators, sat quietly along a roadside near the address Olivia had given them of her ex's apartment. They were dressed in all-black hoodie sweats. It was a little after 1:00 a.m. and not a lot was going on in the seemingly quiet neighborhood they were strangers to. They didn't see the white 5.0 Mustang of her ex in his driveway.

"Them niggas probably somewhere at a club, K," Hammer said softly as they continued to patiently await their targets' arrival.

"They better have a damn good time because, after tonight, their partying will be over," Korey shot back, gripping his burner.

"Oh, for sho', my nigga," Hammer replied, firing up a blunt. Korey didn't smoke. He especially wouldn't do so in the middle of handling his business. Hammer, on the other hand, needed a smoke. He always did to calm his racing nerves before putting in work.

After patiently waiting for about fifteen more minutes of what turned out to be a full hour of waiting for Olivia's perpetrators to show their hand, they saw a white Mustang pull into the driveway.

"That's them niggas right there, yo," Korey said, tapping Hammer's leg and pointing. "Pull up next to them right now." They both could see that there were two individuals in that car pulling into that driveway: one driving and one on the passenger side.

Hammer cruised right up to their targets' car. Korey immediately gripped his burner, equipped with a silencer, and pulled his mask over his face. Before the driver could get out of his ride, Korey was greeting him the thug way. Pop. Pop. He shot the driver, who was the one he truly wanted: Tim, the military cat.

"What the fuck?" the other one said, trying his best to exit the passenger side. It was Olivia's ex, but there was danger on his side as well.

Hammer had quickly made his way around to that area. With the passenger side door open, Hammer aimed his burner, also equipped with a silencer, to his forehead. Also wearing a mask, Hammer said, "I send you greeting from the Queen City, muthafucka. But, moreover, from my niece." Pop. Pop. Pop. He unapologetically squeezed three off in his head, then quickly walked back to his car and got in on the passenger side while Korey pulled off, leaving both their victims slumped over dead in that Mustang, never to treat another woman again as they had Olivia.

They got back to the Queen City a little after 4:00 a.m., cleaned up, and went and lay next to their women and slept like murder had not occurred in ruthless fashion just hours ago at their hands.

By the end of the week, Chapel Hill was in serious mourning over what had happened. Who could have done something so horrible and gruesome to these two victims who seemingly had a lot more living to do, with bright futures ahead of them? That was the major question on the lips of the many who knew them both, as well as what could they have done to have deserved such an execution-styled murder.

Olivia knew the root cause of those cats' early demise, but she wasn't talking. Her father and uncle had taught her well over the years. Nor did she show any sign whatsoever of what she intimately knew. As her school semester ended, she spent her time out of school in the Queen City with family and working closely with Keisha and Kolanda, who were schooling her with all they knew about law and courtroom antics.

What her father and uncle did on her behalf brought her that much closer to them. She knew no one else loved her like them. After graduating with her bachelor's degree from Chapel Hill, she would later go on to law school at Duke University. Meanwhile, Hammer and Korey were continuing to do their music thing and play their thug-gentlemen-like positions in this game called life, where you just never knew what would come at you next.

Like they predicted, Mad Loot and She'Cute blew up like the World Trade Center. Both their CDs were getting major radio play locally as well as nationally. They were even on tour at the moment with the two of them and another of their artists.

Furthermore, Fat Rah's wife, Sheila, slipped back into a coma, causing any real hope of finding who shot her and killed her husband to slowly dampen. And, according to Kolanda's source of information, the guy who provided that sketch of Korey to the authorities had passed away three years after Sheila was shot and her husband was killed. Armed with that news, Hammer and Korey sensed that someone was looking down on them and protecting them from going back to the joint.

Shamika shook her head slowly and shed tears after Korey told her how he and Hammer, unwilling to let Olivia's perpetrators get away, shot and killed them both. Korey didn't mind sharing it with Shamika. He knew that one thing she would never do was go to the cops about his illegal endeavors. Doing something crazy like going to the cops on him would only destroy their relationship forever. Neither of them, who had too much love invested in the other, would chance losing the other under any circumstance.

Shamika, knowing God doesn't like ugly, prayed to Him about the matter. For one can fool man and get away with it, but who can get away with fooling God for the wrongs committed against His divine laws? Shamika knew no one could escape the justice of God. No one. She knew that God's law says, "Thou shall not kill." She asked God to forgive Korey and Hammer. But forgiveness is one thing. God forgetting is another. She loved Korey, and she had love for his ace, Hammer, but she loved God above her love for either of them.

She lay next to Korey with his arm around her, sound asleep, on the night he revealed what he and Hammer had done to Olivia's violators. After silently praying for them both, she began quietly weeping, knowing that what was done in the dark would eventually come to the light. The light is representative of God, most divine and just, who gives to every man according to his deeds and actions.